Heart Stone
By
DJ Edwards

Visit the author's website at www.sethundra.com

First Edition

ISBN: 9781520361024

Cover by Bespoke Book Covers
Edited by writing.co.uk

To Katy and Dylan,
make your dreams reality.

CHAPTER 1

The man drove his car along the winding country road, never once considering that he may be driving a little too quickly around the blind bends, not even glancing at the occasional sign that pointed to some village or another. Curiosity at what might lie down one of the many narrow lanes that branched off his route had died in him long ago. Even the turning that always caught him by surprise failed to register in his preoccupied mind anymore. Often, as a younger man he had wondered what might be down that lane with no signpost, promised himself that next time he would drive down to have a look, but he never seemed to have the time. Besides, he always forgot about it until he had just passed the entrance and there never seemed to be any warning to it coming up. One moment he was looking at an unbroken hedgerow, then it was there, then a second later dwindling away in his rear-view mirror. Next time he would look, next time.

If as younger man he had remembered, although few people ever did, he would have found something that might have surprised him. Down a hill, around a bend, over a ford and then the prettiest village he would likely ever see. The first thing he would come to would be a village green, a flag pole at its centre with the Welsh flag fluttering in a gentle breeze. Picturesque cottages would surround the green, each fronted with a beautiful garden filled with blooms of every shape and colour imaginable. A small pub with no name, only a picture of a great tree on its sign, and around a corner, a tiny church, just big enough to hold all of the village's residents. He wouldn't know the name of the village, there was no sign to greet a traveller and it wouldn't appear on any map. But then his curiosity would grow when he saw a lane leading out of the village on the opposite side to where he had entered. Continue along that for a while and he would find a house; just a typical old farmhouse, but with a garden even more stunning than those in the village. Perhaps he would wonder who lived there, or perhaps he would turn around and go home, or maybe a quick drink and bite to eat in the pub. A shame for him if he did, for if he had knocked on the door of the house and found a welcome there, he may have found that the lane he always drove past, was a very interesting lane indeed.

"Unicorns are very intelligent creatures," Bryn Morgan said, pointing his fork at his grandson, "they're not just horses with horns stuck to their foreheads, they can understand every word you say. But neither are they magical, people only assume that they are because of the intelligence they possess."

Dylan shoved a forkful of chips into his mouth and chewed thoughtfully, considering his response. "If they're not magic why do people hunt them then?"

"Because people are idiots," Grandad responded, his mouth full of peas. "Are foxes hunted because they can pull a rabbit out of a hat, or elephants because their trunks double up as magic wands? No! People see a

4

beautiful creature and try to lock it up, or shoot it and hang its head on a wall, therefore removing the very thing that gave it beauty in the first place. Life, freedom!"

"But all the stories say unicorns are magical, they can heal and stuff," Dylan argued.

Bryn speared a chip and chomped noisily upon it. "Pah!" he said, narrowly avoiding spraying his food across the other diners. "The only stories worth listening to are the ones I tell you, Dylan. Trust me, the truth is more fantastic than the fiction. People hunt unicorns because they look nice, not for magical gain."

"And these people who hunt unicorns," Nanny said from the opposite end of the table to Grandad, "do they speak with their mouth full in front of their grandchildren too?" Dylan's eyes widened, feeling an immediate pang of sympathy for his grandfather. Nanny's deceptively calm tone was always a clear sign that someone was about to get an ear-bashing.

"I am merely instructing Dylan of commonly held myths about unicorns," Bryn retorted, "it might serve him well in the future."

"And good manners at the dinner table won't serve him well in the future, I suppose?"

"I consider unicorn law to be a far more fascinating subject to fill a child's head with than dining etiquette."

"I fail to see why," Nanny said, eyeing her husband dangerously, "I was at the supermarket today and I didn't see any unicorns, the hairdressers yesterday, no unicorns and I'm fairly certain there won't be any at the garden centre tomorrow. In fact, I don't believe I have ever seen

5

a single unicorn in all of my fifty-nine years of life, so I'm struggling to understand why that makes it acceptable for you to SPEAK WITH YOUR MOUTH FULL IN FRONT OF THE GRANDCHILDREN!"

A palpable silence hung over the dinner table as Nanny and Grandad sat locked in a staring match. When she shouted like that, everyone knew that was the point you ceased to argue. The silence was broken by Nanny's hand slamming hard onto the table-top making everyone jump.

"Katy Howard," Nanny said, dangerous calm returning to her voice. Opposite Dylan, his elder sister rested a defiant look on her grandmother. "What have I said about that contraption at the dinner table?"

"If by 'that contraption' you mean this," Katy held up her mobile phone, "you said something about not using it."

"And yet you appear to be doing just that."

"I was looking at something online."

"And is the internet going to disappear in the time it takes you to finish your dinner?"

Katy held Angharad Morgan's gaze a moment longer before shoving her phone into the pocket of her jeans and attacking her plate of food, shooting an angry glare at her brother as it were somehow his fault.

"So, Dylan," Grandad said, changing the subject and making sure his mouth was empty before speaking, "your birthday is almost upon us, the big eleven. Have you decided what you want yet?"

"Skateboard," Dylan said eagerly.

"A fine choice for a young man."

"A stupid and dangerous one, if you ask me," snorted Nanny.

"I'll wear a helmet, Nanny," Dylan protested, "and knee pads. All my friends have got one."

"You haven't got any friends," Katy muttered.

Dylan scowled back. "I have."

"Yeah, but they're all going to different schools after the holidays."

Dylan shifted in his chair, uncomfortably aware of how accurate Katy was. Being small for his age, Dylan often found himself the target of bullies and despite being assured by his grandparents that he would make new friends, losing the companionship of most of the boys he played with was making the prospect of starting a new school terrifying.

"We'll see about the skateboard," Nanny said sympathetically, "and I'm sure you'll make lots of new friends."

Dylan nodded and prodded unenthusiastically at his steak and kidney pie, his appetite diminished to a small and insignificant thing.

Bryn reached across and patted Dylan's arm. "I've got a new story for bedtime, an extra special one. Trust me, you're going to love it."

"More of your nonsense," Nanny shook her head despairingly. "Well I have a meeting in the village this evening, but that's no excuse for staying up later than necessary. Katy, make sure your brother gets to bed on time."

Katy's mouth fell open in protest. "But I was thinking of going out!"

"Thinking about it isn't doing it, so that means you'll be here to make sure Dylan goes to bed on time."

Katy threw her arms in the air. "Fine, whatever." She shovelled a large portion of pie into her mouth, chewing furiously and glaring at her brother.

The rest of the meal continued in silence, just how Nanny liked it, and what Nanny wanted, Nanny usually got. It wasn't as if she was a bad grandmother, quite the opposite in fact, she was always there with open arms when a hug was needed or a sympathetic ear; rules, however, were most definitely not made to be broken and the greatest breaker of rules of all was Dylan's grandfather, Bryn Morgan. Dylan often wondered if Grandad wound Nanny up on purpose, almost as if he got some sort of enjoyment out of it. Not that any argument lasted for very long, life in Nanny and Grandad's house followed a very predictable routine. Grandad would fight with Nanny, Nanny would win the fight, a brief period of peace and then Grandad would fight with Nanny again.

When dinner was finished and everything had been cleared away, Dylan lay on his bed for a while playing on his game console. Nanny soon went out, after reiterating that he needed to go to bed on time, to her meeting in the village. Although what they met up to talk about was beyond Dylan's comprehension. Once, when he had asked why they had so many meetings, Grandad had whispered in a way that everyone in the room could

clearly hear that it was just an excuse for old ladies to have a gossip, which,
unsurprisingly, had caused another row; that Bryn lost.

With bedtime drawing near, Dylan slipped out of his clothes and into his superhero pyjamas and then tiptoed across his bedroom floor. He opened the door a crack and peaked out onto the landing, making sure the coast was clear. Katy always had her headphones on listening to her music, it was only if she decided to go to the bathroom or downstairs to get herself a drink at the wrong moment that she might catch him. Not that it was forbidden for Dylan to have a bedtime story, his grandfather openly encouraged it, even though Nanny quite often muttered about Grandad 'filling the children's heads with nonsense'. It was just that he couldn't stand anymore of Katy's teasing. She was right in a way, at ten years Dylan was a bit old for stories at bedtime from his grandfather, but they were so fantastic, so much better than anything written down in any book that he could never resist them.

There was no sign of movement upon the landing, no sound from Katy's room or the bathroom. It was now or never. He slipped from his room, moving as speedily across the landing as stealth would allow and past his sister's bedroom door. Reaching the top of the stairs he glanced quickly down to make sure that no one was coming up to catch him. Seeing that the stairs were clear he made his way down, remembering to miss out the fourth one from the top with its treacherous creak. He safely reached the bottom and found himself in the hallway, the front door directly before him. He glanced to his left towards the living room. There was no sound from the TV, meaning that Katy was unlikely to be in there, so he turned to his right, and the door to his grandfather's study.

It was a curious door, Dylan had wasted many hours staring at it and no matter how hard he looked he had never found another like it. Whenever he asked where it had come from his grandfather just shrugged and said it had come with the house just like all the others. But the other doors were nothing like this one. Images of plants and trees were beautifully carved into the wood, so lifelike that Dylan almost felt he could push his way into the undergrowth to pick a flower and smell its scent. Seven curious symbols were carved in an arch towards the top of the door and then an eighth underneath the arch. He had no idea what the symbols meant, although he had drawn them several times, usually on a text book in school whenever one of his teachers was being particularly boring. His favourite was the centre one, a seven-pointed star with a circle surrounding it. The others were all wavy lines, crisscrossing patterns and circles, random fancies of the master craftsman who had lovingly made it. There were also eyes in the carvings, hidden within the foliage, camouflaged so cleverly that a casual observer of the door would probably miss them completely. Dylan believed he had found them all, though he couldn't be entirely sure as they were the one thing he didn't like looking at. He always felt they were looking right back at him, and they weren't nice eyes to have staring at you. They were cruel eyes, filled with hatred. Who or what the eyes belonged to was anyone's guess, but Dylan didn't want to find out.

He gave one last quick look around to make sure his
sister wasn't lying in wait to catch him and then pushed open the door and stepped inside.

As always, at this time of the evening the study was dimly lit and slightly musty smelling, much to his grandmother's annoyance. Grandad never allowed Nanny in to clean properly, he always insisted on doing it himself and he never did a proper job of it, if he did it at all. Dylan barely glanced at the hundreds of books that were piled haphazardly upon the many shelves, or the Welsh flag that hung on the wall between two heavily laden bookcases, nor did he pay any attention to the strange and alien looking objects that decorated table tops, hung on spare patches of walls and even lay on the floor where anyone unfamiliar with the room and its treasures could easily trip over. Many of these objects filled Dylan with wonder. The long, slender sword with the golden dragon stitched into the black scabbard that hung over the grand looking fireplace was his favourite, but he was never allowed to touch it, let alone hold it and swing it about, much to his annoyance. *What else are you supposed to do with a sword but swing it about?* Other oddities he was allowed to handle though; cracked vases and plates with odd designs painted on them he was able to pick up, although with great care and under adult supervision. Scrolls with letters he had never seen

before, ornate boxes usually held curious odds and ends and there was one larger chest that, despite his best efforts, he had never been able to open. Then there were the ancient looking maps filled with lands that did not feature in his or any other atlas he had ever seen, Dylan had wasted many a damp afternoon
staring at those.

Wonders to a boy of ten. Rubbish and useless junk to his grandmother. Katy liked the objects too, although she wouldn't admit to it, even when Dylan had caught her trying to reach for the sword once. *Girls are stupid*, Dylan thought. He would have kept her secret if she had let him have a swing or two, but no, she had to start shouting at him and calling him names, as usual.

All the objects in the room told a story, each one more fantastic than the last and each one told a hundred times by the old man who sat in his big, leather armchair in the centre of the room. He looked up as Dylan entered, a smile creasing his already lined face, his bright eyes sparkling with amusement. He wasn't really that old, he'd only just turned sixty, and still strong and fit. Nanny called him old and stupid and lazy and a rascal, but then, that's what Nanny did. Dylan had overheard her explaining to Katy once that it was the best way to keep a man in line and Katy soaked it all up like a sponge, then spent her days practicing her grandmother's advice upon her unfortunate younger brother.

Grandad leant forward in his chair. "Were you seen?" he whispered.

Dylan shook his head. "Nope, I was as stealthy as a cat."

"The best kind of stealthy I've always thought." He leant back and opened his arms. "Time to claim your reward for a well-executed mission."

Dylan jumped up onto his lap and wriggled around a bit to find the most comfortable position, careful to avoid the half-full tankard of beer balanced on the arm of the chair. A clear indication his grandmother was out as Grandad wasn't supposed to be drinking it in the house. If she caught him it would inevitably lead to a lecture about the dangers of drink to a man his age, that he wasn't a teenager anymore, and he should spend a little less time down the pub with his boozy mates and start acting like a grown man. To which Grandad would always respond with a 'yes, dear' and as soon as Nanny's back was turned he would go off and have another quick, sneaky swig of the stuff.

Dylan loved Grandad's stories, even if the old man did insist that they were all true. His grandfather sometimes forgot that Dylan was ten and rapidly approaching his eleventh birthday, so, obviously, he was far too old to believe in the sort of fancies old Bryn Morgan spouted anymore. But the fact that the ten-year-old knew they were all made up did not stop him from enjoying them any the less. On the suggestion of his grandmother, Dylan pretended he believed every word of what Grandad said. Nanny said that it wasn't lying, it was called 'humouring him', which as far as Dylan could tell was just a perfectly acceptable form of grown-up lying.

He looked up into his grandfather's face wondering what tale would unfold this evening. Grandad had the same faraway look in his eyes he always had just before a story began, but then he did something out of the ordinary. He looked quickly away from Dylan and stared at a spot in the study, just in front of one of the bookcases and to the right of the large writing desk. A small smile slowly appeared on his lips as he turned back to face his grandson.

"Have you ever caught a movement out of the corner of your eye, but when you looked, there was nothing there?"

Dylan couldn't recall a particular time when this had happened but he supposed there must have been one, so he nodded that he had.

"There is a secret," his grandfather continued, "known only to a few. It is a secret so great, so wonderful, so fantastic that most people who learn of it do not believe a word. They just laugh. Scoff. Say that it's the delusion of a madman." He looked around the room as if to make sure no one was listening then lowered his voice to a whisper. "Can you keep a secret?"

Dylan had the feeling he was going to be one of those people who didn't believe a word of it, but he nodded his head vigorously anyway, eager for Grandad to go on.

"The secret, Dylan, is that sometimes, in certain places, there *is* something there. And yet not there, if that makes any sense at all. You can't touch them, you can't see them, except in the corner of your eye, that tiny window to the dream world. They're asleep you see,

14

sleeping a sleep that has lasted for thousands of years, endlessly shifting from one dream to the next."

"What are they?"

"Well that's a question that scholars have debated for generations, and yet no one has managed to answer. Some say they are great monsters who used to rule the earth thousands of years ago, or aliens from another world; some say angels, others demons, nobody really knows. But the one thing we are sure of, the one thing that we know to be true, is that they are old, very old. Older than the human race, possibly even older than this world."

"Older than the dinosaurs?"

"Oh yes, much older. If you can keep one awake long enough to ask it a question, then the sethundra would probably tell you exactly how old it is."

"The seth...sef...sefunda?" Dylan said, struggling with the unfamiliar word.

"*Se-thun-dra*," his grandfather repeated slowly, "that's what they're called."

"What does that mean?"

"Mean?" Grandad furrowed his brows and rubbed at his chin before answering. "Well, it means...it means them, it's just their name. We are humans, dogs are dogs, cats are cats and sethundra are sethundra."

"Why have they been asleep for so long?"

"Because long ago a very powerful magical spell was cast, trapping them in an endless sleep. They can never wake up." Bryn beckoned Dylan closer. "Unless someone else wakes them up of course."

"You can wake them up? How?"

15

"By speaking the spell of awakening. It's a magic spell known only to a few, handed down from generation to generation. I taught it to your mother when she was your age, I'm sure she would have passed it onto you if she…" For a fleeting moment Grandad's face took on a pained look. "Well, I'm sure she would have passed it onto you."

Grandad rarely mentioned Dylan's mother, neither did anyone else in fact, everyone avoided the subject. When he was younger he would often ask about her and why she had left not long after he had been born, but either no one knew or they were refusing to tell him. His father wasn't around much, he was great when he was there, but both Dylan and Katy always knew that it wouldn't be long before he vanished, sometimes for weeks at a time. That was never really talked about either, although Dylan always suspected his father was searching for their mother.

"Does Katy know the spell?" Dylan asked.

"She's probably forgotten it. Most people do you know, they forget the spell almost as soon as they hear it. It's part of the magic. The spell decides who is worthy of this knowledge and who is not. After all, you can't have just anyone waking sethundra up whenever they feel like it. Now listen carefully, Dylan, what I am about to tell you is not to be taken lightly. It's not just a funny little poem that you can share with your friends in the playground, it's something that you must keep very secret, only to be spoken of between ourselves. You must promise me that you will never breathe a word of this to another soul."

"I promise, Grandad," Dylan swore faithfully.

"Good lad." Grandad lowered his voice to barely above a whisper. "It is not the words that are important, Dylan, it's what you feel when you speak them. Allow me to demonstrate.

16

Ancient locked within the dream
Held for mortals' sake
I command you now, come forth, be seen
Sethundra, rise and wake."

Nothing happened, not that Dylan had been expecting anything to, but he couldn't help feeling a little disappointed. "Nothing happened," he somewhat needlessly pointed out.

"Of course not, as I said the words are unimportant, they're merely a way of, shall we say, reminding yourself of what to do. A fully trained wizard could easily perform great feats of magic without saying a word, but someone new to the magical arts would need to say the words to practice."

Dylan grinned playfully at his grandfather. "If you're a wizard then why have I never seen you do any magic?"

"Did I say I was a wizard? I don't recall saying such a thing. I thought I was telling you all about the sethundra. I said nothing about being a wizard at all."

"Then how do you know the spell?"

"My father taught it to me, and his to him."

"So, if you're not a wizard how can you remember the spell?"

"Ah, er...well...you know there is such a thing as being too clever you know."

Dylan laughed, feeling he was getting the better of Grandad for once. "Have you ever woken one?"

Grandad's eyes crinkled with mirth. "You are trying to catch me out, young Dylan? I told you, I said nothing about being a wizard."

"Can I try waking one up?"

"If you like. Do you remember the words?" Dylan nodded his head. "Now remember, you must let yourself feel the magic, let it envelope you like a cloak."

"How?" Dylan asked, having no idea where to begin.

"Close your eyes." Dylan closed his eyes. "Now take a deep breath and imagine all the tension leaving your body, let each and every muscle relax." Dylan did his best. "Block out all thoughts from your mind. Focus only on the sound of my voice. Breathe in through your nose and out through your mouth, slowly, not too fast. That's it, well done. Now, imagine a light in front of you, just a small one, not too big, now let it come closer, don't pull, just let it come on its own. Allow it to fill your vision so you can see nothing else but the light, then imagine it surrounding you, covering you completely, drawing ever nearer until it's a part of you. When you have done that, then just say the words."

Dylan did the best he could, although he wasn't sure why he was bothering as it was all rubbish anyway, but he tried to let the light come towards him as he had been told. It took several attempts as thoughts kept getting in the way and the light would vanish, forcing him to start all over again, but in the end he thought he got it. He felt curiously different, his skin tingled slightly and he couldn't remember ever feeling so relaxed. Deciding he was as ready as he would ever be he opened his mouth, and began to recite the spell.

18

CHAPTER 2

"Ancient locked..."

Suddenly the door bust open with a crash, causing an involuntary yelp to escape from between Dylan's lips. His eyes snapped open and he turned to glare at the one he knew would be the source of the interruption.

"Shouldn't you be in bed by now, Shrimp?" Katy said standing in the doorway with that annoying superior look on her face that she had obviously taken such pains to perfect.

Dylan resisted the urge to make a rude gesture with his fingers, but even Grandad wouldn't let him get away with that sort of thing. He hated Katy and the seventeen-year-old hated him back. She always made him so angry, especially when she called him Shrimp. Being short for his age was bad enough at school, but being constantly teased about it by his big sister was even worse. It wasn't like she was perfect, she didn't have many more friends than he did. She was pretty he supposed, at least Nanny and Grandad said she was, and Dylan had often caught the boys at school looking at her, but she was so unfriendly all the time that no one wanted to be near her.

"Don't you ever knock?" Grandad asked Katy, calmly taking a sip from the tankard of beer.

Katy's dark eyes flashed defiantly at her grandfather. "Don't you ever make children go to bed on time?"

Grandad's greying eyebrows came down in a frown at Katy's cheeky tone, but he didn't tell her off for it. It would only lead to one of their legendary rows, Dylan assumed. He often thought that Grandad and Katy's arguments were loud enough to make the neighbours complain about the noise, despite the fact that the nearest house was nearly half a mile away. It looked as though this night wasn't going to be a row night, as Grandad turned to Dylan, an apology showing on his leathery face. "Perhaps it is time you went to bed, Dylan, it is rather late."

"Aw," he complained, "but I wanted to hear more about the sethundra."

"Tomorrow perhaps," Grandad said, letting Dylan slip from his lap, "your Nanny will be home soon and you know what she'll be like if she catches you up. And it'll be all my fault of course."

"And she'd be right," Katy muttered.

Again, Grandad ignored Katy's comment. "Go on, off to bed with you."

"Alright," Dylan said, giving his grandfather a kiss on the cheek, "but I'm only going to save you an ear-bashing from Nanny, not because *she's* telling me to go."

"Then I believe I owe you a favour." Grandad winked and grinned at him.

Dylan pushed past Katy without a word and made his way across the hall towards the kitchen. He hadn't gone three steps beyond the stairs before his sister's voice hissed at him angrily. "Where do you think you're going?" Dylan ignored her and carried on walking through the living room. He had just reached the kitchen door when Katy caught him and spun him to face her. "I said, where do you think you're going?"

Dylan glared up at his older sister. "I'm getting a glass of milk before bed. I am allowed, Nanny and Grandad always let me have one."

"Well hurry up," Katy spat, "I don't intend to look after you all night."

"No one asked you too." He pulled away from her and headed to the fridge.

"Nan, put me in charge. Remember?"

Dylan began pouring some milk into a glass.

"Nice story?" she asked.

Dylan swallowed nervously. Katy's voice had become far too sweet all of a sudden which always made him uneasy, it usually meant he was in store for another bout of teasing. He almost swore as he spilt some of the milk onto the kitchen surface.

Katy shook her head. "Well done, stupid."

"You made me do it," Dylan said putting the milk back in the fridge and getting a paper towel to clean up the mess.

A mischievous smile crept onto Katy's face. "Made you jump, did I?"

"No."

"Was it a scary story? Did it have monsters in it? Is little Dylan scared of the monsters hiding under his bed?"

"Leave me alone," Dylan said taking the milk soaked paper towel to the back door.

"Where're you going now?"

"I'm putting the towel in the bin outside, it'll smell in the inside one. Don't you know anything?"

He opened the door and stepped outside in his slippers. The night was cool and still. In the distance and through the branches of some trees he could just make out some lights from the village of Carreg-y-galon.

"What were they called, those sleeping things of his?" Katy said as she followed him out. "Is that the story he told you? The one about those stupid, invisible monsters?"

"They're not stupid, they're sethundra," Dylan shot back angrily.

21

"That was it, sethundra," Katy laughed, doing an absurd little dance past Dylan and into the garden. "Sethundra," she called, "come out, come out wherever
you are!"

A cool breeze swept through the garden making Katy's long, dark hair blow about her face, and the leaves on the trees rustle like a thousand whispering voices. Eager voices; hungry voices.

"Stop it," Dylan said nervously.

"What's the matter," Katy clapped her hands with delight. "Oh my God, you don't actually believe they're real do you?"

"No."

"Yes you do! You're such a baby."

"No I'm not! They're just a story Grandad made up!"

Katy smiled slyly. "Say it then."

Dylan eyed his sister suspiciously. "Say what?"

"The spell. Say the spell of awakening."

"You're stupid!"

"You're scared."

"You say it then if you're so clever."

"Fine I will." Katy cleared her throat and struck a pose as if she were about to perform poetry on a school stage. She opened her mouth to speak, but instead of reciting the spell she looked back at Dylan with a puzzled frown. "What was it again?"

"Hah! You don't want to say it."

"No, I can't remember it."

Dylan grinned triumphantly at her. "Now who's scared?"

"Fine," Katy spat angrily, "you say it then! Go on, wake up a sethundra!"

The branches of the trees creaked eerily in the breeze. Dylan whipped his head to the right. Had that been a movement he had just caught out of the corner of his eye? No, it must have been branches being moved by the wind. He told himself he was being silly. Glaring balefully at Katy he threw the words out in a rush.

> "Ancient locked within the dream
> Held for mortals' sake
> I command you now, come forth, be seen
> Sethundra, rise and wake!"

He folded his arms and smiled smugly. "There, I did it. Nothing happened, it's all rubbish."

Katy regarded him a moment, then smiled again. "Do it properly."

Dylan held her gaze for what seemed an age, a tiny part of him nervous at what his sister was telling him to do. He shook his head, but as Katy's smile began to broaden anger flared up within him, pushing away his fear. *What am I worried about anyway? It's just a stupid story.*

He closed his eyes, took a deep breath and almost immediately he felt all the tension leave his body. He pushed away thoughts of his sister, emptied his mind of all but what he wanted to do. He pictured a light in front of him, just as his grandfather had told him to. Without even trying the light drew closer and closer towards him. The sound of creaking branches and rustling leaves grew louder as the wind strengthened. Were their excited voices mixed within the sounds of the leaves? The light enveloped him completely, he was one with the light, it was a part of him, or he a part of it, he couldn't tell. He felt as though his whole body was tingling with an energy he had never felt before. And then, without another thought, he began to speak.

"Ancient locked within the dream
Held for mortals' sake
I command you now, come forth, be seen
Sethundra, rise and wake."

The breeze turned into a wind, he was certain he could hear voices now, some whispering with glee, some in anger, others in terror. But the voices didn't frighten him, nothing frightened him in that moment. He had never felt like this before. He felt powerful, as if he could do anything he wished. He didn't know how or why but he was sure he could sense a fear rising inside of Katy. He wanted to laugh in triumph. But instead he spoke again.

"Ancient locked within the dream
Held for mortals' sake
I command you now, come forth, be seen
Sethundra, rise and wake."

The wind grew stronger and Katy's fear grew with it. Was she saying his name? Dylan wanted to laugh out loud. He was smallest boy in his class, but right then he felt like the tallest, the strongest, like he could take on the largest bully with ease. He spoke the spell a third time.

"Ancient locked within the dream
Held for mortals' sake
I command you now, come forth, be seen
Sethundra, rise and wake."

"Stop!" Katy's cried, shaking him roughly by the shoulders. His eyes snapped open to see his sister's fearful face looking down on him. "Stop it, you little freak!"

The light that enveloped him vanished in the blink of an eye and with it went everything else, the feeling of power, the howling wind, he was just Dylan again. He stumbled, suddenly feeling exhausted. "Wh…what happened?" He felt a little dizzy so he put his arm out behind him to steady himself against the wall of the house. His hand brushed against something soft, like some sort of fabric. Had Nanny left washing out overnight? That was unlike her. He pulled his hand back, his dizziness was clearing anyway. He had done it, he had said the spell and Katy had been clearly terrified. *Now it's my turn to tease her! We'll see how she likes that.* One look at Katy however wiped all thoughts of teasing from his mind. An expression of absolute horror was painted on her face; she shook her head from side to side, silently mouthing some sort of denial at whatever she was seeing. And whatever it was that she could see was behind him and several feet above his head. Dylan swallowed nervously, took a deep breath, and slowly turned around.

CHAPTER 3

He had no idea what he had been expecting to see behind him, but it certainly wasn't the creature that stood upon his grandparent's patio.

She, as whatever it was appeared to be female, was tall and slender; taller than Dylan's father by quite a bit and he was at least six foot. His first thought was that it was simply a giant woman that had for some reason wandered into his grandparent's garden, but as he stared up at her in amazement he realised that she was anything but human. Her face was too angular, her vivid, green eyes reminded Dylan of a cat's and he was sure he could see her ears rising to points, poking through her long yellow hair that flowed freely across her shoulders and down her back. Her light, brown skin was smooth and completely wrinkle free, not a single blemish marred her face, almost as if she wore heavy makeup. The creature radiated strength, not just physically as her slender, muscular body suggested, but there was a power to her that Dylan couldn't explain. Her clothes were odd, she wore trousers and soft, knee-high boots, a close-fitting tunic under a short, open jacket with a high collar, all in a reddish-brown colour that gave them the look of leather. There was also a wooden rod, about a foot long hanging from a plain, black belt. Markings appeared to decorate the rod, they might even have been writing carved into the wood, but Dylan couldn't make them out in the dim evening light. A small voice in

26

the corner of his mind was telling him that he should be afraid of this creature, but for some reason he wasn't, in fact he felt oddly calm, even comfortable in its presence.

The creature looked down on Dylan, an expression of curiosity on her strangely beautiful face. "You appear to be a little young to be a…"

She was interrupted by Katy's terrified voice. "It just appeared, one moment there was nothing there, and then there it was!" Katy's face had gone as white as a sheet, her eyes as wide as saucers. "What is it? What the hell is it? Get away from it, Dylan!"

"It?" the creature said in a slightly offended tone. "Has it been so long that we must now be referred to as an 'it'? I am sethundra, child; Artemis I am called. What are you called?"

Dylan gaped at the creature in shock. *The stories are real, there's a real, live sethundra standing in Nanny and Grandad's back garden.* He had a million questions, a billion, but he couldn't even get one out before his sister started screaming.

She didn't get very far before a figure emerged out of the gloom behind her to clamp a huge hand over her mouth. *Another sethundra,* Dylan thought. It looked and was dressed much the same as the other, although this one was male with black hair, pulled roughly back into a ponytail, and he thought it had a mean looking mouth.

"Silence, human," the male sethundra said into Katy's ear, her face white with terror, "there are unwanted listeners."

"Baccus?" The one called Artemis raised a questioning eyebrow.

"Three have been woken this night," the other responded.

"The third? Is it Dardanus?"

Baccus shook his head. "Dardanus still sleeps."

Almost quicker than Dylan could follow Artemis grabbed the odd-looking rod from her waist, it spun in her hand and suddenly was a staff almost as long as she was tall.

"Cool," Dylan muttered, immediately wondering where he could get one and if they built them in his size.

Artemis' catlike eyes scanned the garden as if expecting an attack, suddenly her head whipped to one side and she squinted into the gloom trying to see something.

"She has gone," Baccus muttered.

"But could return at any moment, we must stand ready."

"We should leave ourselves."

"We are bound, Baccus," Artemis said sharply.

"Weakly," Baccus said, a glint in his eye that Dylan didn't like the look of.

"Yet bound still." Artemis held Baccus' gaze for a long time before he finally nodded his agreement. "Release the girl, she is not our enemy."

Baccus glared at the white-faced Katy. "No screaming," he said, not releasing her until she nodded her head.

Artemis glared down at Dylan. "Child, do you have any idea what you have done?"

"I've woken up sethundra," Dylan said, voice full of wonder.

"You have woken three sethundra. Be thankful that Baccus and I found you first, if the third, Melantha had then you would be dead."

"Oh," Dylan gulped, "I'm sorry."

"You will be," Baccus growled.

"Who is Melantha?" Dylan asked Artemis, concluding
that she was the more pleasant of the two.

"That is not a story for this night, all you need to know now is that she is one of the most dangerous sethundra to ever exist. What are you called?"

"Dylan Howard."

"Well, Dylan Howard, you have started this so therefore you must finish it, we must stop Melantha before she can work whatever mischief she might be planning. Where is your Guardian?"

"Guardian?" Dylan wasn't sure what Artemis meant, his mother had vanished years ago, his father away doing whatever it was he did, Nanny and Grandad were the closest thing he had to proper parents, but he didn't really want to get them involved, so he pointed to the one person who always acted as if she were his mother. He pointed to Katy. "Katy's my guardian."

Artemis looked dubious, Baccus even more so. "You are certain?" Artemis raised a questioning eyebrow.

Dylan nodded as Baccus growled, "This cannot be."

"We must trust in the will of the Hearts, Baccus," Artemis said.

"So you have always reminded me, but surely this cannot be correct."

"It is not our place to judge, Baccus. Dylan Howard, are you and your Guardian ready to travel."

"Where're we going?" Dylan asked.

Artemis turned to Baccus. "Baccus, can you track Melantha?"

"I already have. She has gone to Dainnor. Not an unexpected choice, she had a stronghold there during the war."

Dylan was struggling to follow the conversation. "What
stronghold," he demanded, "what war? Where's Dainnor?"

Artemis shook her head disbelievingly. "Dainnor is amongst the stars as is your own world, it is one of the closest to you, although not as close as Tarnasus. Proximity makes little difference to our way of travelling of course."

Dylan couldn't understand half of what Artemis had said, but one thing stuck out clearly in his mind. "We're going to another world?"

"Of course." Artemis suddenly scooped Dylan up into her arms whilst Baccus unceremoniously slung Katy over his shoulder. She didn't resist the sethundra and as far as Dylan could tell she was too terrified to do anything other than give a little whimper. "Lead the way, Baccus."

Baccus glared at Artemis before staring intently at a spot in the garden, seemingly in mid-air. "What's he..." Dylan began to ask, but then something happened that froze the words in his mouth.

Before the big sethundra something appeared that Dylan could only describe as being a hole in the air. It was if everything around it had bent in on itself and plunged into...well, Dylan didn't know what. *It's all the colours of the rainbow,* Dylan thought, *all spinning around and mixing together. It's like one of the water chutes at the pool in Cardiff Bay, only multi-coloured and much bigger, but it's not going down it's going straight ahead.* "What is that?" he said aloud.

"Just how much knowledge has been lost from our time?" Artemis muttered. She looked down at Dylan. "It is a pathway, a shortcut between the worlds, it is how

30

sethundra travel between them. Come, we must make haste, this amount of power will draw eyes."

Without another word Baccus stepped towards the pathway, and then leapt at it. For an instant Baccus and Katy appeared to be frozen in mid-air, then, a fraction of a second later they seemed to stretch towards the opening to be pulled inside before vanishing. Artemis followed immediately, before Dylan could say a word she leapt at the opening. Dylan didn't notice a pause when Artemis leapt, one moment they were flying through the air towards the hole and the next they were being swept along a tunnel made up of a mad kaleidoscope of colours. They sped along at a terrifying speed, there were no twist or turns, it ran in a dead straight line. Dylan tried to watch the colours as they sped past, but within moments of starting he began to feel sick. The only thing that made him feel any better and settle the churning of his stomach was keeping his eyes fixed straight ahead.

He could see Baccus with Katy slung over his shoulder, the sethundra hanging in the centre of the multi-coloured chute, nothing holding him up as he sped along. He couldn't see his sister's face as her head was down, her dark hair covering it completely, but Dylan somehow had the impression that Katy was keeping her eyes tightly shut throughout the whole experience. *That's if she hasn't fainted,* he thought with no small amount of amusement.

It was only because he was staring ahead so intently that Dylan saw what happened next. Just ahead of Baccus he noticed a patch of darkness. He couldn't tell if it was moving towards them or they were moving towards it, but it was definitely getting bigger. He was about to ask Artemis what it was when Artemis herself cried out a warning. "Baccus, lookout!"

Baccus just had time to raise an arm in defence before the darkness struck. For an instant it took the form of another sethundra, possibly female, gowned completely in black, but Dylan couldn't be sure. It hit Baccus hard, knocking Katy from his grasp. Dylan had just enough time to see his sister disappear into the swirl of colours with a scream before Baccus collided with him and Artemis. The world became a spinning, swirling nightmare of tangled legs and arms, so much so that Dylan was sure he was going to be sick. He felt Artemis' grip on him begin to lessen and he reached out and held onto her as tightly as he could.

"Hold on!"

It was all he could do in response to Baccus' cry, the thought of doing anything else terrified him. His arms and fingers hurt from trying to keep his grasp on Artemis, he knew he couldn't hold on much longer. Suddenly there was a blinding flash of light and Dylan instinctively put his hand over his eyes realising too late his mistake. He lost his grip on Artemis and began to fall. He hit something solid and an explosion of pain erupted in his head. He thought he heard someone cry out, his vision was blurred, confused. Was he in a room full of people? He couldn't tell one way or another as the world, or wherever he was, clouded over and he tumbled down into darkness.

CHAPTER 4

"He's coming around, Captain."

"Keep your spears on him. If he makes a move, skewer him."

"But he's just a boy, Sir."

"So he appears to be, but judging by the manner of his arrival I'd rather not take any chances."

Dylan slowly opened his eyes, a throbbing pain pounding in the back of his skull and found himself lying on a hard, cold floor surrounded by several men wearing blue tabards over chainmail armour. In the centre of each tabard was some sort of golden bird of prey, wings outstretched and talons extended: as if about to grab a tasty and unfortunate, ten-year-old meal. Each man wore a long cloak of blue to match their tabards and a tall silver helmet on their heads that obscured most of their faces. These details were lost on Dylan in an instant however as he was more concerned that each and every man, bar one, was pointing a spear directly at him. The one man without a spear was dressed in what Dylan assumed to be an officer's uniform as his bird of prey clutched a spear in its talons. He was armed with a sword and glared at him as if he would like nothing better than to cut his head off there and then, a glare harshened by the nasty looking scar that ran down his left cheek.

"Identify yourself," the scarred one said, placing his sword lightly on Dylan's throat.

He felt numb with fear. *Where am I*, he thought, *what happened to Artemis and Baccus? Where's Katy?* An odd feeling of wanting his big sister around washed over him.

"Answer me, boy," Scarface growled, the sword pressing just a touch more firmly against him.

"Out of my way! Move aside at once!"

Some of the soldiers to Dylan's left were jostled to one side as the new speaker pushed his way through the armed men.

The speaker turned out to be a funny little man not much taller than Dylan himself. Bald, but for tufts of greying hair on either side of his head, and with thin spectacles perched on the end of his nose, he didn't look at all like the sort of person who should be jostling soldiers out of his way, though he did it all the same to great effect. He was dressed in ill-fitting brown coat and breeches that hung off his thin frame, like a scarecrow in a farmer's field. *He looks more like a librarian than someone who should be telling soldiers to move.*

"Captain," the short man said in a dry voice, "I hardly think a young boy is threat enough to warrant a sword at his throat."

"But the manner of his arrival, Professor…"

"Is remarkable indeed, but he is still a boy nonetheless. Please, put up your sword." The captain nodded and removed his sword from Dylan's throat, the other soldiers also visibly relaxed and withdrew their spears, although Dylan noted that the captain didn't actually sheath his sword. The little man knelt beside Dylan, eyeing him quizzically over the rim of his spectacles. "Now then," he said pushing his spectacles up his nose, "perhaps we should begin with your name."

"Dylan Howard."

"Well, Dylan Howard, you may call me Finian. Welcome to the court of Queen Arlana. May I help you up?"

"The court of Queen who?" Dylan asked as he took Finian's proffered hand and climbed to his feet.

"Arlana," said a new voice. The soldiers all snapped to attention as a woman stepped into view. If Dylan had to use one word to describe her he would have used 'regal'. She was everything that he imagined a queen should be, tall, beautiful, blonde hair perfectly arranged to hold the delicate, silver crown she wore, her gown was yellow with touches of lace at the collar and cuffs. Dylan wasn't sure if he was supposed to bow or kneel, the only thing he was sure of was if his grandmother learnt he was standing before a queen wearing nothing more than his superhero pyjamas then his life wouldn't be worth living. The queen looked at Dylan curiously. "I would greatly like to know how, and why, you have appeared in my court, Dylan Howard."

"It's just Dylan. Er…Your Majesty," he added following a sharp look from the scarred captain. He bobbed a hasty bow too, just to be sure of not causing offence. "I'm not really sure how I got here actually. It was something the sethundra did."

The reaction from everyone around him at mentioning the word sethundra was electric. The soldiers close to the queen instantly raised their weapons and began looking around nervously as if expecting an attack, Queen Arlana herself stiffened and drew a sharp intake of breath, whilst someone else in the room that he couldn't see due to the tight ring of soldiers surrounding him, screamed. Finian however merely looked at him thoughtfully.

"Professor," the queen said quietly, "I would appreciate your counsel…Professor!" she said more sharply when Finian didn't immediately respond.

"Oh, er, yes, Your Majesty. Now then, Dylan…erm, which world are you from?"

"He is not of Dainnor?" Arlana gasped.

"It would appear to be the logical assumption, Majesty. The manner of his arrival, his attire, and of course only a Guardian or Apprentice would be able to awaken a sethundra and young Dylan here certainly isn't Dainnor's Guardian or Apprentice. So, therefore, he must logically be a visitor from one of the other worlds. So, which world are you from, young man?

"Planet Earth," Dylan responded.

"That's not one of the Seven," the scarred captain said.

"Thank you, Captain," Finian said testily, "I am aware. Planet Earth is not a name I'm familiar with, Dylan, a local name perhaps. Is it known by another name?" Dylan shrugged that he didn't know. "Oh, well, presumably you are an Apprentice?"

"An apprentice what?" Dylan asked.

"Ah, well..."

"Professor," Queen Arlana interrupted, "the sethundra?"

"Oh yes, of course. The sethundra, Dylan, how many have been woken?"

"Two," Dylan said, "well no, three actually, but I haven't met her yet."

"The Stones preserve us," the queen gasped.

Finian fiddled with his spectacles nervously for a moment. "And where exactly are these sethundra now?"

Dylan didn't have to answer as at that moment there was a loud commotion from the far end of the room. The soldiers parted enough for him to get a view of what was going on. A pair of large ornate doors suddenly burst open and a gust of air wafted several blue banners that were hanging from the ceiling and bearing the same emblem as the soldiers. Two guardsmen went sliding along the floor to land in a heap in front of some finely dressed people and then Baccus strode into the room, twirling a staff much like the one Artemis had held earlier back at home. The finely dressed people began screaming and fighting each other to get away from him, whilst the soldiers surrounding Dylan and the queen nervously raised their weapons.

Baccus eyed them contemptuously. "Mortals," he snorted, "come then if you think you are able."

"That is enough, Baccus," Artemis said coming through the doorway after him. She didn't hold her own staff, it was a foot-long rod again, hanging from her belt. "I do not believe these humans to be our enemies. We have merely come for the boy."

Baccus nodded reluctantly, spun his staff and suddenly it matched Artemis', hanging from his own belt. *I really want one of those,* Dylan thought enviously.

Dylan was surprised when the diminutive professor, of all people, stepped forward to address the two creatures. "Greetings," he said, performing a bow, "you must forgive our lack of ceremony, but we had no prior warning of your arrival. I am Professor Finian, chief advisor to Her Majesty, Queen Arlana."

Artemis bowed back. "Greeting Professor Finian and to you also Queen Arlana. I am called Artemis and my companion is called Baccus. Have no fear, we accept the will of the Hearts."

"How do we know that," Queen Arlana demanded, "are we to just accept your word?"

"If we lie," Baccus growled, "then you would already be dead."

The queen blinked in surprise. Plainly she wasn't used to being addressed in such a tone, the soldiers shifted uncomfortably as if uncertain of what to do, Finian however, chuckled. "He does have a point, Majesty, there would at least have been an attempt on your life if they meant us harm. I am curious however as to what the circumstances are to bring two sethundra to this court. I trust you are responsible for the manner of young Dylan's arrival."

"I am afraid our arrival did not go as planned, Professor," Artemis said, "we were attacked along a pathway by the one we were pursuing. Baccus was caught off guard." Baccus eyed Artemis balefully. "It was not his fault," she said raising a placating hand, "we have slept for a long time, I myself did not notice the attack until it was too late."

"Who attacked you?" the professor asked.

"The sethundra, Melantha."

If Dylan thought there was an electric reaction to him mentioning sethundra it was nothing compared to the reaction of Artemis saying the name Melantha. Two finely dressed women and one even more finely dressed man keeled over in a dead faint, in fact for a moment he thought Queen Arlana might, one soldier threw up whatever he had last eaten and at least half the others looked as though they wished to do the same.

"H...how is that possible?" stammered Finian. "What Guardian would do such a thing?"

"It was no Guardian, Professor. This boy, an Apprentice, is the one responsible."

All eyes turned on Dylan making him feel even smaller than usual. He didn't understand half of what was being said, he had no idea where Katy was, he was all alone on a strange world and a sinking feeling in stomach told him he had done something very bad indeed. "I...I thought it was just a story," he said tears beginning to well in his eyes.

The scarred captain glared down at him, still clutching his sword. "You've doomed us all, boy, you've killed us, all of..."

"Peace, Captain Burgess," Queen Arlana commanded.

"But, Majesty, what this boy has done..."

"Is a terrible deed, one with far-reaching consequences I have no doubt, but I will not have a child attacked in my court. Finian, perhaps it would be wise to continue this discussion in a more private setting."

"Yes, yes of course," the professor nodded.

"We will use my private audience chambers. Captain, double the guard, both here in the palace and the city. And Captain, one word of sethundra in the streets and panic will spread. One word of Melantha...well I wouldn't like to think. See that no one who is not in this room is aware of what has happened here."

"Yes, Your Majesty." The captain finally sheathed his sword, saluted and began barking orders to his men, who in turn began rushing around with a sense of purpose, from running off to presumably double the guard, to picking up fainted, finely dressed people and cleaning up vomit.

The queen addressed the two sethundra. "Artemis, Baccus if you will follow me. Finian, bring the boy." With that she swept away, expecting to be obeyed, leaving the two sethundra, the professor and Dylan with little choice but to follow. Dylan was more than happy to leave, anything to get away from the accusing stares. *Where's Katy?* he thought, wanting his sister more than ever.

They left what appeared to be a throne room by a small door tucked behind a curtain, both Artemis and Baccus had to duck their heads to pass through. They then walked along a short corridor before entering another room via a pair of ornate double doors. This room had a large marble fireplace around which were arranged several uncomfortable looking chairs. The queen took the largest single chair, calmly arranging her skirt before looking to the others in the room. "Please be seated," she said.

Finian indicated a chair for Dylan to sit in whilst placing himself in a chair just to the right of the queen. Dylan was pleased to find that his chair wasn't as uncomfortable as he had expected. Artemis squeezed herself uncomfortably into one next to him, the chair not having been made for one of her size. Baccus merely eyed the chairs dubiously before leaning casually against the wall.

"Now," Arlana said, "can someone please explain to me exactly what is going on."

Artemis inclined her head. "For reasons unknown, the Apprentice, Dylan, has woken three sethundra, I can only assume as he was in the presence of his Guardian that it was a Testing gone awry."

"His Guardian," the queen said incredulously, "if his Guardian was present then why is his Guardian not here? I hardly think this boy is capable of dealing with one of the most dangerous sethundra to ever live on his own."

"We did bring her, Queen Arlana, but she was lost on the Pathway when Melantha attacked. However, there is nothing to fear, she did reach Dainnor, a Guardian, however young should be able to find her way to us without too much difficulty."

Dylan still didn't really understand what everyone was talking about, but he began to get the sinking feeling that his sister's identity had been lost in translation.

"She did not strike me as being particularly capable," Baccus argued.

Artemis shook her head. "I admit she did seem a little unbalanced by our presence, however, I do not believe that standards could have fallen so far. She must have some skills."

"Erm," Finian spoke up, "which world have you all actually travelled from, may I ask? Dylan mentioned, Planet Earth."

"That name is not familiar to me, Professor Finian, but we travelled from Terra."

"Terra?" Finian raised an eyebrow. "Interesting, very interesting."

Terra, Dylan thought, *since when has Earth been called Terra?*

"How so, Professor?" Arlana asked.

"Well, Your Majesty, no contact has been had with Terra since...well, since the Casting. It is thought that they may have retreated from use of the Stones, possibly as a consequence of what is known as The Terran's Sin, but I would have thought that Dylan's Guardian would have transported herself here by now."

Realization suddenly dawned on Dylan and he blurted out, "You think Katy's a wizard?!"

"Wizard?" Arlana said curiously. "What is a wizard?"

"An old term, Your Majesty," Finian said, "not often used and usually by people who have no real notion of what it is they're speaking of. The common term is a "magi", Dylan."

"But Katy isn't one," Dylan said, "she's just a girl, we have to find her."

"Forgive me, Dylan, but are you saying that, um, Katy, *isn't* your Guardian?"

"No, she's my sister, she looks after me sometimes, like a parent if that's what you mean."

"That is not what we mean," Artemis said curtly.

"You said she was your Guardian," Baccus growled.

41

"You didn't say what you meant," Dylan snapped back, "you should have said what you meant."

"Then who is the Guardian?" Finian asked.

"I don't know. I don't even know what a Guardian is. What do they guard anyway?"

"You cannot be serious," Baccus said.

The queen lent forward in her chair and smiled gently. "Dylan, how did you know how to wake the sethundra? Who taught you?"

"It was just a story my Grandad told me. I didn't know it was true."

"Grandad?" the queen mused. "Your Grandfather?" Dylan nodded. "Could he then be the Guardian, Finian?"

"Impossible," the professor said shaking his head, "Guardians are never called from the same family; well, not within the same lifetime anyway. There are records of two from the same bloodline here on Dainnor, but there was nearly five hundred years between them and the claim has never been proven. No, I find it more likely that this boy's grandfather told him a story he had just heard once, perhaps passed down from generation to generation and just by chance Dylan happened to have been called."

"Called by who?" Dylan wanted to know.

"Perhaps we should discuss this with the boy at another time, Your Majesty, when I have had time to consider all the facts. Maybe then we could come up with a best course of action on how to proceed."

"Of course, Professor," Arlana said, "but do not take too much time, Melantha will not wait long before she acts."

"But what about my sister," Dylan said desperately, "where is Katy?"

42

"We do not know, Dylan Howard," Artemis said, "the only thing we do know for certain is that she is on Dainnor."

"But she's all alone, we have to find her"

"Searching an entire world for one single person when we have no clue of where to begin is no easy task, Dylan Howard. Melantha must be our priority. I am afraid that unless your sister manages to finds us then she is lost."

Lost. The word hit Dylan like a bucket of iced water. Katy was lost. He was trapped on a world he knew nothing about, surrounded by strangers and odd creatures from stories. It was all too much for the young boy. He wanted to go home, but had no idea how to get there, he wanted his father, his grandparents, anyone with him that he knew, but there was no one, he was all alone. And so, with that knowledge, Dylan began to cry.

CHAPTER 5

It was the singing of birds that first stirred her from her slumber. A perfectly pleasant sound considering the nightmare Katy had been having. Something to do with two enormous, ugly giants who had loomed over her laughing, waving staffs and thrusting her inside a giant kaleidoscope, the colours of which made her want to vomit up everything she had ever eaten. At least she thought that was what the nightmare had been about. She wasn't so sure now, the memory was beginning to fade.

She wondered why the bird song sounded so close. *I must have left my bedroom window open* she thought sleepily, *they're perched on the branches of the tree just outside.* They often did at Nan and Grandad's house.

She shifted her body to try and get a more comfortable position. Something didn't feel quite right. Her bed felt unusually hard and lumpy; in fact, the more she thought about it the more awake she became and the more un-bed-like it felt.

Katy opened her eyes and squinted up at what she expected to be her bedroom ceiling, but found only more confusion. Green leaves, the sun shining through them, hung before her face. She looked around her in total bewilderment. There was nothing before her, or on either side, but leaves and branches. She sat up with a start, but then her balance shifted and she fell from the tree with a scream, several feet to the ground below.

Winded, bruised, scratched in about a dozen places, but fortunately with nothing broken, Katy pushed herself to her feet, brushing herself down as she stared at the scene before her, trying to make sense of what she was looking at. She was in a wood, but she had no idea where. She prided herself on knowing the woods in the Vale of Glamorgan around her grandparents' house very well, but these were nothing like those. But an even bigger mystery to Katy was how she had actually got there, wherever 'there' was. The last thing she remembered was arguing with Dylan in the back garden. He had said the rhyme that Grandad had taught him, which she still could not remember, there had been a voice, she had looked up, and there had been...something.

But that had been a dream, hadn't it?

She tried to think, tried to sort through the jumble in her head. There had been a woman, but she was too tall in her memory, she was beautiful, but there was something wrong about her, something alien. Dylan had been talking to the woman, and then there had been a man, but again, too tall, too alien looking. One thing she did remember clearly was the fear. She'd been frozen with it, unable to move, to think, to act. Dylan hadn't been afraid, well not as afraid as she had been anyway. She felt ashamed for not doing something, not getting Dylan away, she was the eldest after all, it was her job to protect him. *But from what,* she asked herself, *it had just been a dream. Then how have I ended up here?*

She took a few steps to see if she could find something that she recognized, something that would point her towards home, but she had only taken a few paces before she realised that home could be in any direction at all, and she could have very well chosen the wrong one.

She could hear her mother's voice in her head. *If you don't have to act immediately then don't. Always take the time to think things through. Weigh up all of the alternatives and the correct path will present itself to you.*

Such an odd thing for a mother to say to her six-year-old daughter, but then her mother had often said odd things, at least she had when she became pregnant with Dylan, she'd been a lot more fun before that. It had been one of the last things she had ever said to Katy, just a few days after Dylan had been born. She remembered crying herself to sleep that night, she never knew how, but Katy had known that her mother would leave them that night. And in the morning she had been gone. No word, no note, just gone. For perhaps the millionth time Katy asked herself why her mother had gone, but as always no answer was forthcoming. All she had was the memory of her beautiful, sad face and her strange words of advice. *Dylan will need you, he will depend on you, you must protect him and keep him safe.*

She shook her head, clearing the memory, and tried to think of what to do next. If she was here in the wood, then maybe Dylan was too. "Dylan!" There was no reply, just the sound of birdsong and a gentle breeze rustling through the leafy canopy above her head. "Dylan!" she cried again, but still there was no answer.

Yelling was obviously getting her nowhere. She was just about to try picking a direction and walking until she found a road or something to show her the right way, when the obvious hit her like a slap in the face. "Climb a tree, you idiot!" Of course, if she got as high as she could then maybe she would spot a recognizable landmark. The one she had fallen out of appeared tall enough for the task so she grabbed the nearest branch and began hauling herself up.

She had always been good at climbing and indeed most things physical. She usually ended up on most of the sport teams in school, but whilst that was a guaranteed ticket to acceptance for a boy, for a girl in her school it guaranteed her to be all but a social outcast. She was pretty, she supposed, at least one boy in her school had asked her out once anyway, although at the earliest opportunity he had tried putting his tongue down her throat and his hand up her top. A little piece of advice from her father had swiftly put an end to that idea. It really was quite remarkable what a simple knee to the groin could achieve.

It wasn't long before she got as high as she dared, any higher and she felt sure the branches wouldn't hold her weight but, with a little straining of her neck and pushing a few branches and leaves out of her way, she found she could have a good look around. Although it brought her no comfort to do so.

It was a beautiful warm, sunny day and she could see clearly in all directions. To her right and straight ahead of her there was nothing but the tops of more trees, behind her she could see snow topped mountains in the distance as part of what looked to be some vast range and to her left the trees extended for mile upon mile before ending in what appeared to be a brown haze. She had no idea what it was, but one thing was clear beyond a shadow of doubt, she was no longer in the Vale of Glamorgan. In fact, she was certain she wasn't even in the same country anymore.

Tears welled up in Katy's eyes, as she wondered where she was...and began to sob. She started shaking so much she nearly fell from the tree again.

Take hold of yourself, her mother's voice came in her head, *tears solve nothing. You must be strong.* Katy's mother never liked her crying, she had always swiftly put

a stop to it, but the advice served Katy well at that moment. Taking a deep, steadying breath she managed to climb safely back down to the ground, but when she arrived the tears flowed more freely than ever. She buried her head in her hands, leaning against the trunk as she
sobbed.

"Are you alright?"

Startled at the sudden voice, Katy spun around to face the speaker, but no amount of motherly advice could have prepared her for the creature that now stood before her.

Her first thought was that it was some poor man with a horrible disfigurement, his brown eyes were too dark, his round ears were too large, his huge, flat nose and mouth appeared to be one single piece, protruding slightly from the rest of his dark face. A mop of unruly, curly brown hair flopped over his forehead and around his massive, muscled shoulders. There was something bovine about his features, but the more Katy stared in horror the more she came to realise that this was no disfigured human. It stood taller than any man she had ever met and clutched in its hands a huge axe that Katy felt sure could chop down the tree she had just climbed from with one clean stroke. She didn't want to think about what it could do to her.

Too terrified to scream or to cry for help, Katy began to back away from the nightmare that stood before her. Unbidden, a memory formed in her mind, a memory of sitting on her grandfather's lap, having a story before bedtime. *Minotaurs don't actually have the head of a bull, Katy,* Grandad had said, *but there is something bull-like about them. So a myth was born and man created an image that was untrue.* It made no difference to Katy what minotaurs were supposed to look like at that

48

moment; they weren't real, they were just a story and therefore could not be standing before her watching her back away with a puzzled expression on its face.

I'm dreaming, any moment now I'm going to wake up! Please let me wake up, please, please, please!

She stepped back and Katy's foot unexpectedly met resistance, causing her to lose her balance. Whether it was a rock or a hidden root she couldn't say, all that she did know was that she was falling again. She hit the ground with a bump. The minotaur transferred its axe to its left hand and took a step towards Katy, its right hand reaching out towards her, a hand so big it would completely cover Katy's head. And it was at that precise moment the teenager rediscovered her voice and screamed. The minotaur took a step back looking startled by the sound. Katy screamed again and again, louder and louder, the creature moving further and further away from her.

"What did you do?"

The angry shout came from a blonde haired young man dressed in green running through the trees towards them. *He's gorgeous,* Katy thought distractedly before suddenly remembering there was a seven-foot minotaur standing a few feet away, holding a gigantic axe.

The minotaur turned a terrifying glare upon the young man. "I didn't do anything," he growled in a deep base voice. "I tried to help her and she just started screaming."

"You must've done something; girls don't start screaming for no reason." The young man rested a hand casually on the hilt of a long sword hanging at his waist.

Swords, minotaurs, Katy wondered, *where the hell am I?*

"Well this one started screaming for no reason. I only asked her if she was alright."

49

"Then she probably knows the reputation of one of your kind."

"My kind?! Mind your tongue, human."

"Mind your own, *minotaur*, you stand in the presence of a prince in his own lands."

"You too stand in the presence of a prince and my own lands are not so far away, in case you've forgotten."

The young man gripped his sword tightly as did the minotaur his axe. Katy felt certain it was about to come to blows when the sound of horses approaching broke through the tension. All three of them looked in the direction of the sound to see a company of riders coming towards them through the trees. All but one were armed men, soldiers by the look of them, dressed in green much like the young man beside her and armed with bows and short swords. The other stood out from the rest and couldn't have looked more out of place if she had tried. It was a woman, a few years older than Katy wearing a dress that looked more suitable for a royal ball than riding through a wood surrounded by armed men. And the word beauty didn't quite cover how she looked. *All the makeup and hairstylist in the world couldn't make me look half as good as that,* Katy thought enviously as the woman reined in and regarded them all with a cool, superior expression.

Her gaze lingered on Katy a moment, before turning back to the young man. "Your Highness," she smiled and dipped her head a fraction in his direction, "we heard raised voices. I do hope everything is in order and you were not about to start a war by squabbling with Prince Hrolf."

The woman's tone was condescending, but even so she expected the young man to be ogling her as most young, and indeed old men, would, but instead he glared at her with even more dislike than he did at the minotaur. "I have been instructed by the Queen to listen to your council, Oriana, not your insolent tone."

"Of course, Your Highness, please forgive me." This time Oriana went so far as to bow in her saddle, although Katy noted that little had changed in the way she addressed the prince. "However, I do believe your mother also instructed you to put aside your prejudices and make peace with the minotaurs. Forgive me, Conall, but it almost looked as though you were about to come to blows," her gaze settled back on Katy, "over a girl."

The prince ignored the woman this time and turned to one of the soldiers, this one older than the others, a grizzled looking veteran. "I thought I ordered you to remain in the camp, Captain."

"My apologies, Your Highness," the man replied, "Lady Oriana said she was going for a ride and if I intended to stop her then I would have to sit on her. I could hardly let her go without an escort."

"Indeed you could not, Dunham. Though next time you have my permission to sit on her." Oriana laughed at the thought whilst Dunham looked a little ill. Conall then turned his attention back to the minotaur. "Prince Hrolf, please forgive my hasty words. No harm appears to have befallen the girl, my accusation was inexcusable."

Hrolf regarded the young man a moment before nodding his huge head. "Apology excepted."

"With regards to the girl," Oriana said from her saddle, "is anyone going to help her up, possibly ask her who she is and maybe find out why she is wandering these woods alone so far from any settlement?"

The prince's cheeks reddened a little in embarrassment as he held out a hand to pull Katy to her feet.

"I assumed she was one of your camp," Hrolf said.

"In that attire," said Oriana, "I think we would have noticed her before now."

Katy looked down at her clothes, a short sleeved top and black jeans. What was the woman talking about? The jeans weren't that tight.

The young man smiled at her. "We appear to have forgotten our introductions, my name is Conall, and you are?"

"Katy," she said in a quiet voice. "I'm sorry, but where am I?"

"About one hundred miles south of Aldarris, roughly fifty miles north of the border to the minotaur kingdom." The name Aldarris rang a bell in Katy's mind but left her none the wiser. She shook her head in confusion. "And where are you from, My Lady?"

"I...I don't understand."

"It's a simple enough question, child," Oriana laughed, "where have you come from?"

"I'm not a child," Katy shot back at Oriana.

"Then answer the question. Where are you from?"

"My grandparents' house near the village, Carreg-y-galon, in the Vale of Glamorgan. It's in Wales," she added when this fell upon blank stares.

"Where's Wales?" Hrolf asked.

"The same place it's always been," she snapped, national pride momentarily making her forget she was talking to a minotaur, "in Great Britain." More blank expressions. "The United Kingdom? Planet Earth?"

That got a reaction out of all there. The soldiers all began muttering to each other, Hrolf nodded to himself as if the whole situation suddenly made perfect sense to him, Oriana stared at her as if nothing else in the world mattered at all, but Conall looked at her with a face full of wonder and excitement. "You're from one of the other worlds?"

52

"Other worlds? Where am I?"

"You don't know? You're on Dainnor."

Katy felt as if Conall had just slapped her face. Suddenly the name, Aldarris, that had rang a bell inside her head made sense. *Aldarris, capital of the kingdom of Lors. Bloody hell, I'm in one of Grandad's stories!* She was suddenly assaulted with memories of the previous evening, everything came crashing back. "Dylan woke the sethundra," she said in amazement.

Conall, Hrolf and the soldiers all drew their weapons, eyes searching the woods nervously, as if expecting an attack. As for Oriana, she merely stared at Katy so intently her eyes could have bored holes into her head. "Who is Dylan?" she said quietly, in a tone that Katy did not like at all.

Katy raised her chin defiantly, trying her best not to wither under the stare. "My brother"

Oriana held her gaze before she began barking orders. "We will return to the camp at once! Put up your weapons, fools! If the sethundra intended to attack you would already be dead."

"Oriana," Conall snarled angrily, "need I remind you again that I command here not you."

Oriana's eyes blazed as she spat angrily at the prince, "Then perhaps you could advise us all on how to deal with awakened sethundra, Your Highness. Perhaps you could hit them with your little sword? I have no time for your foolishness, Conall, I must consult with my Order. As you appear to have forgotten your horse you can walk back to the camp with Prince Hrolf. Do try not to start a war. Captain, bring the girl!"

Without waiting to see whether she would be obeyed Oriana spun her horse around and galloped off back through the trees. The Captain, Dunham, waited for

Conall's angry nod before trotting up to Katy, reaching down and hauling her up into the saddle behind him.

He was just telling half the soldiers to remain behind with the two princes when Conall interrupted. "No, Dunham, Prince Hrolf and I will be safe enough. Take the girl back to the camp, see that no harm comes to her. Do not allow Oriana to speak to her until my arrival."

Dunham saluted and he and the rest of the soldiers rode off after Oriana with Katy bouncing uncomfortable behind the soldier. She just had time to catch a glance at a worried looking Conall before she lost sight of him and the minotaur in the trees.

CHAPTER 6

He had no idea how long he had cried but Dylan was exhausted, struggling to keep his eyes open by the time he had finished. It had been the queen who held him the longest. In the instant that the tears had begun to fall she had lost her commanding presence and wrapped her arms around him in a motherly embrace. Well, grandmotherly to Dylan, he had never been held by his mother in his memory, but the queen held him in the same way his grandmother would whenever he was upset, stroking his hair soothingly.

At some point he got passed on to another woman, dressed in what looked like servant's clothes, who he hadn't noticed entering the room. As he moved over he saw that his tears had left a wet patch on Queen Arlana's dress. He had mumbled an apology and received a light kiss for his good manners.

His mouth stretched open into a huge yawn as he rubbed at his eyes and he looked around to find that the others had all gone.

"There now, My Lord," the new woman said kindly, "feeling better are we? Why, you look tired enough to fall asleep right where you sit." She stood up from her seat and held a hand out. "Come now, My Lord, I think it's time we found you a room of your own so you can have a nap."

Dylan took her hand, taking an instant liking to the woman, only partly because she kept calling him "My Lord". She had a kind, smiling face, so much so that Dylan had a hard time trying to imagine her frowning. Bretta, for he soon discovered that was her name, did not stop talking as she led him through a maze of marble corridors. Dylan quickly gave up trying to follow what Bretta was talking about: it involved a lot of names of people and places that he had never heard of and she jumped from one topic to the next so often that even if Dylan had heard of anything he still doubted he would have followed the continual stream of chatter. He decided to study his surroundings instead. As horrible as everything was with Katy being missing, he was in another world after all.

He decided that he was in a palace rather than a castle. Grandad had often taken him to castles and even the ones that didn't look as though they were about to fall down were cold and draughty places of bare stone. This building was much finer; more what he thought Buckingham Palace must be like. The floors were white marble and polished so finely that Dylan could see his reflection walking along with them when he looked down. Tall arched windows lined the walls with beautiful tapestries and splendid suits of armour standing between. He tried to get a look out of the windows as they walked past, but the only thing he could tell was that it was day outside. He could see nothing of the city that must be out there and, judging by the speed the chattering Bretta marched, he doubted he was going to get a close enough to a window to get a good look.

I wonder if anyone else has ever travelled here, he thought curiously, *I suppose someone must have as everyone seems to have heard of my world.* A thought occurred to him so suddenly that he blurted it out aloud before he could stop himself. "I wonder if Grandad has ever been here?"

"I find that unlikely, My Lord," Bretta answered without appearing to even pause from whatever topic she had been talking about. "The way I understand it no one has visited Dainnor in hundreds of years, maybe

56

even thousands. Not that I know about these things you must understand, I'm just a serving maid. But the way my pa taught me is that you can't travel without a sethundra anyway. There are stories that the Guardians could do that sort of thing back in the old days, but if they could then why don't they, that's what I say. Not that anyone here knows who our Guardian is of course, well some say they do, though I'm not so sure, it don't seem right, surely a Guardian should be bigger, stronger…"

"What are the Guardians?" Dylan interrupted.

"What are the Guardians? What are the Guardians? Well I heard tell once that the Terrans were a funny bunch, not that I think that of course, My Lord. It's like my pa always told me, "never judge one by the actions of another", he was full of stuff like that was my pa, but I would've thought you'd know what the Guardians are at least? Especially as you go travelling with sethundra. But never mind, if you don't know then you don't know. Now here's how I understand it, they might do more, but that's not for the likes of me to question, but Guardians look after the Heart Stones."

"What's a Heart Stone?"

He had moved several paces down the corridor before Dylan realised that Bretta was no longer beside him. He turned to see her standing outside a door, staring at him, mouth agape. "What's a… what's a…" She was in such shock that she couldn't get the words out. She shook her head in amazement. "The Stones preserve us. Your room, My Lord," she pushed open the door and curtsied rather unsteadily.

Dylan walked back to Bretta and stuck his head through the open doorway and gasped. The room was huge, at least three times as big as his grandparents' room. It was dominated by a massive four-poster bed that he felt sure would accommodate his entire family.

"It's all for me?"

"Of course, My Lord."

Dylan ran to one of the tall arched windows that stood on either side of the bed and gaped in wonder as he got his first proper look at a new world. A city like nothing he had ever seen lay before him. Tall towers of white stone rose majestically from a sea of red tiled rooftops, broken occasionally by magnificent looking palaces, each one trying to outdo the others in grandeur, and atop them all flew banners bearing the golden bird of prey, fluttering proudly in the breeze. Directly below him was a walled courtyard, where smartly dressed guards and servants rushed about on whatever errands were set for them, some moving to and from the tall golden gates that led out of the palace grounds and into the city. To his left, far in the distance, rolling hills could be seen beyond the city; to his right he could make out the masts of great ships that must have sat in a harbour beyond his vision. Dylan longed to go out and explore, he was about to ask if he could, when he suddenly remembered his attire. People did not go exploring cities in their superhero pyjamas.

"Can I get you anything else, My Lord?" Bretta asked.

Dylan looked down at himself ruefully. "Not unless you can find me some lord's clothes to go with this room."

"Very good, My Lord," Bretta said, curtsying before exiting the room and shutting the door behind her.

Grinning at the wonder of it all, Dylan turned away from the door and continued looking out of the window. He thought he probably should try to get some sleep, technically it was his bedtime after all, at least it was at home, here it appeared to be the middle of the day. Through the window he caught glimpses of people moving about cobbled streets, ships masts pulling in and out of the harbour, at one point a group of men on horseback, looking resplendent in their armour and blue capes, each holding a long white lance held at precisely the same angle, rode through the courtyard and out into the city. His thoughts began to drift back to home. It was the school holidays there and he was supposed to write an essay for his new school about what he had done. Dylan doubted very much that his teacher would believe him if he actually told the truth. Perhaps he could get Grandad to try convincing his old teacher, Mr Jones, that he really had travelled to another world, they were good friends after all. *It would be a holiday to brag about. Way better than going to America or Spain like the other kids do. At least it would be if I knew where Katy was.* He still found that thought strange, he hated Katy and the way she always bossed him around. Didn't he?

He jumped when he heard a polite cough behind him and turned to see the funny, little Professor, Finian, with Artemis and Baccus standing to either side of him; Artemis regarding him with interest, Baccus wearing his customary scowl. *This room seems a lot smaller with those two standing in it.*

"Dylan," the professor began, "might we have a word."

Dylan nodded and turned from the view outside to sit on the window sill, his feet dangling over the edge whilst Finian jumped up to sit on the bed. Dylan was amused that the professor's feet dangled too. The two sethundra had to make do with finding a place to sit on the floor. He found his eyes beginning to feel heavy again, but he forced them to stay open and tried to concentrate on what the little man was saying.

"Tell me, Dylan," Finian said, "what exactly do you know about the sethundra?"

"Only what Grandad told me, they've always been asleep and you can't see them…oh, and I know how to wake them up."

"Evidently," Baccus muttered.

"Erm, yes, indeed," Finian scratched his chin thoughtfully. "And earlier you claimed it was your grandfather who taught you how to do it?"

Dylan nodded. "Grandad taught me a rhyme, a spell I suppose, but the words don't really matter, you can say anything really, they're just to remind you of what to do, to help you practice."

"A Focus."

"What? I mean pardon?" Dylan asked, remembering his manners.

Finian smiled. "What you were describing is called a "Focus". It's used in the training of magi."

"Oh, well, he didn't say that, but it sounds like it might be the same thing, but anyway, he then told me how to do it properly, by relaxing and breathing and imagining a light and letting it come towards me."

"That proves it then," Baccus growled, "his grandfather must be the Guardian."

Finian shook his head. "Impossible. The Stones do not call people from the same family, "Heart of Stone"; remember the Terran's Sin."

Heart of Stone? That tickled something in the back of Dylan's mind, but it was gone before he could grasp it.

"But he appeared to be doing a Testing, Professor," Artemis argued. "If he is not Terra's Guardian why would he be teaching Dylan Howard how to wake us?"

"He could very well be a magi, even one actively looking for someone who has been called, but I find it more likely that this man is doing no more than telling his grandson a story he was probably told by his own grandfather. Tell me, Dylan, have you ever before witnessed your grandfather casting?"

"Do you mean doing magic?"

"Yes, yes magic," Finian said waving his arms impatiently.

"No, never."

"You see; what grandfather wouldn't delight in performing feats to entertain his grandchild. No, this man is not Terra's Guardian, he probably isn't even a magi."

"Then it was an accident, the boy was without fault," Artemis said.

"Indeed, so with no clue on how to find Terra's Guardian then I must myself educate the boy enough to be able to send him back to Terra safely."

"You're a wiz...er, a magi?" Dylan asked.

"Yes I am, young Dylan, that and more. I am in fact Dainnor's Guardian. Most people are aware of this, or suspect at least, but even so, it is not a thing to be talked about openly. Do you understand? You must keep this thing a secret." Dylan nodded. "Good, boy. Now, I suggest you get some sleep, you look just about ready to fall off that window sill. Come now, into bed. Tomorrow we will begin your training."

Dylan found he was too tired to argue and got down from the window, crawling into bed as Finian moved towards the door with the two sethundra.

"And Melantha," Baccus said, "what are we to do about her?"

"Well finding her would be the first course of action," the professor said as he opened the door, "I'll leave that to the two of you, but be careful as..."

Dylan didn't hear the rest of the conversation as his eyes slid shut and he fell into a deep sleep filled with dreams of his grandfather performing magic tricks for an audience of excited sethundra.

CHAPTER 7

Katy was glad the ride through the woods didn't last long as holding onto a soldier upon the back of a trotting horse was not the most comfortable experience of her life. But any relief that the short journey had ended vanished the moment she caught sight of their destination. Tents dotted a wide clearing in a seemingly haphazard fashion, mainly dull greens and browns, but a large blue one stood proudly at its centre, a banner bearing a golden bird flying atop it. A wide path of hard-packed earth sat on the edge of the camp and disappeared off into the trees with several empty carts lined up along what appeared to pass for a road upon Dainnor. A stream meandered into the trees on the other side of the camp where several men and women wearing blue livery were filling buckets from it. But it was the figures with them that filled Katy with despair. Minotaur servants mingled with the humans, apparently performing similar chores and where human soldiers rested or tended to weapons and armour, fierce looking minotaurs did the same. Huge, scarred beasts that made Hrolf look like a cuddly, friendly giant in comparison. One minotaur had been terrifying enough for Katy, a whole camp of them made her want to curl up somewhere and weep. To make matters worse, she immediately sensed a tension within the camp. A look here, an unnecessarily wide berth there. The humans and the minotaurs were travelling together, but many of them weren't happy about it.

Dunham swung down from the saddle and held up a helping hand for Katy which she gratefully accepted. She slid down off the horse, her feet landing lightly upon springy turf and nervously eyed a particularly large brute armed with a spear as he lumbered past.

"Don't worry, Miss," Dunham said. He nodded towards a group of minotaurs at her questioning look. "It'll take time for old wounds to heal, but they're as committed to peace as we are."

"You've been at war then?"

Dunham chuckled. "With the minotaurs? We've been fighting so long most of us can't even remember why we ever started."

"So what's making you stop?"

"Three years ago there was a battle, a pretty messy one at that. Our King, Corann, Prince Conall's own father and Conall's elder brother, Conyn died. So did both of Prince Hrolf's brothers; a tragic, bloody affair. And for what? Some disputed border miles from any of either side's settlements. Queen Arlana sent an envoy to ask for peace and now here we are. It seems the minotaurs are as sick of war as we are. At least most of the clans are. Best you stay nearby though, Miss; until the prince returns anyway. Oh, and er...probably best if you keep your origins and how you got here to yourself too." The soldier gave her a friendly nod and began tending to his horse.

Katy walked about a bit in an effort to ease the soreness out of her legs, heeding Dunham's advice about staying nearby. She actually found herself to be more worried about meeting the woman, Oriana than the minotaurs. She had not liked the way Oriana had looked at her one bit. Fortunately, she could see no sign of her,

Katy supposed she must be inside one of the more colourful tents that were dotted around the place.

"I haven't seen you in the camp before."

Katy spun at the sound of the voice to find, to her despair, another minotaur looking down on her. *How do such large creatures keep managing to sneak up on me like that?* This one was female, and she was smiling at her pleasantly.

"Er, I...I'm new," Katy stammered.

"I thought so," the minotaur said clapping her huge hands with delight, "humans are so difficult to tell apart, but I've been trying so very hard. Are you pretty?"

"What?" Katy looked indignantly at the soldiers chuckling nearby.

"Sorry, I didn't mean to be rude, I just want to learn as much about humans as I can before we reach the city. It's so difficult to tell what's what with humans. Are you pretty?"

"Well, I, er..."

"Yes, Freya," Dunham said, "she's pretty."

Again the soldiers laughed. "Very pretty," one called out. "Aye, and the prince seemed to think so too," said another, "going by the way he was looking at her."

Katy couldn't help but grin at that. *The prince thinks I'm pretty?* "Are...are you pretty?" she said aloud. It felt like a stupid thing to be asking a minotaur, but she could think of nothing else to say.

The minotaur looked away shyly a moment. "Oh, I don't think so. At least no one has ever really said I am anyway. Apart from my father," she smiled sadly, "but I don't think he really counts."

Katy unexpectedly found herself warming to the huge creature. Far from being fierce she looked quite gentle, at least in comparison to the other minotaurs she had seen. She studied her face thoughtfully for a moment.

65

There was an odd delicateness to her features that hadn't been present in Hrolf's, her eyes were large and brown her skin dark and smooth, her hair fell in glossy, black waves across her shoulders and down her back. *A pleasant face,* she thought. "Well I'm no expert, you're only the second minotaur I've ever met, but you look pretty to me."

The minotaur's smile widened considerably. "I'm Freya," she said.

"I'm Katy," Katy smiled back.

"Could we be friends," Freya asked, "I've tried making human friends but without much success, and I would so much like to have a human friend."

"I...I suppose so." Freya's grin grew even more. *I've just made friends with a minotaur. I wasn't expecting that when I got up this morning.*

"So who was the first minotaur you met?"

"Oh...er, Hrolf, Prince Hrolf, in the woods earlier with Prince Conall."

Freya began smoothing down her plain, brown dress, looking around a little nervously. "Oh, Prince Hrolf. He's handsome, very handsome."

"Do you like him then?"

"Oh yes, but he's never even looked at me. Not that he would. I'm just a servant and he's a prince. Conall's handsome too, isn't he?"

"Yes, I suppose so," Katy replied as casually as she could manage.

"I hear some of the women in the camp talking about him, they all like him." Just then Katy saw Oriana emerge from one of the tents. She surveyed the camp until she spotted Dunham and his men, her eyes quickly locked onto Katy and she began striding purposefully towards them. "Is she pretty?" Freya whispered.

"Yes, very."

66

"That's a pity. I don't like her at all."

That makes two of us.

Dunham moved closer to Katy and Freya, his hand resting easily on the pommel of his sword though Katy could see nervousness in the soldier's eyes. "My Lady Oriana," he said as she drew close, "is there something I can help you with?"

"I doubt that, Captain," Oriana replied without taking her eyes off Katy's face, "I would speak with our guest."

"I'm sure that can be arranged with the prince when he arrives back at the camp."

"I see no reason to await his arrival, anything the girl can tell me I will pass on to His Highness."

"I have my orders, My Lady."

Oriana turned her gaze onto the soldier. He held it well, though his discomfort was palpable. "Very well," Oriana finally said, "we will await the arrival of the prince." She strode away without another word, disappearing off into the camp. As soon as she had vanished from view, Dunham visibly relaxed. He nodded to Katy and Freya as he went back to tending his horse.

"Why is everyone so scared of her?" Katy asked the minotaur.

"She's a shaman, or magi as you humans call them. Quite powerful I believe."

"You mean she casts spells?"

Freya looked at her curiously for a moment. She was about to speak when the two princes marched into the camp. Katy couldn't help but notice that they walked several feet apart from each other and the silence between them was almost tangible. Spotting them, Conall began making his way in their direction, Hrolf following behind. Katy gave a start as Freya grabbed her arm with one of her huge hands just a little too tightly to be comfortable.

"He's coming over here," Freya said, breathing heavily in excitement.

Conall smiled warmly at her, and Katy felt her heart
skip a beat. He then turned to Dunham. "Any trouble, Captain?"

"Nothing I couldn't handle, Highness."

"Good man. Get your men fed and rested, I expect a long ride in the morning."

Dunham saluted and began seeing to his men. Conall frowned at Freya's grip on Katy's arm. "Is there a problem here?"

"N...no, Your Highness," Freya said snatching her hand away, much to Katy's relief. She had begun to get pins and needles. "I was just talking to my new friend."

"New friend?" The prince raised an eyebrow. "With a minotaur?"

"Yes, Freya's nice," Katy said defensively, "she made me feel very welcome. And Dunham tells me that you and the minotaurs are at peace now."

"It's a work in progress. Forgive me...Freya? But I meant no disrespect. We must all try to be friends now."

"Oh I hope we can, Prince Conall. War's terrible. My father died in the same battle yours did."

"I'm sorry to hear that, Freya," Conall smiled sadly. "If you will excuse us, I must speak with Katy alone."

Freya did a rough approximation of a curtsy, grinned at Katy and walked off into the camp, trying her best not to stare at Hrolf who in turn appeared to look everywhere other than at Freya.

"Katy," Conall said, "we need to talk, alone."

"Not alone," Hrolf said, "I have questions of my own." Conall turned a glare on the minotaur. "The sethundra concern my people as much as yours, Conall."

Conall held the minotaur's gaze before nodding his consent, then leading them to the blue tent in the centre of the camp. Katy followed Conall inside; Hrolf, uncomfortably close behind her, had to duck to get through the entry flap.

The interior was comfortable, neat and tidy. A made-up camp bed lay at the far end and a writing desk with chair sat in the centre, two other stools sat near the wall of the tent. Conall offered Katy the chair whilst he himself sat on the edge of the bed, Hrolf who hadn't been offered a seat sat cross-legged on the floor.

"Tell me everything you know about the sethundra," Conall said.

Katy shook her head. "I don't really know anything about them, only that my brother woke them up."

"Them?" Hrolf asked, startled. "How many have been woken?"

"Two, no three, at least they said there was a third, but I didn't see the other one."

"And where are they now?" Conall asked.

"I don't know. Everything went blurry, it made me feel sick, so I closed my eyes. There was some shouting, and I woke up here. Please, we have to find my little brother, we have to find Dylan."

"We will, we will," Conall said soothingly, "but first we need to know where to look."

"We should speak to the Guardian," Hrolf said. "The Guardian will know how to find the sethundra. Who is it?"

"That's a secret of the crown."

"One that should be shared with my people."

"That's not something I can decide on alone, it will have to be agreed with the queen and she is in Aldarris. As is the Guardian."

"We leave at first light then and no more leisurely stops at pretty camping sites."

"Agreed." Hrolf looked surprised at Conall's consent. "I don't argue when you talk sense."

Hrolf turned back to Katy. "Did either of the sethundra give a name, Katy?"

"I remember that. The female was called Artemis and the male Baccus."

"Do they mean anything to you, Conall?"

The prince shook his head. "What about the third? Did they say that one's name?"

"Yes, and they weren't happy she was awake. They said she was one of the most dangerous sethundra to ever live and she had a stronghold here on Dainnor. Her name was..."

"Melantha," a voice said. Katy looked up to see Oriana standing just inside the entry flap. A man was with her, he looked to be in his fifties, tall, solid looking, a bald head and a grizzled face, not used to smiling. "This girl's foolish, little brother has awoken Melantha."

"So it would seem," the man said. "Highness, I should have been informed the moment you learnt of this girl's arrival."

"I wanted to..."

"It is not a question of what you want to do, it is a question of doing what you need to do. It is about time you learnt that."

The prince did not look pleased at being interrupted. "I am doing what I need to..."

"This girl has apparently arrived with news that could be the greatest threat to be faced by not only our world, but by all the worlds in two thousand years and you decide to secrete her away into your tent because she has a pretty face. Your first course of action should have been to summon your advisers to interview the girl and in this camp that is myself and the Lady Oriana, not your

minotaur friend who is as unprepared to rule as you are."

"It is for my father to decide who his heir to the clans will be," Hrolf said, a dangerous note to his voice, "not yours, General Macklyn."

"And it is for the clan chiefs to approve that heir, if they do not then your father will have to choose another and if the chiefs cannot agree then the clans will split and a war of succession will follow. Many of your people will die and the fragile peace that currently exist between our two peoples will almost certainly shatter. And if Clan Chief Alberich's opinion is anything to go by then you have a lot to learn before even half of the clans will accept you."

Hrolf opened his mouth as if to respond, but then closed it again, shifting uncomfortably on the ground. "Now that your advisers are gathered," the general continued, "we will discuss the matter at hand." Macklyn picked up the two stools and placed them both down, indicating Oriana should sit before sitting himself. "Prince Hrolf, would you like Chief Alberich to be present?"

Hrolf scowled back at Macklyn a moment before answering. "I'd rather he wasn't. My people's history with Melantha is not one I would care to have repeated. Alberich often talks of the "glory days" of the minotaurs."

"You believe he would turn to her?"

Hrolf shrugged. "I'd rather not find out."

"All the minotaurs were allied to Melantha during the Sethundra War," Conall said

"Our allegiance was bought with lies. We no longer worship the dark sethundra and haven't for over a thousand years."

"Look," Katy butted into the conversation, "I haven't
got a clue what any of you are talking about, I'm still not entirely sure if I'm dreaming or not, but will someone please tell me who Melantha is."

It was Oriana who answered. "Some call her the bride of Zotikos, the sethundra lord, others say she was the queen of the sethundra and that Zotikos was answerable to her. The truth is we don't really know who answered to who, the only thing that all the tales agree upon is that short of Zotikos himself there isn't a more dangerous sethundra your brother could have woken up. Zotikos, Melantha and their allies hated humanity, they believed they should rule over all the worlds and that any who would not serve them should be destroyed. I doubt she has changed her mind."

"We can take heart in one thing," Conall said, "these other two sethundra, Artemis and Baccus, they were not happy at Melantha being woken. They must serve the will of the Stones."

"Unless that is what they wanted Katy's brother to think, take him to Melantha and then force him to awaken others of her cause. Why were they in the proximity of Melantha when the Casting took place?"

"They could have been fighting her," Hrolf offered.

"It is possible. But just two sethundra, not powerful or noteworthy enough to be mentioned in the histories and battling Melantha alone? It seems a little desperate."

"Sethundra aside for a moment," Macklyn said, "can we deal with the issue of which world the girl is actually from."

"The *girl* is called Katy," Katy said acidly, "and I'm from Earth."

"Earth is not a name we're familiar with."

"Another name, perhaps," Oriana queried, "we know them as Tarnasus, Lagannia, Terra, Set'ia…"

"Terra," Katy interrupted, "I think that's the Latin word for Earth."

"Terra? Interesting. Aside from Palmora, Terra is the last place I would have expected you to be from. I had assumed you to be from one of the twins, Set'ia or Set'ta."

"Why?" Conall asked curiously.

Oriana shook her head. "It does not matter. She claims to be from Terra so we must assume she tells the truth until proven otherwise."

"But why would such a powerful sethundra as Melantha be on Terra at the time of the Casting," Macklyn mused, "surely she should have been on Palmora trying to prevent the Casting from taking place."

"It makes no sense," Hrolf said, shaking his head.

"There was another sethundra still asleep," Katy said, "I think they said his name was Dardanus."

"Another un-noteworthy," Oriana said thoughtfully, "hunting one of the most powerful of the sethundra? An intriguing mystery."

"But not one for us to solve," Macklyn said. "We could stay here all evening debating this and we would still be none the wiser at the end. I want everyone to get some sleep, we ride at first light."

"I've already given that order," Conall said sullenly.

"I know, one of my captains informed me. A sensible decision I grant you, but one that you should have consulted with me first."

"Isn't he your prince?" Katy asked, feeling that Conall needed someone to fight his corner.

"Yes he is," Macklyn said, turning a piercing gaze upon her, "but his mother, the queen, gave command of this mission to me. Conall is here for diplomacy and to learn. Now, we need to find you somewhere to sleep."

"Katy will sleep here tonight," Conall said, "I'll sleep

with the men."

"How very gallant, Your Highness," Oriana smirked.

"Very well," the general said rising. "If you will excuse me, I must see to the preparations."

General Macklyn left the tent whilst Oriana stared intently at Katy, making her shift uncomfortably, before getting up and leaving without another word.

"I don't think General Macklyn likes you two very much," Katy said.

"He likes me fine," Conall said, "he just has no sense of humour. And he despairs of me as heir to the throne of Lors...I was never meant to be king," he added quietly.

"Neither of us were," Hrolf said.

Conall glared at Hrolf a moment before standing up from the bed. "I'll have a meal sent over for you," he said to Katy. "Try not to fear for your brother, I suspect Artemis and Baccus have taken him to Dainnor's Guardian to ask for his advice. Believe me, your brother couldn't be in safer hands."

"Thank you."

The prince smiled and left the tent, without even a glance at the minotaur. Hrolf got to his feet and looked down on Katy. "I agree with Conall." Just before he exited the tent he turned back to her and winked. "Don't tell him I said that though."

It was only a few minutes later when Freya, entered the tent carrying a tray of food. "The prince said you might be hungry." She didn't say which prince, but judging by the fact she didn't seem to blush or sigh when saying it she assumed in was Conall.

The smells wafting off the tray made Katy realise just how famished she was. She wasted no time in attacking the food vigorously, stuffing warm bread and stew into her mouth as fast as she could. Whilst she ate, Freya chatted away as if they had been friends for years rather than being two people who had only just met. Katy didn't have a clue what Freya was talking about, but made polite noises between mouthfuls. Freya mainly talked about camp gossip that she had overheard, but Katy found it comforting listening to her anyway. She even felt a little sorry for the minotaur, she got the impression no one else really talked to her. The human servants were nervous around the minotaurs and the servants of Freya's kind were all much older than she. Soon Freya had exhausted even her wealth of gossip and bid Katy a goodnight, taking the now empty tray with her.

Katy lay down on the bed listening to the sounds of the camp outside the tent. It was still daylight, she guessed late afternoon and people were busy making a great deal of noise as they went about whatever duties they had. As she stared up at the canvas ceiling worrying about where her brother was and how she was to get him home, her eyelids soon grew heavy and before long she drifted off to sleep.

It felt like only a few minutes since she closed her eyes when she was gently shaken awake. It was now dark and the camp silent, she could just make out the form of someone standing over her.

"Get up," came Conall's hushed voice, "we're leaving."

"Leaving," Katy whispered back, "but it isn't morning yet."

"It will be soon, but we're not going with the others."

"What? Why?"

"I'll explain later. Here," he dropped a pile of clothing into her lap, "put these on, they're better for travelling and we've got a long way to go. Hurry up, I'll meet you outside. And be quiet, we're trying to avoid notice."

It turned out that changing your clothes in the dark when you had no idea what the clothes you were going to be wearing looked like was no mean feat. The trousers she managed to put on backwards and she did the same with the tunic too. She was impressed that everything fit perfectly, especially the boots, though it took her a while to work out that what she thought was a blanket was actually a cloak and hood that fitted together with a broach, the pin of which she managed to prick herself with, twice.

Bloody princes and their night time excursions, she thought sucking the blood from her thumb, *would it have killed him to bring just one lamp.*

There was also a belt on which hung a long knife and a pouch. Remembering she still had her mobile phone in the pocket of her jeans she tucked it securely into the pouch and fastened the belt around her waist.

Finally, she was ready and she tiptoed out of the tent into the night to find Conall waiting impatiently outside. There was just enough moonlight for her to see him put a finger to his lips before indicating that she should follow him. Silently the two of them stalked through the camp of sleeping soldiers and servants. For the most part it was

76

silent, but Katy noticed a constant rumbling sound coming from the minotaur section. It took her a moment to realise it was the sound of them snoring. The camp wasn't large, so it wasn't long before they were outside and moving swiftly through the trees.

After ten minutes or so of silence, Katy was about to ask where they were going when she heard the whickering of a horse. Stepping around a tree they found six horses, three with riders, two with empty saddles and one laden with provisions. It was then that Katy noticed how much lighter it was getting as she could clearly make out the solid features of Dunham on one of the riders. The other two she didn't recognize, but they were so alike they must have been brothers.

"Any problems?" the prince asked.

Dunham shook his head. "None, Highness, though I daresay the general will have my hide when we get back."

Conall grinned. "Not too late to turn back, Captain."

"And leave you to go off on your own? Then the general will *execute me*; after the queen has finished with the torture, that is."

"Will somebody please tell me where we're going," Katy urged.

"The Deadlands I'd imagine," came a deep voice behind them.

Conall and the soldiers all spun towards the sound, swords drawn, eyes searching the gloom. A large shadow moved and emerged into the form of Hrolf, a large pack on his back and his huge axe resting easily on one shoulder.

Conall eyed the pack on Hrolf's back. "Planning a trip of your own?"

"I've always fancied seeing the Deadlands, apparently they're quite pretty in the right light."

The soldiers chuckled quietly as they put away their weapons. Conall was slower, but he did eventually sheathe his sword. "What gave us away?"

"I wouldn't have known if I hadn't thought the same thing myself. Add that to your reputation for recklessness and all I had to do was wait for you to fetch the girl."

Conall snorted. "Rumour has it that you have your own reputation for recklessness."

"Would I be here if I didn't?"

"We'll be riding hard."

"Any minotaur can keep up with a horse."

Katy folded her arms irritably. "This male bonding is all very touching, but will someone tell me what the bloody hell the Deadlands are and why exactly we're going there?!"

"Melantha had a fortress in what is now called the Deadlands," Conall explained. "The place still exists, apparently. Trolls inhabit it now. Considering where we found you there is a good chance that Melantha went there. It's possible your brother's there too."

"I thought you said he would be in the city?"

"And if he is he'll be in safe hands, but if he isn't then he'll be in the Deadlands with Melantha. As to what the Deadlands are? Well, I think it'll be easier if we just show you."

And so, Katy found herself trotting through the trees on horseback with a human prince riding to one side of her and a minotaur prince loping along on the other. Dunham brought up the rear leading the packhorse whilst the other two, who she learned were twins called Bevan and Brennan rode some distance ahead.

Dawn was soon upon them and she could now see clearly. She frowned curiously when Bevan and Brennan suddenly both raised their hoods over their heads, Conall did the same as did Hrolf, she turned in her saddle to see Dunham do the same just as the trees came to an abrupt end.

It was as if someone had drawn a line on the ground over which vegetation was no longer allowed to grow, in its place was a land of bare earth and barren rock. An unpleasant, brown fog hung in the air; she could still see, but it was like looking through a dirty net curtain.

It's the brown haze that I could see from the top of the tree yesterday, she thought looking around in astonishment.

And then, with no warning, the madness began.

CHAPTER 8

The long column of blue cloaked guardsmen marched out of the gates as Dylan watched from his window, munching on the last of his breakfast of crusty bread, dripping with honey. Bretta had woken him that morning with a tray laden with food in one hand and a selection of clothes in the other. He now wore a fine pair of polished black boots, beige trousers, a silk shirt and a short blue coat with gold thread. *I feel like a prince.* In fact, Bretta had informed him that the clothes had actually belonged to Queen Arlana's son, Prince Conall.

A soft knock at the door turned his head away from the window. "Come in," he said jumping down from the window sill.

A young woman, just a few years older than Katy stepped into the room and smiled at him. "Hello," she said brightly, "you must be Dylan. I'm Olwyn." She stepped up to Dylan and shook his hand vigorously. "I am so very pleased to meet. I can't tell you how long I've wanted to meet someone from another world, and one from Terra too. Fascinating, absolutely fascinating."

"I'm pleased to meet you too, Olwyn," Dylan said taking an instant liking to her and trying not to stare at what appeared to be a smudge of ink on her chin. There were also ink stains on her fingers too. "I'm sure I would have loved to meet someone from another world too, if I'd known there had been other worlds with people on them of course."

Olwyn threw back her head and laughed, sounding a bit like a barking dog. "Oh it's going to be fascinating getting to know you, Dylan. I never would have thought that Terra could have forgotten so much. But then we

80

know so little about the other worlds nowadays, most of our information is hundreds of years old. Will you tell me about Terra?"

"Of course. Firstly, we don't call it Terra, we call it Earth."

"Earth." Olwyn mulled over the name for a moment. "Yes, yes, I think I like it. And if that's what you call it, then that's what I'll call it. Come on, you can tell me more about Earth on the way."

"On the way to where?"

"Oh, sorry, I forgot to mention, I'm a student of Professor Finian, I'm to escort you to his study."

"Is he going to teach me magic?" Dylan asked excitedly.

"Magic? Oh, you mean how to use the power of the stones. No, well, I'm not sure actually, but casting takes many years to master, many hours of study."

"Are you a magi?" Dylan asked as they stepped out of the room and began making their way down the marble corridor.

"Yes I am, well, training to be one that is. Top of my class actually." Dylan liked the way she just stated her position without a hint of boasting. She was the top of her class and that was that. "I'm not entirely sure what's going on, the professor doesn't reveal much, but I'm guessing as you're here at all then you must have woken a sethundra. Professor Finian must want to teach you enough control so you can put it, or them, back to sleep again."

"Why doesn't Professor Finian just do it?"

"Because he can't. When a Guardian wakes a sethundra that sethundra is bound to that Guardian forever, unless he releases it, puts it back to sleep or the Guardian dies. Any sethundra woken by you are yours to control."

"You mean Artemis and Baccus have to do as I tell
them?" Dylan gaped, his mind whirling with possibilities of two obedient sethundra at his command.

"So those are their names. Not sure I've seen them in the records, they must be lesser sethundra. Only the more powerful names or ones that did anything noteworthy during the Sethundra War were recorded. But yes, if you have enough control of your own power you can control sethundra. However, the more powerful the sethundra the harder it is to control."

"It will be even harder to control Melantha then."

Olwyn stumbled a little at that. "Melan…Melantha?" she said breathlessly. "Oh…oh my…oh dear. Right then. Fascinating, yes fascinating."

They walked on in silence after that as Olwyn appeared to process the ground shaking news. Fortunately for Dylan the silence didn't last long as they soon arrived at the professor's study.

"Here we are," Olwyn said opening the door and leading Dylan inside.

He had expected to see something like his grandfather's study, perhaps a little larger, but what he found was not what he had expected at all. The room was massive, row upon row of shelves stuffed full of books and scrolls lined the walls the only break the tall arched windows running along one side. The shelves were so high that anyone wanting to reach a book from the top would need ladders to reach them. Down the centre of the room was a long table with benches on either side. On the table were more books and scrolls, many of which lay open as if someone were in the middle of reading them and had gone off to take a break. He could see the diminutive shape of Professor Finian sitting hunched over one such book at the far end of the room.

Nobody else was present other than a sullen looking lad about Katy's age sweeping the floor with as little enthusiasm as he could muster.

Olwyn led Dylan over to the professor, pointedly ignoring the sweeping teenager as she passed him. Dylan tried smiling a friendly greeting at him, but the lad just glared back at him and went back to his sweeping.

Olwyn cleared her throat when they reached Finian. "Professor, I brought Dylan as requested."

Finian looked up at the young woman frowning at her as if she were a problem he couldn't quite figure out, before looking to Dylan with an even more puzzled expression. "Ah yes, Dylan, of course. Take a seat, there's a good lad. Alanson!" The professor's shout made Dylan jump as he was settling onto a bench. It was the teenager that appeared to be the target of Finian's shout. "When I told you to sweep the floor I meant with gusto boy! Put some effort into it or I'll have you sweep the entire palace, you see if I don't." Alanson, paled visibly at the prospect and immediately put renewed effort into his sweeping. "Now then, Dylan, what to do with you."

"Olwyn said you were going to teach me how to control the sethundra."

"Did she? Did she now?" Finian eyed her over his spectacles. "And does Olwyn not have studies of her own to see to."

"Of course, Professor, of course." Olwyn scuttled off to one of the open books further up the table and set to work, looking a little embarrassed.

"Now," Finian polished his spectacles with a rather grimy looking rag and then perched them back onto his nose. "Controlling a sethundra, full control mind, not just waking one up or summoning one to your side, is no easy feat. Years of study are required before a magi can maintain that level of control for any amount of time, even with the lesser sethundra. Unfortunately, I don't have years to train you, mores the pity, I'm afraid I can only really teach you enough so when the time comes you at least know how to put Melantha to sleep. Considering your question about controlling the sethundra, I trust Olwyn has explained that only you can put Melantha, or indeed Artemis and Baccus to sleep again?"

"Yes," Dylan said nodding, "but why were they asleep, Professor?"

"Ah, an excellent question and an excellent place to begin. It can't hurt for you to have a little knowledge of our history. Now, around...yes, what now?!"

Dylan jumped and looked up to see a liveried servant had entered the room. He stood about halfway down the long table looking nervous. "Th...the...Her Majesty, Queen Arlana has requested your presence, Professor Finian," he stammered.

"Can't you tell her to wait?" The servant turned a rather alarming shade of green at the question. Finian, appearing to realise what he had suggested to the poor man, jumped up from the bench. "No, of course you can't, what am I thinking. Dylan, you can make a start by studying that book in front of you. Yes, yes that one." Dylan pulled the indicated book towards him. "Well don't just stand there, man, lead on, the queen awaits!" With that Finian left the room, hustling the poor servant ahead of him.

Dylan looked down at the book before him. It had no title, but seven simple designs dominated the otherwise plain brown, leather cover. They were arranged neatly in a half circle, like an arch of some kind, it took Dylan just a moment to realise where he had seen them before. *The door to Grandad's study. These are all carved into the wood.* Firstly, there was the horizontal line with two diagonal lines, fanning out above it, next a vertical line in the centre with four diagonal lines, two on either side pointing downwards. The third was two vertical lines, each with a diagonal line pointing slightly downwards and reaching for the other, not quite touching. Two of the symbols were very similar, a large circle with a smaller circle offset inside it, one symbol the offset circle was to the right, the other, the left. The sixth was two identical wavy lines, one atop the other and finally there was the vertical line with a long diagonal line on either side, pointing downwards and then two more diagonal lines fanning out from the top of the centre line. "But where's the eighth?" he said out loud. "Where's the star and the circle?"

"Eighth? There isn't an eighth," Dylan looked up to see the sullen teenager, Alanson, peering over his shoulder.

"Yes there is," Dylan argued, "there should be an eighth symbol right here." He pointed his finger at the centre of the front cover. "On my grandfather's door there are eight symbols, not seven and the eighth is here in the middle, the other seven cover it like an arch."

Alanson smirked. "Those are the symbols of the seven worlds, stupid. There isn't an eighth world, there are only seven. Your grandfather probably just carved a new symbol onto his door, unless you're suggesting he knows of another world the rest of us don't know anything about?" Finding this extremely funny, Alanson went back to sweeping the floor.

Dylan sighed, he decided he didn't like Alanson very much, but he had to admit he had a point. He opened the book and groaned in dismay. As far as he could tell it was just pages and pages of writing, not a single picture to break it up. And the book was huge, like the bible in the village church. *I'll be here forever reading this! This is so unfair. I should be exploring Dainnor and looking for Katy, not sitting around reading some boring, old book.* Flicking through he noticed that the book was arranged into seven chapters, one for each world. *I'll learn the names of the worlds, Finian can't say I haven't tried then.*

Dainnor was the first chapter, the world he was currently on, then came Palmora, followed by Terra. The next two chapters were Set'ta and Set'ia, followed by Lagannia and finally Tarnasus. He recited them over and over in his head until he could do them without looking at the book. Feeling pleased with himself he decided to have a look at some of the other books lining the shelves.

The books that actually had titles didn't really interest him at all. They appeared to be mainly stuffy history books of Dainnor. A book entitled *A Study of the Political Structure of the Minotaur Kingdom* caught his eye, but he soon put it back on the shelf again. He'd been hoping for pictures of the minotaurs but, like the book Finian had given him, it was sadly lacking. Another book called *Myths and Legends of the Lost Knights of Lors* looked as though it may have been interesting, but being slightly out of reach he left it and moved on. He arrived at one of the windows and found it looked out on some very pretty gardens. A pang of homesickness hit him as he thought how much Nanny would enjoy looking at them. She was always pottering around in the garden, it was the prettiest garden in Carreg-y-galon, which was saying something considering how many keen gardeners lived there. A few people were pruning and weeding in the flowerbeds, but as there was nothing else going on to hold the attention of a ten-year-old boy, he left the window and continued with his exploration.

The light from the windows didn't quite reach a corner right at the back of the room so, naturally, he wandered over to have a look. He found a plain wooden door tucked in between two massive bookcases. Appearing to be the only door besides the entrance in the entire place, Dylan could hardly miss the opportunity for a quick peek inside. He looked back to see if anyone was watching him. Olwyn was engrossed in her own studies; Alanson, who appeared to be taking Finian's threat of sweeping the entire palace seriously, was attacking the floor vigorously. He felt sure the door would be locked, but as he grasped the handle it swung open easily on silent hinges. Dylan darted inside, shutting the door behind him.

He found himself in a small, unremarkable square room. From the layers of dust on the floor no one had been in there for some time. There were no windows, no pictures or tapestries decorating the plain stone walls, and no furniture. And yet light. *How can I see?* Dylan thought looking around for a light source. He spun around in a circle, looked overhead, pushed aside the dust on the floor with his foot, but still he couldn't find the source of the light.

For perhaps the tenth time his gaze passed over what he had thought to be a blank wall when he snapped his eyes back to one spot in confusion. Directly in front of him was a door, a door he would have sworn had not been there earlier. And it wasn't just any door, but a door he had seen many times before, or one just like it, on another world. The entrance to his grandfather's study. It appeared to be made of wood and carved with vegetation so life-like he almost felt he could reach out and pull it away; and the eyes, the eyes were there too, hiding amongst the trees and branches, staring out at him, filled with hatred. And in the centre of the door were the symbols, the ones that he now knew to represent the worlds, but there was an eighth, exactly the same on his grandfather's door at home, seven in an arc rising over an eighth. A circle with a seven-pointed star at its centre.

Come.

Dylan turned at the sound of the voice, expecting to
find someone ready to berate him for entering somewhere he wasn't meant to be. But there was nobody there, he was alone in the room.

Come.

"Who said that?" he said aloud, his own voice sounding thin and frightened.

Come.

Again he pivoted around, again there was nobody there. But now the curious door stood open. There was nothing to see through the opening, whatever light illuminated the room it wasn't strong enough to penetrate the blackness through the doorway.

Come.

He found himself standing in the doorway staring into the blackness, yet he had no memory of walking to get there.

Come.

Fear gripped him, but he could no more deny the voice than stop breathing. With a deep breath, he stepped through the doorway, into the darkness. There was a brief moment of panic when he didn't immediately feel ground beneath his foot, but then his boot struck solid stone and he breathed a sigh of relief. Looking around in surprise he saw that the darkness had moved away from him; he could clearly see where he stood. He was on a stone stair leading down, there were only a few steps ahead visible before they disappeared into more darkness and a quick glance behind revealed the doorway was gone, there were only a couple of steps to be seen behind him before they too vanished into the gloom. Rough stone walls rose up on either side of him, but by how far he couldn't tell, as looking up revealed only more black. *Well I've come this far.* He carried on down the stairs, curiosity just having the edge over his fear. With each step that he took the darkness retreated away from him, as if he were carrying a torch that couldn't penetrate more than a few feet ahead. He continued on for about ten minutes before he finally reached the bottom of the stairs, a few feet of stone floor stretching out before him. *I must be deep underground by now.* He took a single step, and then it all changed.

The darkness retreated away from him, a lot further this time and the walls, whilst still made of stone, were no longer bare. Trees, shrubs, flowers, vegetation as life-like as that decorating the door far above were carved into the hard rock walls rising up on either side of him. Dylan felt as though he stood on a dead straight path that led through a silent, stone forest. As he began to move forward he almost imagined that the leaves were blowing in an unfelt breeze. And, just as with the door above, the eyes were there too, but now they felt closer, hungrier.

Come. It is time.

He moved forward along the path, but this time the darkness ahead didn't retreat from him, but stayed still, waiting for Dylan to come to it. He reached the end of the path, standing before it, wondering what to do next. And then, without warning, it enveloped him. He was surrounded by blackness, but oddly when he looked down at himself he could see his own body as clearly as if it were a bright sunny day.

It is time.

He could see something. He wasn't certain at first whether it was his mind playing tricks, but slowly something came into view.

It looked a little like a misshapen egg, one that pulsed with a white fire. But it wasn't whole, it wasn't perfect. Black, crusted lines of stone crisscrossed over the surface, obscuring a little of the brilliance that shone beneath. It hung in the air, just out of arms reach of the ten-year-old.

It is time to wake.

Whatever the thing was, Dylan knew it was the source of the voice in his head. He was afraid of it, more afraid of anything than he had been in his young life, but he also wanted it. He wanted to take it in his hands, hold it close to him and never let it go.

It is time to wake.

He found himself reaching for it, not with his hand, but with his mind. He didn't know how he did it, but he suddenly felt connected to the object. There was power in it, more power than he could imagine.

It is time to wake.

His body relaxed. Unbidden, a light appeared in his mind and swept towards him until it enveloped him completely. Power poured into him, a tiny trickle at first, then it became a raging flood. He felt dizzy, a small part of him knew it was too much, but he didn't care, he wanted it all.

It is time to wake.

"Ancient locked within the dream..." *No, this is wrong, I mustn't!* His head began to hurt, a dull throb at first, but then more power rushed into him, and with it, the pain grew.

90

It is time to wake.

"Held for mortals' sake…" He couldn't stop, he wanted to, but couldn't. As he continued the spell; the power, and the pain, grew.

****

The Apprentice walked down the silent corridor, her bare feet slapping on the smooth floor. Her robe had already consumed the last of the moisture from her body, but her thick, dark, curly hair would take a more determined effort to dry. Firstly, she had chores, and Grand Mistress Rozamond was anything but forgiving if Lina missed a chore. Particularly for something as trivial as hair.

She reached the double doors to the Central Chamber and pushed them open. She stopped and stared, shock, terror and confusion freezing her in place.

As the Heart Stone flared.

****

His eyes watered as the pain become unbearable. "I commanded you now, come forth be seen…" He screamed in pain, he felt his head exploding, he couldn't bear it anymore, he had to stop but he couldn't. "SETHUNDRA…!" he screamed in agony just as he felt a hand grab his shoulder.

And suddenly it was gone. The power, the pain, everything. His head span, he was going to be sick. He had a brief image of a huge shape and Finian's study and then blackness consumed him, and he knew no more.

****

Lina stared, still rooted to the spot. The Heart Stone pulsed with a pure white light, just as it always had, nothing more, nothing less. But there had been a flare, for the briefest of moments it had shone as brightly as the sun. *But why?* She could find no answer. Perhaps Rozamond could provide answers, perhaps there would
be clues into what had happened in the Grand Library.

Slamming the doors behind her, Lina ran as fast as she could to find her mistress. And inside the chamber, hidden in the shadows, a figure wept.

****

"Come."

Commander Dryden stepped through the doorway, taking a moment to locate the First Minister staring out of the window onto the city below. Despite the First Minister having his back to Dryden he saluted anyway, the First had an odd way of knowing when you hadn't done something that you should have.

"What is it, Commander," the minister's voice was quiet, barely above a whisper.

"There has been an...incident, First."

"An incident? It must be one of some significance to trouble me with, Commander," the First said, a slight hint of a threat in his voice.

"The Starbridge, First. It...it...fluctuated." The word didn't seem right somehow, but it was the best that Dryden could come up with.

"The Guardians?" A note of urgency entered the First Minister's voice.

"Are secure, First. But there were people on the Starbridge when it...well, they were Set'tans, First, but they did not emerge. They're gone."

Commander Dryden had no love for Set'tans, few did, but even so he found the First Minister's reaction odd. The minister's shoulders shook as if sobbing with grief at the loss of hundreds of lives, many of them children, but as he got louder Dryden heard that the First wasn't sobbing; the First was laughing.

CHAPTER 9

Freya let herself fall a little further behind the humans, General Macklyn, Oriana and the minotaur chief, Alberich, who walked beside them. They were arguing again. They had done little else in the three days since the two princes had disappeared with Katy and the last time Freya had tried listening in she had received an extremely public scolding from Alberich when he had caught her. The last thing she wanted was to risk another.

They weren't very far from the city now, and there had been a steadily increasing number of human settlements to show that. Farms were dotted about everywhere, the only thing standing between them were villages and the occasional small town. There were more travellers on the road too, though they all quickly made way for the band of armed human soldiers, not to mention the fifty or so minotaurs in the group.

Freya noticed that many of the humans, particularly the servants, were beginning to look tired at the punishing pace that Macklyn had set them. He was eager to reach the city as quickly as possible and left little time for rest. Freya felt a fierce sense of pride that her own kin showed no fatigue at all. *I bet we could have reached the city a day ago on our own.* The humans were certainly weaker than the minotaurs, Freya could see that clearly, it was the sheer number of them that she found staggering. All the farms, villages and towns they had passed in just the last two days had held thousands of humans between them and from what she understood the city held more than all of those put together.

If humans can do one thing well it's breeding, Freya thought, bringing on an involuntary giggle. A mounted soldier looked at her curiously and she smiled back. He returned a friendly nod. Freya found it odd that the soldiers appeared to be more friendly than the human servants, they all looked at her as if she were about to eat them. *Humans and their overactive imaginations.* The very thought of it made Freya feel a little ill.

"Finc, together then!" Macklyn's voice snapped at Alberich, fortunately loud enough for the entire party to hear, at least Freya couldn't be accused of eavesdropping.

"I wonder what that argument was about?" Freya said to no one in particular.

"How to tell the queen her son is missing." It was the mounted soldier who answered. "The General will want to have a private audience no doubt, but your man, Alberich will almost certainly want to be present, if for no other reason than to ensure no blame is directed his way."

"But it was nobody's fault, Prince Conall and Prince Hrolf left together."

"Trust, Freya," the soldier said, "it is not the way of the great and powerful to trust each other."

Freya blinked in surprise. "You know my name?"

The soldier laughed. "Of course. We all know the name of Freya, the curious minotaur. We have a wager as to whether there are any secrets left in the camp," he laughed good naturedly at Freya's embarrassment. "Fear not, there are many more secrets left for you to learn." The soldier nodded ahead of them, "we're here."

Freya looked ahead to see that they had just rounded a bend in the road and Aldarris, the city that she had heard so much about, had come into view. Whatever she had been expecting vanished at the sight of the city before her. Thirty-foot-high stone walls stretched out in either direction behind which could be seen the tops of hundreds of buildings. Towers soared into the sky, the pinnacles of some Freya felt sure would be hidden in the clouds if the day had not been so bright and clear. On a hill in the centre of the city she could make out the huge shape of what must be the royal palace shining in the sun so brightly she could almost believe the legend that it was made entirely of gold. To the left, she could just make out the great river that led down to the sea and the tiny shapes of the ships sailing upon it. Freya had never seen the sea; it was one of the things she desperately wanted to visit on this trip. *All that water and none of it drinkable. What do the humans do with it?* she pondered. A steady stream of humans was going in and out of the main gate to the city upon a larger road that their own was about to connect with. Merchants carrying their wares on large wagons, farmers, either with carts full of crops or empty if they were returning to their farms; travellers, adventurers, many armed with swords, axes and bows rode or walked one way or another through those gates. *So many humans, how can there be so many?* It occurred to Freya just how good the new peace treaty would be. *If the humans decided to destroy us we wouldn't stand a chance against so many.*

They soon joined the main road and the flood of traffic heading towards the gate. Freya expected everyone to move out of the way of their party, but it quickly became apparent that the sheer number of people, wagons and horses made it impossible and they soon slowed to a crawl. The soldiers, obviously a common sight this close to the city, barely received so much as a glance from the people, but many stopped and stared, mouths agape and eyes wide with fear at the minotaurs, which, unfortunately, only served to add more to the congestion and chaos of moving in and out of the city.

Freya did her best to try and look friendly in an effort to counteract the grim looks of the minotaur warriors, but it appeared to have little or no effect. *They only see a child eating minotaur,* she thought sadly. *I hope I live to see a day when we're all friends.* She even tried waving at a couple of small children, but they just cried and clung tightly to their mother who appeared to be burdened enough with a large bundle. She briefly wondered if she should go and ask if she could carry it for the woman, but quickly dismissed the idea. If the children cried at her waving at them she didn't want to think what would happen if she went over and spoke to their mother.

Finally, they reached the gates and an impatient looking Macklyn halted the party as he began speaking to one of the blue-cloaked guards. The guard disappeared into the crowd leaving Macklyn glaring at the press of people, almost as if he wanted to draw his sword and hack his way through. Oriana appeared to be lost in thought, whilst Alberich tried his best not to gape at the sights as much as the rest of his kin. After several minutes the guard returned, a number of identically dressed comrades in tow. They immediately formed up in front of the party, spears at precisely the same angle, shields bearing the Golden Hawk of Lors held across their chests.

"Make way," roared the commanding officer over the din of the crowd, "make way for the royal party!"

That had a remarkable effect. Immediately people moved to the sides of the street that stretched into the city before them. It took a while to get the carts out of the way, but after a fair bit of huffing, puffing and some rather colourful language, a clear path began to open up before them. Freya was impressed, particularly as there wasn't actually anybody royal in their party anymore. The commander then began marching forward yelling at people to make way as he went. Soon the other guards moved forward, closely followed by their own party. And so it went as they marched through the city, the shouting commander, people squashed up against the sides of buildings, other people hanging out of windows to see what all the commotion was about and an eerie silence from the humans.

How many lost loved ones in the wars? She was uncomfortably aware of just how many humans there were, and how few minotaurs. If the people decided to attack they would be swiftly overwhelmed. She turned to the mounted soldier beside her to ask him a question, but the words faded on her tongue when she saw the grim look on his face. His eyes scanned the crowd constantly, one hand gripping the hilt of his sword. Looking around she could see that the other soldiers were doing the same, whilst the minotaur warriors were struggling not to reach for axes and war hammers.

"We need the prince," the soldier beside her muttered, "they can't see their prince and they're worried."

They came upon a group of men standing outside a building with a picture of a bulls severed head on a sign. Many of the men were heavily scarred, some even with missing limbs, others held tankards of ale, and all stared balefully at the minotaurs. Freya nervously eyed the sign, remembering that some humans actually believed that minotaurs had the heads of bulls.

The tension was unbearable. One of the warriors glared at the men outside the tavern as one of them spat on the ground. The warrior growled, a rumble emerging deep within his chest, his huge muscled arm moved a little closer to his war hammer. A man with a tankard clutched in his single hand turned to the others and shouted in a voice loud enough to be heard over the whole street. "Looks as though beef's on the menu, lads!"

The silence that suddenly descended on the street was
deafening. Every one of the minotaur warriors came to an immediate halt, every hand moved a little closer to a weapon.

"Damn," the mounted soldier growled. His hand gripping his sword hilt so tightly his knuckles turned white. The minotaurs hands also now gripped weapons, a few even went as far as to draw them, the tavern men began squaring up, whilst the other soldiers in the party looked around indecisively. Some looked towards Macklyn, uncertain which side they should be on. The general muttered something angrily under his breath before trotting between the party and the veterans. Oriana looked back at the unfolding scene with a look of annoyance on her face and Alberich stepped towards his warriors. The blue-cloaked guardsmen hefted their spears, some even edged towards the men at the tavern, as if they had already chosen their side.

Dread filled Freya's heart, she could see a slaughter of hundreds of innocent people in the street, her own kin dying, as her father had, for no reason and no one was there to stop it. But then Freya heard a baby cry. She looked across to the opposite side of the street and saw a group of terrified women, almost all with children clinging to them, many of them babies, the largest coming no higher than their mothers' waists. It did nothing to ease the tension, but something snapped inside Freya.

"STOP," she cried as loudly as she could. All eyes swivelled to stare directly at her, making Freya feel as though the entire city was watching her, but she went on anyway, words just pouring out. "I loved my father, he was everything to me. I remember how he used to carry me on his shoulders when I was little. He would tell me stories, silly stories that could never be true, but I loved every one. He was a farmer and every day he would go to work in our fields and every night he would come home with another story to tell me. But one day he didn't come home and there were no more stories. He died in a silly war for no reason. And...and I don't want that to happen to anyone else..." She trailed off at the end, suddenly feeling awkward and self-conscious.

"So get back in line!" Macklyn roared. The soldiers and the guards scrambled to obey. The general then glared down at the tavern veterans. "The minotaurs are guests of our Queen Arlana. Never in the history of our kingdom has a guest of the crown been assaulted in the streets of Aldarris, and never will it happen whilst I draw breath. Do you understand?"

The one-armed man who had first shouted paled under the general's glare. "Sorry, General," he stammered, "meant no offense. I...I just lost some friends to minotaurs, that's all. But the girl minotaur there lost her pa to us, so I...er...suppose that make us all square. At least so I reckon it"

Macklyn stared at the veteran for a moment before nodding and riding to the front of the party, indicating that the guards should continue to clear the way.

The clan warriors relaxed visibly, although Freya noticed that a few of them gave her appraising looks that made her blush more than a little.

"You are destined for great things I think, Freya," the mounted soldier next to her said, nodding to her respectfully.

Freya smiled at him. She noticed the men at the tavern slinking away, many of them looking shamefaced. Glancing across to the women with the children she saw they had all begun talking quietly amongst themselves, occasionally pointing in her direction. Freya began to feel self conscious again until one of the women smiled and waved at her. Freya's own smile nearly split her face in two as she waved back and continued on with the party. Her grin vanished when she noticed the flat stare Oriana gave her.

The rest of the journey through the city went without incident and they soon found themselves passing through tall arched gates, into the grounds of the royal palace itself. Freya was a little disappointed to find that it wasn't actually made of gold, but found it to be an impressive sight nonetheless. Made primarily of white stone it was decorated with huge stone columns, stretching out to either side, each one topped with gold that had been modelled to resemble fearsome looking winged beasts. Tall, arched windows stood proudly between the columns, the sun shining off them so they sparkled like crystals. A pair of huge doors stood open in the centre of the building, white stone steps leading up to them with liveried servants standing on either side. Twin lines of guardsmen stood to rigid attention, halberds held at exactly the same angle, forming a pathway for the royal party to the open, welcoming doors. At the top of the steps stood a woman looking resplendent in a golden gown with a delicate silver crown on her head, and she did not look happy.

She thought she was becoming better at distinguishing one human from another and Freya felt sure that even without the crown she would recognise the woman as Queen Arlana. There was clearly something of Prince Conall in the woman's face. Unnoticed before, Freya saw a man, small even by human standards, standing a little behind the queen. Dressed all in brown and looking more than a little out of place amongst all the splendour, he had a thoughtful and somewhat concerned expression on his face; although, going by how little attention he appeared to be giving the royal party, Freya doubted his concern had anything to do with them.

Oriana dismounted from her horse, a groom appearing from nowhere to take the reins as she proceeded towards the queen on foot, Macklyn and Alberich following closely behind. She curtsied gracefully, Macklyn and Alberich bowed. An odd move by Alberich. Minotaur clan chiefs didn't even bow to their own kings let alone other peoples.

"My Queen..." Oriana began.

"Where is my son?" the queen said, her voice so cold Freya half expected Oriana to turn to ice on the spot.

"The prince decided to take leave of our company without our knowledge, Majesty."

"I asked you where he was, I did not ask you if he informed you of his travel plans."

Oriana stiffened at the queen's tone. Clearly she was not used to being spoken to in such a way; at least not in public. Oriana stared back at the queen and Arlana held her gaze. The tension was suddenly almost as bad as it had been earlier in the street with the men at the tavern.

Macklyn cleared his throat, causing both women to turn their eyes upon him. "We believe he may have entered the Deadlands, Majesty."

On the mention of the Deadlands the small, brown man looked up sharply.

"For what purpose?"

"We can only guess, Your Majesty, however, I believe it is something that should be discussed in a more private setting."

"And you, Chief Alberich, did Prince Hrolf inform you of his plans?"

"No," Alberich growled. "And I would like to know what makes General Macklyn think the princes have gone to the Deadlands too, as he or the Lady Oriana have not mentioned this to me before."

"It appears we both have questions that require answering, Chief Alberich. We have set aside quarters and refreshments for Prince Hrolf's retinue, but I would like you to join us in council." Freya began to leave with the other servants and warriors until the queen's voice pulled her up short. "Not you." All eyes, including the queens rested on Freya and she swallowed nervously, wondering what trouble she was in now, but then Arlana smiled warmly at her. "Word travels swiftly in this city and it appears I have you to thank for averting a bloodbath in my streets."

"I...I didn't really do anything, Your Majesty," Freya stammered. "It was General Macklyn really, he made the men stand down."

"But it was you who began it. You helped to avoid a conflict with words, the very thing we have gathered to try and achieve. Join us."

"But she's just a servant," Alberich spluttered in outrage.

"We are all servants, Chief Alberich."

"Majesty," Oriana said, "this girl fetches and carries, she cannot be present at such an important council."

The queen raised an eyebrow. "Do you now command here, Oriana? General, I would hear your thoughts."

Macklyn regarded Freya thoughtfully. "A wise commander should always judge a man on his capabilities rather than his birth. I believe she should attend. Besides, with Freya's reputation for eavesdropping she would almost certainly know exactly what we've discussed by the end of the day anyway."

"It is decided then. If you will all follow me."

Without another word the queen turned and walked back into the palace, leaving Macklyn, Oriana, Alberich and a shocked Freya, with no choice but to follow. The small man wordlessly fell in beside her, the distracted expression returning to his face.

After moving down several marble corridors, lined with fine looking paintings and tapestries they eventually reached a small room. Freya saw that someone had been kind enough to provide seating fit for a minotaur, for which she was extremely grateful, though it did mean she had to sit uncomfortably close to the scowling Alberich.

"Now," Queen Arlana said when all were comfortably seated, "perhaps you could explain your theory for my fool son entering the Deadlands."

"I believe he and Prince Hrolf mean to try to locate a sethundra; Melantha to be precise," Oriana stated as simply as if she were discussing the weather.

Freya gasped in shock as Alberich lurched from his seat, reaching for a weapon.

"I feared as much," the small man said, waving Alberich back down into his seat, who, for a wonder, did as instructed. "The boy was always spirited, much like his father at that age. Tell me, Oriana, what exactly led him to believe that Melantha was even awake."

"We met a girl," Oriana continued, "from Terra, or so she claims."

Katy, Freya thought, *she must mean Katy.*

"She says her brother awoke three sethundra, one being Melantha. I take it from your lack of surprise, Professor Finian, that you have the brother here? Perhaps with the other two sethundra?"

Freya blinked in surprise on hearing the little man's name. Professor Finian was said to be Dainnor's Guardian. She had expected someone taller.

Finian ignored Oriana's question. "The important thing now is to locate the two princes and bring them back here before they do anything foolish."

"I believe they already have done something foolish," the queen said dryly. "I would like to know why you didn't go into the Deadlands to drag him back, General Macklyn."

"You gave me command, Your Majesty," Macklyn replied, "however, Conall is my prince and your heir, and a little old for 'dragging', particularly in front of men and women that he will rule one day. He has Captain Dunham with him, who is more than capable, and two of my finest scouts. Such a small party should be able to avoid detection. However, if I had led our party into the Deadlands I have little doubt we would have been spotted by trolls and fighting for our lives right about now. And that's if Melantha didn't turn up to aid them."

"He's right about that," Alberich huffed, "we're a peaceful delegation, not a war party."

The queen sighed heavily. "You are right, of course. Forgive me, General, I should not blame my son's wrongheadedness on you. You acted correctly. Could Artemis and Baccus find the princes, Finian?"

"No doubt, if they have a rough idea where they entered the Deadlands and where they're going. The question is, will they? To them their task is a simple one, put Melantha back in her cage before going back into their own. I'm afraid they care little for anything else."

"Are Artemis and Baccus sethundra too?" Freya asked.

"Yes, Freya" Arlana answered, "Artemis and Baccus arrived here a few days ago."

"Well, I…erm…I'm sorry I don't know much about it, but couldn't the Guardian who awoke them just command them to find the princes?"

"A very sensible suggestion, Freya," Finian said, "but unfortunately it is not an option open to us at this time."

"Why, has something happened to the Terran girl's brother?" Oriana said sharply.

Finian and the queen exchanged a long look before Arlana answered. "We will leave this for now. We at least have an idea where my son and Prince Hrolf are, and if the sethundra will not aid us then we must trust in them to see to their own affairs. I see no other way of helping them than allowing Artemis and Baccus to continue in their task of putting Melantha back to sleep, at least then Conall and Hrolf will only have trolls to deal with. Chief Alberich, if you are willing I would like to continue with the peace talks with yourself in the prince's absence."

"I am, Your Majesty, though my own people will have talks of our own. I doubt Hrolf will be a prince much longer, given his behaviour."

"Very well. We will begin in the morning. We have prepared a feast in your honour this evening, it will be a more sombre affair than I would have liked, but given the

106

circumstances, it cannot be helped. In the meantime, Freya, I wonder if you would be so kind as to have tea with me, I would like to hear more of your father and his stories. I will then in turn tell you of my husband and eldest son."

"Of course, Your Majesty, I would love to," Freya said, her cheeks reddening.

And with that the meeting was over. Finian, Macklyn, Oriana and Alberich quietly left the private audience chamber whilst Freya, the nosy servant, began chatting to the most powerful monarch on Dainnor as if they had been best friends for years.

CHAPTER 10

Oriana ignored Alberich's polite farewell as he was led away by a serving man to his quarters, she also put out of her mind the queen's somewhat ridiculous notion of inviting servants to councils and then having tea with them, she was more interested in what Professor Finian and General Macklyn were talking about in hushed tones. Whatever it was, it was a conversation that they clearly did not wish her to be a part of, much to her irritation.

They talked briefly before departing in different directions without speaking a word to her. Oriana's eyes followed the diminutive form of the professor as he trotted off down a corridor. She lifted the hem of her skirt slightly and followed him. She was surprised that it took her quite a while to catch him. He moved quickly for a man with such short legs, and she flatly refused to run. She finally caught him just as he was opening the door to his study.

"Professor Finian," she said, annoyed that her voice sounded a little breathless, "I must speak with you."

"Concerning?" Finian said opening the door to the study. He stepped inside, barely glancing in her direction.

"The sethundra of course," she snapped, "and Terra's Guardian. Or is it the apprentice?" She noticed Olwyn, the young woman widely assumed to be Dainnor's own apprentice with her head buried in a book. A young man polishing some ornaments looked up at their entrance and gave her such a leer that she had to resist an urge to march over and slap his face.

"Alanson!" Finian barked. The young man jumped almost knocking a valuable looking vase off the table he was working at. "Keep your mind on your work and if you break anything I'll skin you alive and feed you to the dogs!" Abashed, the young man began polishing with a renewed vigour. Finian turned his gaze on Oriana, looking up at her over the rim of his spectacles. Oriana always felt uncomfortable under that look, most men had one thing only on their minds when they stared at her, Professor Finian was one of the few who appeared to have no interest in her as a woman whatsoever. Something she always found a little disconcerting. Finian was worse however. Something about him always made her feel she should immediately confess her every wrongdoing. A thing that Oriana was less than willing to do.

"The boy," Finian said quietly, "is none of your concern."

"Be that as it may," Oriana said, refusing to back down, "the sethundra concern us all. I am a magi of not insignificant ability, as well you know. If Melantha were to attack the city you would want me at your side. And these other two, Artemis and Baccus? I have studied much on the sethundra and their names are unknown to me. How do they stand?"

"They accept the will of the Stones."

"And yet they slept extremely close to Melantha. Do you not find this curious?"

Finian shook his head, finally averting his gaze. "Very curious. I believe both Artemis and Baccus to be of considerable strength, but I can find no record of them in the archives."

"And the other sethundra, the one who remains asleep, Dardanus?"

"Again, another whom I have not heard of. However, this is a curiosity not a concern, if they sided with

Melantha then they would hardly have delivered the boy to me."

"Unless their intention was to gain your trust to discover the identity of your own apprentice." Oriana couldn't help but glance in the direction of Olwyn. "Two young apprentices under their control and on Dainnor of all places. It could be disastrous."

"An interesting theory," the professor mused, "but I fail to see what advantage they would gain by having two apprentices, one would suffice if they merely wished to awaken more sethundra to their cause. No, I believe in my heart that whatever mysteries surround Artemis and Baccus they accept the will of the Stones and will aid us in the stopping of Melantha."

"And by stopping Melantha do you mean putting her back into the Casting or destroying her?"

"Neither an easy task, but I would prefer to keep my options open at this time."

"The boy lives then?"

"The boy lives, and is protected. Now, if you will excuse me, Oriana, I have a lot of work to do."

Finian began ushering Oriana towards the door.

"Where is the boy, Professor?"

Finian's hard stare returned instantly. "As I have already made quite clear, the boy is not of your concern." The Professor firmly shut the door in Oriana's face.

Oriana pursed her lips in irritation, but didn't waste a moment longer. She began making her way as quickly as she could, without looking as though she were hurrying, to her own apartments in the palace. Getting anything useful out of Finian was always a struggle, but she had at least gained a little information. The boy was alive, something had happened that much was certain, possibly something that threatened his life, but he definitely lived. The very fact that Finian was considering attempting to destroy Melantha suggested that the boy might yet die, or at least be incapable of sending her back into the Casting. And if he did die? What then for Artemis and Baccus? Two free sethundra, powerful ones too, would have consequences that would shake all the worlds, not just Dainnor.

She was nearing her apartments. She hadn't visited them in some time, but she knew they would be untouched. The last time she had caught a maid cleaning without her consent, some chattering fool called Bretta, Oriana had given her such a tongue lashing that every servant in the palace knew that her rooms were strictly out of bounds. Her rooms were safe, there was no chance of anybody stumbling on anything they shouldn't.

Oriana reached her door and pulled out the key from under her blouse. A small smile creased her lips. *Keep your little secrets, Finian,* she thought as she placed the key into the lock, *I have plenty of my own.*

****

Finian lent against the door, listening to Oriana retreat down the corridor. A useful skill. With a little extra effort he could have followed her progress to see exactly where she went, unfortunately that would mean she would instantly know what he was up to. A puzzling problem that one, one he had never been able to successfully find a way around. Even non-magi would have a sense of being watched if you weren't careful.

He feared he had given too much away to Oriana, although he had never managed to get to the bottom of why exactly he didn't trust her. One of his finest students and of considerable power, he had expected her to be called as the apprentice, as had she no doubt. But when she had failed the Testing the bitterness within her had grown, as had her lust for power. Finian often had the impression that Oriana blamed him for her failure. Preposterous of course, but since that day a rift had opened between teacher and student, one that Finian had never managed to close. Now he found her far too curious for her own good and he feared greatly where that curiosity was leading her.

He shook his head. Three times during his time as Guardian he had been certain he knew who his Apprentice would be. Three times he had been wrong. Oriana had been the second, the first he had lost in a tragic accident and the third continued to baffle him to this very day. One of his students, Olwyn, looked up from her book and smiled in his direction. A puzzle that one, not a problem as such, but a very intriguing puzzle nonetheless. Alanson, on the other hand, was a problem, one that he had no choice but to face. Unfortunately, as always seemed to be the case, he had other, more immediate concerns at that moment.

Dylan lived, but for how long he was not sure. The consequences if he died was something he did not want to dwell upon, but like many things in his life he found himself forced to do the one thing he didn't want. *If he dies, Melantha, Artemis and Baccus will be free.* He doubted he was strong enough to defeat one, let alone all three and he had serious concerns as to whether he could rely on Artemis and Baccus to help him defeat Melantha. Baccus especially. That one's acceptance of the will of the Stones was grudgingly given at best. Artemis he had more faith in, to her the Stones were sacrosanct, or at least so it appeared. But if the boy died would freedom be too tempting for Finian to rely upon her? *Perhaps I should confide in Oriana, but how far can I trust her?*

He rubbed at his temples, feeling a headache beginning to emerge and, not for the first time, questioned the path that had led him to Guardianship. His people, warriors, men and women both, Finian had never fitted in. Slight of build and weak of limb, the magi of his people had nevertheless recognised the power in him and sent him, away from his family, to Aldarris for training. It hadn't been long before he had passed the Testing and become Dainnor's Apprentice. An appointment that never ceased to baffle him. A burden he had never wished to carry.

Shaking his head, he opened the door and left the study. Despite his feelings, Dylan was his main concern right now. Whatever happened the boy must live. Something told the professor that the fate of all the worlds might depend upon it.

****

She was ancient beyond the comprehension of the mortals, her knowledge spread over eons, even before the Dream. Empires had risen and fallen by her hand. Worshipped as a god, feared and loved in equal measure. They knew her name, but no mortal could begin to understand what she was. And yet, despite her vast knowledge, a thing now puzzled her. She sensed something, but she couldn't understand what. There was something on Dainnor that she had never experienced before, it concerned her, but she had no idea why. There should be nothing in all the worlds to concern Melantha,

Queen of the sethundra, but now there was, now there was a power that threatened her somehow. That should not be.

She was still reeling from what had happened. The Casting was supposed to have failed. What had gone wrong? How had Zotikos been defeated? She should have been at his side, if she had then their victory would have been assured, she had always said that. But what Zotikos wanted, Zotikos got. So she had found herself on Terra, and Zotikos had failed; and at such a cost. Melantha had never wept before in her long life, but she had wept when she learnt of Palmora's fate.

Proof that the Hearts were wrong, the mortals should never have been chosen. They are weak, inferior in every possible way. We were right. The mortals should either serve or die.

Melantha rose from the throne that was carved into the rock itself, her shimmering black gown trailed behind her, a golden circlet held back her long sable hair as she moved to a window to survey what had become of the world she had once known. Below her she could see several hundred of the mortals that she had already gathered to serve her. Trolls, the least intelligent but the easiest to persuade to her cause. Besides, their strength had always impressed her, they would be useful. She would prefer to use the minotaurs, as she had during the war, but that had taken a lot of work to turn them. Another miscalculation of the Hearts. No Guardian had ever been called from the minotaurs, a snub guaranteed to bruise their warrior pride. But one that Melantha had been able to exploit. Human allies would also be useful, weak of body but strong of mind they were much more versatile than the trolls and subtler than minotaurs, they would seek her out in time, once word had spread of her return. The cryn were impossible to turn, to them the will of the Hearts was sacred, they were healers, not warriors, and besides given Palmora's fate, it was unlikely any still lived. The mer were as varied as the humans and equally useful, she would find allies amongst them also. Dragons were by far the most powerful, but also the most dangerous, she couldn't possibly approach them in her present state. The dragons had never been ruled by fear, it was an equal alliance, or there would be no alliance. She smiled, a rarity for her. Allies would come and then, in time, all would serve.

Her smile turned to a frown while she studied the brown haze that covered the land a mile or two from her fortress. A curiosity, one that she would get to the bottom of once more important matters had been attended to.

Something had happened, the Apprentice had been in desperate peril, so desperate she had had a hard time resisting the urge to leap to his aid. He had almost died. She had been within a hairsbreadth of being free. *What had he been trying to do?*

Her thoughts turned to the other two sethundra who had been awoken on the same night as she. The traitor, Baccus, and the other one, the self-righteous Artemis. If it hadn't had been for her Melantha would have risked approaching Baccus as soon as she had woken up, the Apprentice was young and inexperienced. Surely he couldn't be Terra's Guardian? But with Artemis there, the risk had been too great. Melantha had no idea which way Baccus would turn. And there had also been that unknown threat. She had sensed it on Terra too.

But what concerned her the most, was that the unknown threat, whatever it was, was slowly coming closer.

CHAPTER 11

Flicker.

Without thinking Katy spun her head in the direction of the movement, swearing as her peripheral vision was assailed with a barrage of flickering images. She pulled her hood lower over her eyes in irritation, tugging it sharply until the inside of her hood was the only thing visible.

"Just how many sethundra are there here anyway?" she asked to no one in particular for perhaps the hundredth time.

"Thousands," Conall responded wearily from the horse beside her, "no one knows for sure."

In the three days of travelling through the Deadlands not one of her companions had given her a different answer to that question. In fact, if she had wanted to know anything she doubted she could have picked a worse group of men. *The Deadlands,* she thought, going over the few things she had learned, *are called the Deadlands because there was a massive battle between the sethundra here and, for some reason, stuff doesn't grow anymore and they think that's because the number of sethundra is so great, but nobody knows for sure. The battle was going on when a thing called the "Casting" happened, which as far as I can tell was the thing that put the sethundra to sleep and that's why I keep seeing stuff out of the corner of my eye every time I lower my hood. But no one knows why I can see them out of the corner of my eye, but not when I'm looking straight at the damn things. Oh, and the Deadlands are not actually dead, there are trolls here and many patches of land that things will grow in, presumably because there are no bloody sethundra in those bits, but no one knows for sure. Ask one of this lot how to swing a sword and they'll give you a lecture lasting several hours before they let you go near the sodding thing! Ask something genuinely quite interesting? They don't have a bloody clue!*

In fairness, the last point about the areas where things did grow was almost certainly areas with no sethundra. There was no movement out of the corner of the eye when they entered into one. They took advantage of every area they found to rest for the night, or even to stay several hours of the day, making their progress through the Deadlands painstakingly slow. During these periods of 'rest', Conall and the others took the opportunity to bash her around the place with a sword or make her shoot arrows with a bow until she collapsed in exhaustion. She had proven to be quite good with the bow. When shooting at unmoving trees anyway, but the sword was proving a little more challenging. Hrolf told her that she was doing quite well, that she was merely practicing against very good swordsmen, particularly Conall, but she couldn't shake the feeling that he was just trying to be encouraging.

Katy found it odd that of all her companions she enjoyed Hrolf's company the most. He was generally interested in getting to know her and making friends, probably because Katy was the only human in the party without any prejudice towards minotaurs. Dunham talked about nothing but soldiering, Bevan and Brennan barely said anything at all and Conall, whilst very nice to look at, seemed incapable of taking anything seriously apart from his dislike for Hrolf, although a part of Katy was convinced that he didn't dislike the minotaur half as much as he wanted everyone to believe.

Other than the odd oasis of vegetation and a little animal life they had seen no evidence that anything else lived here, although everyone said they needed to keep a wary eye out for trolls. Not an easy thing to do when keeping a hood pulled low over your eyes to avoid seeing too much. A part of her desperately wanted to see a troll, many of Grandad's stories had featured such creatures and she was keen to see what one actually looked like. Back home there appeared to be as many descriptions as there were stories. *Surely one of them must be accurate.* On the other hand, trolls never seemed to be particularly pleasant creatures and judging by her companions' feelings towards them she guessed Dainnor's trolls were no exception.

"Ok," she said to Conall, "you don't know how many sethundra there are, what about trolls? Are there many?"

"Trolls tend to move around in small groups, maybe half a dozen or so," the prince said. "They might band together to form a raiding party into our lands, but it's rare."

Hrolf who was marching tirelessly on the other side of Katy added his own voice. "They haven't formed anything remotely resembling an army for at least three hundred years. Trolls are stupid creatures; they don't have what it takes to hold a large force together."

"So what happened three hundred years ago?" Katy asked curiously.

Hrolf shook his head sadly. "One of my own people. He and a band of followers gathered the trolls under his banner in an effort to conquer Lors. They invaded quite deeply into the kingdom before the humans were able to defeat them. They almost reached the gates of Aldarris itself."

"And entire towns and villages were destroyed," Conall said, his anger rising, "not just the buildings, the people too. Women and children included."

"A dark time in my people's history, a shameful time, but we must not allow the past to control the present, Conall. If we stand together we can prevent these crimes from ever happening again."

"I don't disagree with you, Hrolf and I will work with you to achieve this, but it will not return my father or brother to me." Conall dug his heels into his horse's flanks taking him ahead of Katy and the minotaur.

Hrolf sighed heavily. "He sees no difference between one minotaur and another."

"He lost his father and brother, he's angry, he's probably been angry about it for a long time. I don't think he hates you, Hrolf, I think he just needs to get used to thinking about minotaurs in another way."

"You're probably right, but our two peoples need their princes to put aside their differences now. We must lead by example."

Hrolf let himself fall a little behind, lost in his own thoughts, marching between Katy and Brennan who was bringing up the rear. At least Katy thought it was Brennan, three days of travelling together and she still couldn't tell the difference between him and his brother. She dug her own heels in and caught up with Conall. He looked across to her and smiled. *A girl could lose her head to smile like that,* she thought unconsciously patting her hair and getting a new barrage of flickering out of the corner of her eyes as she knocked her hood. She tugged it firmly back into place again.

"Sorry," Conall said, "I know it's not his fault."

"Perhaps you should try telling him that."

Conall sighed and nodded. "I'll do it when we next make camp."

They rode on in silence for a while before the prince spoke again. "I miss my father, but I miss my brother even more. He was only a year older than me, we used to do everything together. We would spar with each other, race our horses," he chuckled, "avoid Finian's lessons. Everything." Katy winced a little at the mention of racing horses. Her ride through the Deadlands was turning her into quite a good rider, but she didn't fancy the idea of racing yet. She still felt saddle sore and dreaded to think what her bottom looked like. "Every time I look at Hrolf, or any minotaur, I find myself wondering, "was that the one that did it, did that one kill them". And to lose my father too. People don't know what it's like when you lose a parent so young."

"I do. I lost my mother."

"I'm sorry, I didn't know…How did she die?"

"I've no idea. Some people, well my grandparents and my father, think she's still alive, but she's dead. She has to be."

"What happened?"

"A few weeks after Dylan was born she vanished, she just went out one day and didn't come back. At first I thought that maybe she'd had an accident, even murdered, but she knew. The way she spoke to me before she left, the advice she used to give me, she knew she was going and not coming back, she knew she was going to die. She had an illness or something and went somewhere to die alone."

"That's very sad. You must miss her."

"She was a selfish coward," Katy snapped.

"Why do you say that?"

120

"She left us, kept her illness, whatever it was, to herself. If she had told my father then he could have grieved and moved on and we could have been a proper family. Instead he spends every moment looking for her. She's dead, but without a body he won't accept it."

"It may not have been the right decision, but I'm sure she meant…"

"What? She meant well?" Anger flared up within Katy. "She wanted to spare us pain? Well she didn't! We had as much pain as anyone else, more, because we've never been able to move on." She brushed a tear from her cheek and looked away from Conall, not wanting to talk anymore. Thankfully, the prince seemed to understand, and didn't press her.

They rode on in silence for some time after that until Bevan, or was it Brennan, came riding back to have a hushed conversation with Dunham. They waited until the others had caught up with them.

"What is it, Captain?" Conall said.

"A large area of woodland, Highness, just over the next ridge. Brennan believes it's just an hour or so from Melantha's ancient stronghold."

"I can't be sure though, Your Highness," Brennan said, "I've only got old maps to go by and I don't have one with me, I'm just working from memory see."

"It's alright, Brennan," Conall said, "you're doing the best you can. We'll stop for the night in the woods and then go on to the fortress in the morn…" Conall looked to Hrolf. "At least that's my advice, what do you think, Hrolf?"

Hrolf, momentarily taken aback at being asked his opinion, paused before answering. "I agree, best we're all as fresh as we can be when we enter the old fortress, daylight will also work in our favour if we encounter trolls."

"Why's that?" Katy asked.

"Trolls don't like the sunlight much," Conall explained, "they'll move about in it if they have to, but their eyesight isn't great in the day so they prefer the dark. It's agreed then, we'll make camp in the woods. Lead the way, Brennan."

The scout nodded and began leading the way, the others following silently behind. It wasn't long before they reached the top of the ridge and could clearly see the large area of woodland some distance ahead of them. It stretched out for about a mile in either direction and, as far as Katy could tell, about half that deep. At the far end of the woodland it looked as though the ground rose up to meet a cliff face, it was hard to tell for certain through the brown haze. There was something different to the wooded area that Katy couldn't quite put her finger on at first, but as they began moving closer it suddenly came to her.

"The edges are ragged," she said drawing curious looks from the others. "All the other areas of vegetation we've seen had straight edges, these are ragged, more natural looking."

"She's right," Hrolf said.

Conall nodded his head. "Yet another mystery of the Deadlands."

They continued on for a short while before they reached the trees, Brennan quickly finding what looked to be a path and leading them inside. Instantly Katy noticed the difference. Outside the air was dry, arid; here it was damp and cool. Moss grew on rocks whilst mushrooms and toadstools sprouted between the exposed roots of trees. Ferns scattered the woodland floor and ivy wrapped around branches to hang like serpents above their heads. Like the others, Katy gratefully pushed back her hood and breathed in the refreshingly cool air.

"No sethundra," she said, looking around her in relief. It was then that she noticed something odd about the rocks. Where the trees looked more natural than any they had seen so far, the rocks looked less so. The edges were a little too straight, the angles too precise. Many of the trees had twisted into odd shapes, wrapping around the rocks like a protective mother hugging her child. She was about to mention it to the others when Conall spoke.

"This was a settlement of some kind, that must be why there're no sethundra here. This area wouldn't have been part of the battlefield."

"It may have been for the minotaurs," Hrolf said nodding, "during the sethundra war many of my people lived in this area under the direct rule of Melantha. If I remember my lessons correctly it was in a settlement just outside of her fortress."

"That at least confirms our location. Find a good place to make camp, Brennan."

"Somewhere defensible," Hrolf added clutching his axe and looking around nervously.

"What's wrong? We haven't seen a single troll so far," said Conall

"Exactly; doesn't that strike you as being odd, three days in the Deadlands and not one troll?"

Conall frowned, plainly he hadn't thought of it and had just put it down to good fortune.

"I think Prince Hrolf may be right, Your Highness," Dunham said, "the Deadlands are too quiet. Normally I would just accept that as good luck and think nothing more of it, but with the return of Melantha, I'm not so sure."

"You think they're being gathered?"

"It seems logical, Your Highness. If she wanted to re-establish her power, gathering the trolls would give her a formidable army."

"That we're quite possibly walking right into. By the Stones, I'm a fool!"

"No more than the rest of us, Conall," Hrolf said, "none of us really thought this through properly, but I still say we made the right decision to come. We have to find out what has happened to Katy's brother."

"Let's proceed with upmost caution from now on. Do as Hrolf said, Brennan, find us somewhere defensible. And keep your voices down from now on everyone, no unnecessary talking."

It didn't take Brennan long to find somewhere. Katy guessed it used to be some sort of building, the front was fairly open but for many large rocks scattered around at random. To the rear and either side there looked to be a fairly solid wall, though covered with a lot of ivy and an open space in the centre. With a little difficulty they managed to get the horses through the jumble of rocks and into the centre. Katy noted uncomfortably that if they had to escape in a hurry they would have to climb and leave their mounts behind.

They had barely settled in when Bevan, who had been scouting the area, ran back into the camp, his face grim with the news they had all been dreading.

"Trolls! And they're coming this way."

CHAPTER 12

He ran through a forest of stone; stone leaves that felt the same as normal leaves, branches moving as freely as if made of wood and the underbrush parted for his legs just the same as in any natural forest. He didn't know how long he had run, he couldn't remember starting, he couldn't remember a time when he hadn't been running. It felt as though he had been running his whole life. But no matter how far he ran, he couldn't escape the voice.

It is time to wake.

Whenever he caught a glimpse of the sky through the stone canopy above his head, he saw dark, boiling clouds, so black he felt sure that rain should be pelting him hard enough to draw blood.

It is time to wake.

On he ran through the stone forest, never seeing another living creature, but unable to shake the feeling of being watched. Watched by thousands of eyes, malevolent, full of hate for this small, pathetic, lost creature.

It is time to wake.

He knew the voice; he didn't know how he knew it, only that he did. He wanted it to stop telling him the same thing over and over again, but it wouldn't stop, it wouldn't...he came to a halt. Everything had suddenly changed.

Dark clouds still dominated the sky, but the forest was gone, vanished in the blink of an eye. He now stood upon a barren plane, featureless, but for a single hill standing before him and upon that hill stood a lone figure, shrouded in a dark cloak and hood. The figure

made him feel afraid, but he found himself moving towards it
nonetheless.

It is time to wake.

Closer and closer he came, each step seeming to cross more ground than a natural step should take. He didn't remember climbing the hill, but before he knew it he stood at the top, the shrouded figure standing with its back to him.

It is time to wake.

Slowly it began to turn around, terror filled his heart, he turned to run, but someone stood behind him, blocking his path. A young woman, in elegant looking armour and holding a long, silver sword, he didn't immediately recognize her face for it was horribly scarred. An empty socket where her right eye should be, jagged lines running across her cheeks, her hair burnt away along the left side of her head. He screamed in horror at the grim face, turned away so he didn't have to look at it, only to come face to face with the shrouded figure before him.

Another face that he knew looked down on him, another woman, this one older, but very similar in look to the scarred one behind him. She looked down at him, confusion clearly showing in her eyes. He had never really met her, but he knew her, he had seen pictures, had dreamed of her many times before.

"Mummy?"

It is time to wake.

The woman's eyes opened wide in shock and fear. "No!" she cried. "Not him, leave him!"

It is time to wake.

"Noooooo!" This time her cry turned into a scream as she threw her head back in agony, she flung out her arm towards him, trying to reach him, he tried to reach her too, but something held him back. A slender armoured hand. He looked back into that face and saw it was grimmer than ever, tears pouring down the ruined cheeks. He turned back to his tortured mother, her mouth opened wide and fire burst out of her mouth, her eyes, until she was completely engulfed in flame.

"Mummy!" Dylan cried out sitting up in bed. The sheets, soaked in his sweat, fell down to his waist.

"Oh thank the Stones, you're awake!"

Dylan turned to see Bretta looking relieved, holding a damp cloth in her hand that she had been pressing to his forehead. He couldn't help himself, it had been such a horrible dream, he burst into tears and flung his arms around the plump serving woman. She held him tightly, rocking him and making soothing noises.

"What did you dream, Dylan Howard?"

He looked up to see the towering form of Artemis standing beside the bed, Baccus was also there, he sat on the floor with his back to the wall watching him curiously.

"Hush now," Bretta scolded, "sethundra you might be, but the young lord's upset and he doesn't want to be questioned right now."

"It could be important," Artemis responded, showing no hint at what she thought about being told off by a serving woman, "the boy is an Apprentice, a dream could be a message from the Heart Stones."

"Well I'm sure it can wait until he's finished his sobbing."

"We do not know that until we know what the message is. Dylan Howard, you must tell..."

127

Bretta suddenly turned on Artemis, her finger jabbing forward, pointing at the sethundra like a dagger. "Now you listen to me, this young boy has just come back from the brink of death and something's upset him terribly. Now I know I'm just a serving woman, but Queen Arlana herself and Professor Finian, told me to look after the young lord so look after him I will! Your questions can wait! You're an immortal, show some patience!"

Artemis stared at Bretta for a long while and for her part Bretta held the gaze defiantly. The silence in the room was deafening. Finally, after an age, Artemis inclined her head in agreement. "We will wait."

Bretta nodded satisfactorily, although Dylan couldn't help but notice that the arms holding him relaxed by quite a bit. He also noticed that he had stopped crying, but he found the cuddle from Bretta comforting, so he didn't move. He felt incredibly weak, his belly as hollow as if he hadn't eaten in days. Soon the door opened and Finian entered.

"Ah good," he said brightly, "you're awake. How're you feeling, young man?"

"The serving wench says we are not allowed to ask," Baccus said dryly.

"I said nothing of the sort..." Bretta spluttered.

"It's okay, Bretta," Dylan said, "I'm feeling better now. I'm really hungry though."

"I'd imagine you are," Finian said studying him over the rim of his spectacles. "Bretta, would you be so good as to fetch young Dylan some dinner."

"Yes, Professor," she said, settling Dylan back into bed. "But don't be exhausting him, he still needs rest." She left the room, but not before giving both Artemis and Baccus a sharp, warning look.

"A curious woman," Artemis said, "either she has a Dragon Knight's courage or a troll's sense."

"What's a Dragon Knight?" Dylan asked excitedly.

"The Dragon Knights are…"

"A tale for another time," Finian interrupted.

Dylan crossed his arms and heaved his shoulders in disappointment.

"So, Dylan, how are you feeling?"

"A little tired, but ok."

"Headaches, nausea, any pain?" Dylan shook his head. "Good, then we can have a little talk before Bretta returns with dinner, after which you can get some rest."

"More rest? I feel like I've been sleeping forever. How long was I asleep anyway?"

"Three days. Now, Dylan…"

"Three days? I've been asleep for three days? I can't have, what happened?"

"I assure you, Dylan, you have been asleep for three days and if you'll just stop interrupting me for a few moments then I will tell you what happened." He sat down on the edge of the bed, took a rag out of his pocket, and began polishing his spectacles. "You have no idea just how lucky you are, young man, you very nearly died. In fact, I'm quite surprised you are alive. What you did, or attempted to do anyway, was to directly access the power of a Heart Stone. Few Guardians in history have been powerful enough to do such a thing. An untrained Apprentice, such as yourself, most likely would kill himself, drive himself insane or even…well, you could have levelled half the city with whatever it was you were trying to do. What were you trying to do anyway?"

"I don't know," Dylan answered truthfully, "I can't really remember."

"Well in that case we must proceed as if you were acting in pure ignorance, which you were. But Dylan, I cannot stress enough that you must never, never try to use a Heart Stone in that way again."

"But what is a Heart Stone?"

Finian shook his head despairingly. "My, my, it's a wonder that Terra still exists at all. A Heart Stone, Dylan, is, well it's complicated, but I'll try to be brief. They are the living heart of a world; they are, in fact, what gives a world life. Without them I wouldn't be here, neither would you, Artemis, Baccus, or indeed any living thing."

"Are they alive?"

"Oh yes, very much so."

"Can they talk?"

"They can communicate to a degree. Which is where you and I come in. Guardians and their Apprentices are people whom the Stones have chosen to communicate with and to protect them of course. We are, if you like, their hands to do the work that they cannot."

"Can sethundra be Guardians?" Dylan blinked his surprise when Baccus made a sound in his throat almost like a growl.

"Ah, well, that brings us to a rather sensitive point considering our two companions here." Finian watched Baccus thoughtfully for a moment before turning back to Dylan. "However, it is that very point that we need to discuss. There are, or were, seven Heart Stones, therefore seven worlds..."

"I learnt their names from your book, Terra, Dainnor, Tarnasus, Set'ta, Set'ia, Lagannia and Palmora."

"Good, that's very good. Now, let us go back to your question, "can sethundra be Guardians?" and the answer is, no they cannot." Dylan caught Baccus shifting uncomfortably out of the corner of his eye. "There are several theories as to why, one being that there are no magi amongst them, another is that the Stones can't actually communicate with them."

"I do not believe that to be true, Professor Finian," Artemis said, "the sethundra are closer to the Hearts in nature than any of the mortal races, and although we have no magi we do have certain natural abilities that you do not, the opening of pathways for example. The Hearts do not communicate with us because they choose not to, perhaps it is because we are that much stronger, and therefore harder for them to control."

"Possible," Finian mused, "but whatever the reason many of the sethundra were deeply unhappy about it."

"A great understatement, Professor Finian, aside from the Hearts themselves, we are the superior of all the races. To have weaker mortals placed above us and even given a degree of control over us was a bitter blow for my people."

"Indeed it was, Artemis and even I myself question the wisdom of the Stones, for whatever the reason for their decision it led to a terrible conclusion."

"What happened?" Dylan asked.

"War," Baccus said quietly, his eyes staring into the past, his face full of grief, "the war of the sethundra."

"A terrible, terrible business," Finian said, shaking his head. "It stretched across all seven worlds and raged on for hundreds of years. Entire civilizations were wiped out, Guardians and Apprentices fell as sethundra who refused to accept the will of the Heart Stones tried to gain control of them, it split the mortal races as they too went to war, choosing sides, some even worshipping individual sethundra and forgetting the will of the Stones altogether. The war threatened everything, the very existence of all life and it seemed as though there could be no victor, until one day a particularly powerful Guardian was called. She hatched a plan and gathered all the Guardians and their Apprentices together on her home world of Palmora and together they did something that had never been done before. They combined the power of all seven Heart Stones for a mighty casting, to hide the sethundra, wherever they may be, trap them in an endless sleep, only to be awoken at the will of a Guardian. Thus, ending the war in one single blow."

"It worked then," Dylan said excitedly, "the sethundra were all put to sleep."

"Yes, Dylan Howard," Artemis said mournfully, "but at too great a cost. One of the Hearts, Palmora, died in the casting."

"So now there are just six worlds," Finian said, "the casting was too great an ask."

"But there is another world," Dylan said, "an eighth, or seventh I suppose, I saw it carved on a door in Grandad's house."

"Olwyn told me you had been talking to Alanson about the symbols. I'm not sure what you saw carved on your grandfather's door but it wasn't another world, Dylan. There are just six worlds now, Terra has fallen so far that I expect any knowledge they have is just considered to be folklore, fireside tales to entertain the children."

"But I saw the door again, in your study."

"I assure you there is no door carved with fanciful symbols in my study, Dylan, I would know if there was."

"But…"

"Accessing the Stone directly as you did could conjure up all sorts of images. Most likely the Stone attempted to communicate with you, you would have been flooded with visions that you didn't understand. Put it from your mind, boy, you're safe now and we have to think about our next course of action regarding Melantha."

"You know where she is?"

"We do, Dylan Howard," Artemis said, "she is in the very place we believed she would go to when she came to Dainnor. She is at her ancient stronghold in what is now known as the Deadlands, no doubt she is gathering some of her old allies to her as we speak."

"What about, Katy?"

"We have found no trace of your sister, neither have we looked."

"But you have to," Dylan said desperately until a sudden idea occurred to him, "I order it. You have to do as I tell you, so I order you to find Katy." Nothing happened. Artemis just stood looking at him, doing nothing, Baccus actually smirked. *I don't understand, they're supposed to do as I tell them.*

"It's not as simple as just telling a sethundra to do something, Dylan," Finian said, "it's much like casting, you could just say the rhyme your grandfather taught you and nothing will happen but if you prepare yourself properly first you can of course wake up the sethundra. I must teach you how to focus, but I must also teach you some degree of responsibility as well." As he said this, Bretta entered the room bearing a large tray laden with food. "Ah, excellent, your dinner has arrived. I think that's our cue to leave you to get some rest." He hopped down off the bed and headed for the door. "Eat as much as you can and then get some sleep, we'll talk some more in the morning." He left, closing the door behind him, neither Artemis or Baccus moved a muscle as Bretta placed the tray on his lap.

The smells wafting up from the tray reminded him that he hadn't eaten anything in three days and he attacked the tray enthusiastically, before long though, his eyes began to droop and just as Bretta moved the tray away he fell into a deep sleep, filled with dreams of talking stones arguing with giant beings and wizards.

CHAPTER 13

Freya rather liked staying in the palace. She'd risen from an extremely restful night in a bed that, for a wonder, was large enough to comfortably accommodate a minotaur. Not that she was particularly large by minotaur standards, but she was certainly a lot bigger than the average human. She had woken to a delicious breakfast and given the run of the palace and its grounds by the queen herself. The queen had even said that she could explore the city if she wanted to. She would be quite safe, Queen Arlana had assured her, news of "Freya the Peacekeeper" had spread throughout the city like wildfire. She giggled to herself when she imagined what Prince Hrolf would think of that. *Maybe he'll notice Freya the Peacekeeper more than he notices Freya the Servant,* she laughed to herself. Thinking of the prince soured her mood slightly, feeling a pang of worry for Hrolf and Conall out in the Deadlands. *Keep them safe, Katy. They need a good woman to keep them on a straight path.*

She was now exploring the palace itself after she had just finished a lovely morning stroll in the gardens. The gardeners had been delighted to be told by her that the flowerbeds looked beautiful and even more delighted when she showed a genuine interest in the names of the different plants. One young man had even given her a flower to wear in her hair, she'd forgotten what he had called it, but it had perfect peach coloured petals and

135

was the prettiest thing she had ever seen. She wondered if Hrolf would think her pretty with it.

At one point she had seen Chief Alberich coming towards her and had half expected another public scolding, this one about neglecting her servant duties, but instead he had just given her a respectful nod and continued on his way. Apparently, according to a chatty serving woman by the name of Bretta, everyone had been told that all the minotaurs were guests of the queen so no one had servant duties to perform for the duration of their stay.

Freya rounded a corner and came to a halt, watching curiously as a small human boy peeked around a suit of armour, checking the corridor ahead of him like he didn't want to be seen. He looked far too finely dressed to be servant, although his dark hair needed a good brushing, a young lord perhaps, trying to hide from his lessons. Freya smiled warmly. *Human children are so cute.* Seeing that the corridor ahead was empty the boy rushed out from his hiding place, running down the corridor a few paces before ducking behind a plinth with an amber vase sitting upon it, then peeking down the corridor again. Filled with curiosity, Freya trotted to catch up to him.

"Hello," she said, "can I help you?"

The boy started at the sound of her voice, his eyes rising up and growing wider and wider until they reached Freya's face. He screamed and leapt back, bumping the plinth, the amber vase wobbling precariously. The boy then flung his arm out as if throwing something at Freya. "Fireball!" he shouted, flinging his arm back and forth. When nothing happened he brought both his arms up together, pointing all of his fingers rigidly at Freya and crying out, "Lightning!"

"What are you doing?" Freya asked, politely trying her best not to giggle.

The boy flung his arms wide before pointing one single finger at her. "I banish thee, demon!"

Freya could contain herself no longer and laughed loudly at the ridiculous display. "I'm not a demon, silly, I'm a minotaur. And why would you want to banish me, I only came over to say hello."

The boy glared at his finger in frustration before looking up at her suspiciously. "You're a friendly minotaur?"

"I like to think so. My name's Freya, what's yours?"

The boy squinted at her for a moment before answering. "Dylan."

Freya clapped her hands in delight. "You're Katy's brother! They said you were in the palace. Are you well? I heard you had been taken ill."

"You know Katy," Dylan said eagerly, "where is she, is she alright?"

"I do know her, yes. I'm not sure exactly where she is, but I know she's with two princes, so she should be fine."

"Two princes?" Dylan rolled his eyes. "I'll never hear the last of that. I'm glad she's alright though. Are you really a minotaur, Freya?"

"Yes, of course."

"It's just that I've never heard of a girl minotaur. Grandad told me a story once about a minotaur in a maze, I'm pretty sure that was a boy, but I suppose there must be girl minotaurs otherwise how would you get baby minotaurs. Do you know the story of the minotaur in the maze?"

"No, I'm afraid I don't, sorry. What are you doing anyway?"

Dylan shifted uncomfortably. "Oh, I er, was trying to sneak out of the palace to go exploring. I wanted to see some of the city."

"Aren't you allowed?"

"Well, er, nobody said I couldn't. Artemis did say it would be 'inadvisable' but she's no fun at all, and Baccus just snorted, but then Baccus doesn't really say much, so I sort of snuck out, but as I said, no one said I couldn't. They think it won't be safe on my own and the queen doesn't want sethundra being seen in the city."

"I was just going out to explore the city myself, you could always come with me."

"Really? I could explore the city with a real, live minotaur?! That would be cool!"

"Cool?" Freya asked, confused.

"Really good I mean. That's what we say on my world when something's good, well some of us do anyway. Can we go now?"

"I don't see why not. Now, unless I'm mistaken the main entrance is just down this..."

"No," Dylan said urgently, "not the main entrance. Isn't there a back door we could go through?"

Freya smiled, "There's a small gate near the servants' quarters we could use; I don't think it gets used very often."

"That sounds great, let's go," Dylan said, sounding relieved.

They started off together down the corridor, heading
for the servant quarters, Dylan watching suspiciously for anyone who might drag him off back to his room. Whenever he did see someone he didn't like the look of, which appeared to be everyone, he would move to whichever side of Freya obscured him from them. On more than one occasion Freya had very nearly stepped on him as he dodged around her, it led to the two of them doing a somewhat inelegant dance. It made conversation with the boy impossible too, which was a pity as Freya was desperate to find out more about his world. She hoped she would get a chance to visit it one day.

They reached the servants quarters, somehow managing not to trip each other up and ending as a tangled mess on the floor. It was fairly quiet, with all the servants being out and about performing whatever duties were required of them. They met three young serving girls who were sat down catching a break and gossiping about some young man or another. They waved and smiled at Freya in greeting and frowned at the well-dressed boy who hid unsuccessfully behind her skirt, but whatever mystery surrounded the pair it wasn't as interesting as the gossip they were sharing, so Freya and Dylan were allowed to go unchallenged.

The minotaur led the boy through a door that found them standing in a small yard, ahead of them was an open gate that led into the streets of the city. Freya had feared the gate would be locked and they would have to find another way out, but a couple of burly looking men were carrying sacks and crates of goods through the gate from the back of a cart that stood just outside. The men appeared even less interested in Freya and Dylan than the serving women inside had been, Freya assumed they merely wanted to get their work done as quickly as possible so they could have a break of their own. Again unchallenged, the pair stepped out of the palace grounds, out into the city.

"We did it," Dylan exclaimed, punching the air of all things, "well done, Freya, you're a genius! Where should we go first?"

Freya shrugged. "I don't know; this is my first visit to Aldarris too."

"Well let's see what we can find then. Come on, Freya, it's about time we had a proper adventure." And then he was off down the street so quickly that Freya had to trot to catch up with him.

The streets near the palace were wide and relatively quiet, not many people had business there and the buildings seemed to be mainly fine looking houses owned by one lord or another, each building trying to outdo the other in grandeur. None came close to the splendour of the palace itself though so they failed to hold either explorers' attention for long. They soon found themselves in the more populated areas of the city. Taverns and shops lined the street selling everything, from bolts of cloth to tools and fine weapons. Hawkers cried out their wares announcing to the world the fabulous quality of their goods, each one claiming that you wouldn't find better anywhere else. Music and laughter floated from the taverns which Dylan badly wanted to go into, but Freya insisted he was too young to frequent such places and beside neither of them had thought to bring any money to buy a drink. Some street entertainers amused them for a while; jugglers tossed rings and brightly coloured balls in the air whilst a young woman wearing a scandalously revealing outfit did back flips and walked up and down the street on her hands, then a man wearing just his breeches, his entire upper body covered in tattoos, stepped forward and breathed fire to the delight of everyone in the crowd.

Freya herself attracted a lot of attention as they moved about the city. People would point her out to others, some would wave in friendly greeting, whilst others, mainly men who looked as though they might have fought in the wars at some time, looked at her with expressions that ranged from thoughtful curiosity to outright hatred. Fortunately, nobody attacked them, verbally or otherwise, and on more than one occasion she caught the name 'Freya Peacekeeper' being spoken. She thought Dylan might have had something to do with keeping potential attackers at bay, a small, laughing boy pulling a minotaur excitedly by the hand from one site to another was surely an image to soften even the hardest of hearts.

Humans fascinated Freya as a rule, but the little boy from another world never stopped surprising her. He was constantly using what Freya considered to be the wrong words, 'cool' meaning 'good' for one, and from the way he kept using the word 'awesome' she took it to mean very good. At one point when the juggler started tossing knives into the air he referred to it as being 'wicked' which really confused her, as that, on clarification, apparently meant he liked the display. As for the fire-eater; Freya spent a long time looking for a misbehaving donkey before Dylan, between uncontrollable bouts of laughter, tried explaining that 'badass' was something else entirely, although even he himself appeared to have trouble explaining what exactly it was.

"Conversation on your world must be very confusing, Dylan," Freya said when Dylan had finally stopped laughing.

"We get by," he said with a grin, "though Nanny struggles with it sometimes too. Let's go down there!" And again Freya was dragged off down a side street by the boundless energy and enthusiasm of the strange, but likeable, ten-year-old boy.

The side streets were dark, narrow and twisting and it wasn't long before Freya began to worry that this may not be the safest environment for the two of them. She was about to suggest to Dylan that perhaps they should find their way back to the more open and populated streets when he let go of Freya's hand and darted off with an excited, "Come on, Freya, keep up!"

He sped off round one corner, forcing Freya to lengthen her stride to keep pace. She just had time to see him take a left before losing sight of him again. When she caught up he was galloping down some narrow, stone stairs, the buildings rising up ominously on either side of them. Freya being that much larger than Dylan, and growing up in the wide, open lands of the minotaurs, began to feel claustrophobic, a feeling that wasn't helped by a growing fear of the type of people that might inhabit such an environment. Cutpurses, muggers and the like were the sort of stories she had heard about. She could only hope that her physical size would frighten any off. She just wished that Dylan would slow down.

"Stop, Dylan," she called out as loudly as she dared. "Don't go too far ahead."

Dylan poked his head around a corner. "Come on, Freya, I thought you were cool. You sounded just like my sister then." His head disappeared back around the corner with a laugh.

Freya ran to catch up, slipping slightly on a muddy patch as she went. She caught herself on the corner of the wall and saw Dylan running along the path ahead of her, narrowly dodging an old woman carrying a basket of washing. The woman swore loudly at the boy as he rushed past her, before turning back to continue on her way. Her eyes went wide with terror at the sight of a nearly seven-foot minotaur charging towards her. Muttering an apology for the boy's behaviour and any fright that she herself might have caused, Freya edged past the woman as carefully as she could. The old woman just stared up at her as if all her nightmares had been made flesh and magically appeared before her in the alley.

On Freya went, trying to catch the boy who, in her own estimation, was becoming less likeable by the second and more and more wicked; although not in the way that Dylan would use the word. They were now in a more residential part of the city and with that came more obstacles for Freya to navigate herself around. Washing hung on ropes between the buildings, easy for Dylan to duck under, not so much for the minotaur. She pushed past one sheet, ducked under another, nearly barrelled down a group of women who then began screaming in terror. Freya backed away, apologising as she went, turned to run after Dylan and crashed into a pile of rubbish standing beside someone's front door.

Picking herself up and dusting herself down, she looked up in sudden fear. Dylan was nowhere to be seen. She hurried forward to a crossroads in the alley, looking frantically down each street, but she couldn't see him anywhere. She wrung her hands in worry as she tried to think what she should do.

Suddenly, down the left-hand alley there was a crash, some angry shouts and a boy's cry. With a roar of anger, Freya hurtled herself down the alleyway, determined that if anyone had hurt the little boy from another world then they would have Freya Peacekeeper to answer to.

CHAPTER 14

Dylan wiped off some of the beer that now covered his face and clothes, admitting to himself that he probably should have been paying better attention to where he had been going. He smiled as innocently as he could at the angry looking men standing over him. Well, two were standing over him, the other three were untangling themselves from each other, picking themselves up off the ground and spouting swear words that Dylan hadn't known existed.

An alleyway is a silly place to have a pub anyway, he thought, looking up at the sign that showed a picture of a pig being roasted on a spit. He noticed he was no longer in an alley, it had opened out into a small square with buildings looming up around them, blocking out any view of the rest of the city. The door to the tavern was up some steps, raucous laughter drifted out through the open doorway.

He spat out some of the beer that had trickled into his mouth and grimaced, it tasted even worse than the stuff his grandfather drank. Nanny had been furious when she had caught him tasting it, although, in truth, she had shouted mostly at Dylan's grandfather as if it had all been his fault.

A particularly ugly looking man with a huge boil on his nose glared down at Dylan. "What're you playing at..." He didn't get to finish his sentence as Freya suddenly came

145

bellowing around the corner, her head lowered as if ready to charge. Shocked, the men scrambled away from the angry looking minotaur, two of them picked up chairs to use as weapons, the one with the boil just looked as though he wanted to be anywhere but where he was.

"Leave him alone," Freya shouted, oddly her voice going quite high-pitched and even sounding a little fearful. "He's just a boy! You harm him and you'll...you'll have me to deal with, yes you will!"

Dylan had never imagined a minotaur defending him in battle, but he felt that if he had it would have made a far more impressive picture than the one currently before him. She looked almost comical.

"Get back, minotaur," one of the men growled, "I've killed your kind before and not above doing it again."

"We're not here to fight," Freya said, "we're here to make peace!"

"You don't look like you're here to make peace," another man said, "you look like you want to bash our heads in!"

"Well I will if you try to harm him!"

Dylan wasn't at all convinced. *She sounds terrified. I thought minotaurs would be fearsome.*

"Peace!" All eyes turned to the source of the new voice. A slender man stood in the doorway to the tavern. His clothes were mainly black, but his long coat was richly embroidered with a variety of coloured flowers and golden thread lined the cuffs and collar. His black hair was pulled back into a short ponytail and a neatly trimmed goatee covered his chin. "Peace," he said again, "don't you lads know who it is you address? This is Freya Peacekeeper, Princess of the Minotaur Kingdom."

146

Freya blinked in surprise at that.

Princess? Dylan thought. *I thought she said she was a servant.*

"I don't care who she is," the one with the boil said, "a bashed head, is a bashed head, it don't matter who bashed it."

The man in black laughed loudly, revealing straight rows of perfectly white teeth. "Wise words, Gelban, Doyle never took you to be a philosopher. Doyle never knew such wisdom was to be found in the sewers. Perhaps Doyle should find himself work there too, then Doyle will be as wise as Gelban."

"Shut your mouth, Doyle. We were just having a quiet drink is all. It's the damned boy who spilt our ale, charging about like he was. Who's going to buy us another?"

"Barman," the one called Doyle roared back into the inn, "drinks for these men! There! Doyle has solved Gelban's problem, Gelban and his friends have drinks, Gelban and his friends no longer have a quarrel with the princess and the young lord. Is Doyle not correct." Gelban nodded his head reluctantly and he and the others began straightening the tables and chairs, though a couple of them kept a wary eye on Freya who stood with her arms folded, glaring back suspiciously. "Well, my young lord," Dylan looked up to see the black clad man standing over him, a ring covered hand outstretched, "might Doyle lend you a hand?" Dylan took the man's hand and was heaved to his feet. The man then gave both Dylan and Freya a flourishing bow. "Kelvin Doyle at your service, forgive Doyle's companions here, they are not used to those of higher birth like yourselves."

"There's nothing to forgive, sir," Freya said politely, "it was us that disturbed their drinking, it is we that should be apologising."

"Think nothing of it, Princess Freya. Perhaps Doyle
could offer you and the young lord some refreshment at the Spitted Boar. A cooling drink and a bite to eat."

"Yes please," Dylan said eagerly, his stomach rumbling hungrily.

"I'm not sure," Freya said, "maybe we should go back to the palace."

"Oh come on, Freya, it must be lunchtime by now, I'm starving. We won't stay long; we can go back to the palace later."

"The young lord is correct," Doyle said, "the palace is not going anywhere, but Doyle rarely stays in one place for long. Come, it is rare for Doyle to have such fine company. Dine with Doyle."

The minotaur sighed. "Very well, but only for a short time. I'm not even sure I can remember the way to the palace from here anyway."

The man smiled broadly. "Again, Kelvin Doyle provides the solution when a problem arises. In return for good conversation, Doyle will guide you back to the palace. Then the princess and the young lord will part Doyle's company and our lives will be richer for it. Please, come!"

He stepped through the doorway and before Freya could object, Dylan scrambled after him, finding himself in a dark and dingy, and not the nicest smelling, common room. Rough looking men sitting around tables talking and laughing suddenly went quiet at the sight of a minotaur standing in the doorway. Some hands even drifted toward belt knives as a tension suddenly descended upon the room.

"Fear not friends," Doyle said loudly, "this is Freya Peacekeeper, princess of the minotaurs and her young, lordly companion. They are guests of Doyle."

Conversation slowly resumed as Doyle led them through the common room. Dylan heard Freya mutter, "I'm not a princess, I'm a servant," but he couldn't see what she was worried about. He wasn't exactly a lord either.

Doyle had a quick whispered conversation with the barman who was cleaning a tankard with a rather filthy looking rag, before leading Dylan and Freya through a door at the back of the tavern.

If the common room had been in need of good clean this room had at least seen a cleaning cloth before, if not very recently. A single large table dominated the room with an assortment of mismatched chairs and stools surrounding it. There was only one window decorating the otherwise bare walls and that, rather worryingly, had bars on it.

Doyle indicated they should sit. Dylan grabbed the only chair with a cushion whilst Freya perched herself precariously on a wobbly stool, never taking her suspicious eyes off Doyle for a second. Doyle himself sat in a large, high-backed chair at the head of the table, regarding his guests over the top of his ringed fingers, like a king waiting to pass judgement from his throne. He said nothing, just allowed his gaze to switch between the two of them, lingering on Dylan a moment longer than on Freya. The door shortly opened, admitting a rather haggard looking serving girl carrying a large plate with some gristly, fatty meat and overcooked vegetables on it in one hand and two battered tankards with some unpleasant looking liquid inside, in the other. She dumped them unceremoniously in the centre of the table, tossed an unpleasant look in Doyle's direction and exited the room, shutting the door firmly behind her.

"Eat, my friends, eat," Doyle said as soon as the serving girl had left. Dylan sniffed the liquid suspiciously and eyed the gristly meat, swiftly coming to the conclusion that he wasn't as hungry as he had first thought.

"I really think we should be going back to the palace now, Master Doyle," Freya said politely. "Thank you for your hospitality, you are most generous."

"Doyle is very curious," he said, appearing to ignore Freya, "as to what brings a young lord and a minotaur princess into this part of the city. Doyle is thinking that the Warren is not a place for princesses and young lords."

"We were exploring," Dylan said.

"And I am not a princess," Freya said insistently, "I'm just a servant and Dylan's not a lord either, at least not on this..." Freya swallowed what she had been about to say, much to Dylan's relief. Revealing he was from another world to a stranger could have gotten them into a whole heap of trouble.

"A servant is it," Doyle smiled unpleasantly, "and the young man here is no lord? Doyle supposes he's a servant too then. Why else would he be staying at the palace?"

"That's right," Dylan said, "I'm a servant and I have to go back to work in...er, the kitchens."

"A little finely dressed for working in the kitchens, aren't you? Dylan, is it?" Dylan looked down at himself, realising he was still wearing the prince's old clothes. "Doyle doesn't like to be lied to, especially when Doyle went to such a great trouble to protect you from the men outside. Rough men, they are, not very nice at all. Doyle took a great risk protecting you from them."

"I'm sure if you show us the way back to the palace the queen will repay you for your kindness," Freya said a little nervously.

150

"Now why would she do that for a couple of servants?"

Freya stood up abruptly. "We really must be going now, Master Doyle. Come, Dylan." Dylan, feeling uncomfortable with the situation, jumped up from his chair, taking Freya's outstretched hand.

Doyle didn't move. He just sat where he was, staring at them. "Doyle is afraid you won't be going anywhere. At least, not for a while."

"We'll be going, right now."

Freya led Dylan to the door, but came to an abrupt halt when a knife whizzed past her to land with a solid *thunk* in the wood. The pair whipped back to face Doyle, their eyes wide with fear. Another knife was in his hand and he casually picked the nails of his other hand with it as he spoke. "Now Doyle has many friends, he buys them drinks, looks after them and they look after Doyle. But all of this costs coin, much coin. Now what's Doyle and his friends to do when a rich lord and a princess comes running into their world? Why, they take advantage is what they do. They see an opportunity to make much coin. Now the minotaur claims she's not a princess, just a servant; maybe that's true, maybe not, Doyle does not know, but what Doyle does know is that when someone dresses a young man as well as they dress young Dylan, then that someone is willing to pay much coin to get him back when he falls afoul of Doyle and his friends. So you will both be staying with Doyle and his friends for some time. When Doyle and his friends hear the names of those that are looking for the prettily dressed Dylan, then Doyle and his friends will know who to speak to in getting the best price for his safe return. The longer it takes for Doyle and his friends to hear the proper names, the longer Dylan and the minotaur will be Doyle's guests. So why don't you be a good boy, tell Doyle the proper names."

"People will come looking for us," Dylan spat defiantly.

"Of course they will, but why would anyone be looking for a young lord and his minotaur in the Warren? The Royal Guard do not come here, they do not know here, even the city watch tread warily in Kelvin Doyle's world." Doyle stood, casually twirling the knife with his fingers. He gestured Freya and Dylan away from the door. "Now you two have a little think about how long you would like to be the guests of Doyle and his friends. Just remember, the longer it takes you to tell Doyle the proper names, the more uncomfortable your stay will become. Enjoy your meal."

He smiled cruelly as he retrieved his other knife, opened the door and stepped through. With a click he locked it behind him, leaving Dylan and Freya alone in the dingy room at the Spitted Boar.

CHAPTER 15

Arlana paced back and forth across the plush carpet of her audience chamber, anger and frustration clearly visible on her face had anyone actually been present within the room to witness it. Which was, in fact, the whole reason for her anger and frustration.

Chief Alberich was late. Half an hour late to be precise. She had supposed to be meeting with Prince Hrolf, but as he had gone gallivanting off with her son she was stuck with a tribal chief who considered it to be diplomatically acceptable to keep a queen waiting in her own palace.

With some effort, she resisted the urge to pick something up and throw it, settling in the end for giving the wall a good kick instead, earning herself a sore toe that did little to improve her mood. She opened her mouth to scream out her frustration when a knock on the door forced her to bite it back at the last second.

Finally!

Trying her best not to hobble, she walked to the centre of the room, smoothed down her dress and following a deep breath said, "Come," in the calm, controlled voice she had perfected so well during her years as queen.

The door opened, admitting a sheepish-looking General Macklyn, followed closely by the hulking form of Alberich who didn't look in the least bit apologetic. Along with the rough leather and fur traditionally worn by the minotaur people, he wore a challenging expression, his eyes flashing fiercely, almost as if daring the queen to berate him for his tardiness.

Arlana responded by flashing her warmest smile, the one reserved for family, friends and anyone she desperately needed something from, opened her arms and said, "Chief Alberich," she stepped up to the minotaur, standing up on tiptoe to kiss him on both cheeks, "good of you to come."

She felt an enormous burst of satisfaction when Alberich, clearly taken aback, performed a jerky half-bow and stammered, "My apologies for my lateness, Your Majesty."

"Arlana, when we're alone, Alberich, please," she said, managing to keep the smugness she felt out of her voice "won't you take a seat."

Alberich nodded, off guard, sitting down in one of the minotaur sized chairs she had had brought up. The queen sat opposite him, whilst Macklyn took another chair, a hint of a smirk forming on his lips, clearly remembering several other people of importance, himself included, who had fallen afoul of Arlana's ability to disarm a political opponent.

"I trust you are finding your stay comfortable?" she began politely.

Alberich snorted. "I am sure your hospitality is fitting for human dignitaries, but it's too soft for warriors of the minotaur clans. Even kings and queens will sleep and sit on the ground at times."

"We do have a greatly different way of living Alberich, the simpler lifestyle of your people was always greatly admired by my late husband, the king. He often said how

154

much stronger the minotaurs were for it." *Take some away, give a little back.*

A fierce pride entered Alberich's eyes. "An honourable man your husband, a great warrior."

Arlana inclined her head at the compliment. "He always wanted to live alongside the minotaurs rather than fighting them. It was safer if nothing else," she added with a smile.

Alberich barked a laugh. "And for my kind too. You must allow us to return the honour of this visit by returning with me to our halls for a time."

"I would be honoured."

Alberich smiled. "We will find you a soft bed fitting for your kind."

Arlana smiled back through gritted teeth. "Thank you, that would be most considerate of you. General, will you pour us some wine."

"Of course, Your Majesty," the general said, getting up and filling some goblets from the table in corner of the room.

"Have you yet received news of the princes?" Alberich asked, when he had taken his wine.

Arlana shook her head. "None, I'm afraid. The sethundra refuse to look for them, the safety of the boy being their only concern and I dare not send a force into the Deadlands to look for them. Such an action could cause the trolls to gather with or without Melantha. To risk thousands of lives for one..." A lump caught in her throat, but she forced it down. "Well, it's not something I can condone."

Alberich nodded. "A hard decision, harder still for a mother, but the right one. A ruler must make hard decisions for the good of his people, a thing Hrolf has not
yet been able to learn."

"Will the tribes support his claim?"

"Doubtful. He was not born to be king; his brothers were more suited to that task. Hrolf is still a reckless boy, his head full of dreams of adventure. The time of succession draws near, but he is not nearly ready. His father, Asger, is not long for this world I fear."

"And if the chiefs will not support Hrolf, what then? Will the tribes be at war?"

"Maybe, there is no clear favourite amongst possible claimants. Dreng, of the Blood Spear Tribe has a strong claim, but he is young and too fond of war for the liking of many. Asger is committed to peace, has led us far along that path and there are many who wish to continue upon it."

"I remember Dreng during the wars," Macklyn said, "a brutal opponent who led the charge that broke our lines. A charge that cost the life of the king and Prince Conyn. I cannot see the peace holding if he won the Horned Crown. Will you not press your own claim, Alberich?"

The minotaur shook his head. "I have no male heirs, they died in the wars. If I took the crown it will only delay a war of succession for another time. If the tribes would support me at all, that is." He growled in frustration. "I had hoped that this journey would ground Hrolf, that he could learn to be the king our people need, but this jaunt into the Deadlands...Pah! If his brothers lived I would drink to his courage, but now he has merely shown he is unready."

Arlana shook her head. "It appears that the heirs off our two kingdoms have much in common. Conall is also not ready to rule."

Alberich eyed her shrewdly. "But your people will

accept him anyway, where mine will only accept a strong king. You could soon find the minotaurs an uncomfortable neighbour if the wrong chief wins the Horned Crown."

Arlana glared dangerously at the minotaur. "I still have many years left in me yet, Alberich and Conall will learn. He might not like it, but by the time I'm through with him he'll be as fine a king as ever sat upon the throne. Even if I have to nail him to the bloody thing myself."

The chieftain threw back his head and roared with laughter. "I like you, Queen Arlana, there is a fire in your belly. Many of my kin say that human women are weak, they are wrong I think. Asger was right, this peace will benefit both our peoples."

"You will argue it is kept to Asger's successor then?"

"More, I will only support the claims of those who support peace. But I warn you, Arlana, not all of my people will be sorry Melantha has returned. There are those who would see us return to our former strength when she was our ally."

"Ally?" Arlana raised an eyebrow. "Were any allies to Melantha, or merely servants to her cause?"

Alberich nodded his head. "You are right, of course, but there are those of strength and influence who will not see it that way. Dreng being foremost amongst them"

Macklyn shifted uncomfortably in his seat. "Then we must hope she is put back in her cage swiftly."

Alberich turned to the general, a grin spreading across his dark skin. "As do I. I have grown to like you General Macklyn, it would be a shame to kill you on the field of battle."

The general smiled back. "I would weep as my sword removed your head."

Arlana rolled her eyes. She opened her mouth to interrupt the pair when the door suddenly banged open. Both Macklyn and Alberich leapt to their feet, chairs flying across the room behind them as they reached for their belt knives. Arlana merely regarded the wide-eyed serving woman that stood breathing heavily in the doorway. "Bretta," she said calmly, "I trust you have a very good reason for bursting in like this?"

"Forgive me, Your Majesty," Bretta said, dropping a hasty curtsy, "but it's the boy, Dylan. He's vanished!"

****

The troll crashed against the wall; it's now broken, lifeless body sliding to the ground in a heap.

Stupid creature, Melantha thought angrily, flicking her staff back onto her belt. That had been the third that had come to her offering protection in the last hour. The other two she had allowed to live, but now her patience was wearing thin. *Do they honestly believe I am not capable of defending myself?*

"Get that thing out of my sight," she snapped at two other trolls who stood cowering in the doorway, "and the next one of you to disobey me will beg for death before I am finished."

They scrambled to obey, picking up the dead troll from the floor easily between them and fleeing the throne room as quickly as they could. She pushed the hulking brutes from her mind and allowed her thoughts to retreat back to the boy.

She could clearly sense him from this distance, could even be at his side in an instant, though she dare not. Surely the boy was being guarded. He could be surrounded by a hundred magi. Even Dainnor's Guardian and Apprentice would be more than a match for her; at least they should be. So much had changed since her time, anything was possible. She couldn't take more than a couple of trolls with her, only Guardians could transport more. The boy had to come to her and if he came in force then she would open a pathway and flee, find herself stronger allies. Not for the first time since being woken, Melantha considered returning to Terra.

The boy was young, could only recently have been called. The negligence that must have been displayed by his Guardian to allow him to awaken three sethundra unaided astounded her. *Could they have become so weak, fallen so far?* Yet more proof that the will of the Hearts was wrong. Only the sethundra should hold the Heart Stones. Only the sethundra should rule. She shook her head. Attempting to overpower a Guardian alone was too great a risk. Just one magi that she could trust and she would take that risk; retreat from Dainnor, attack Terra. But three thousand years of sleep left her with no clue as to how to find a trustworthy magi, the world had changed so much, the sethundra gone too long. She would have to wait for someone to seek her out.

Another thought pushed its way to the forefront of Melantha' s mind. That vague threatening feeling that wouldn't go away. It was closer now, just hours away. It felt familiar somehow, she had a sense that she had felt something similar before, long ago, before the Casting. It puzzled her. It was no sethundra, she would have sensed one so close, like she could sense the thousands that slept in this lifeless land. But if the threat was not a sethundra then what could it be? Few, if any, sethundra were of any real threat to her. Surely no mortal was her match. A magi perhaps? But she had faced powerful magi before and none had ever made her feel as she did now.

She shook her head, finding no answers, and walked to the window, looking out on what remained of her once glorious fortress. The trolls were busy in the courtyard; they would soon be ready. The sethundra smiled cruelly. Her enemies would come to her, the boy would come to her, and when they did, Melantha had a nasty surprise awaiting them.

****

160

Oriana stalked down the busy corridor, narrowly avoiding a collision with yet another servant running about like a headless chicken.

Five hours had passed since the boy, Dylan, had gone missing. The queen had ordered a search of the palace the moment she had found out, causing a huge, and unnecessary, panic. If she had only stopped to think for a moment then she would have known that the sethundra could have found him instantly, linked to him as they were. But by the time she had thought of that, or rather Finian had explained it to her, the damage had been done.

She reached the door to Finian's study, and without pausing to knock marched straight inside. She had expected to find the two sethundra there, but meeting them for the first time was still something of a shock. She had often imagined what the sethundra would look like. *They look quite human, only...better.* One, the male Baccus, sat crossed-legged on the floor, back straight, his eyes closed as if in meditation, his black hair pulled back into a ponytail, leaving his angular, handsome face clear. The female stood by a window looking out onto the gardens. She turned at Oriana's entrance and looked at her without any expression showing on her breathtakingly, beautiful face.

Oriana curtsied deeply. "It is an honour to meet you, ancient ones, long have I wished to gaze upon the immortal glory of the sethundra."

"Don't you knock?" She turned to see Finian rising up from a chair, the girl, Olwyn sat next to him whilst the boy, Alanson, stood gaping open mouthed at the sethundra, an unused broom held limply in his hand. "Have manners completely fled this palace along with senses," Finian continued irritably. "I trust you have good reason for barging in here, Oriana. Whatever it is, make it quick, I have more than enough to do and little enough patience left in me."

Oriana glared at the diminutive man. "The boy isn't in the palace; I trust you have located him."

"I know the boy isn't in the palace, I'm not a complete idiot! As to locating him, Baccus is following him as we speak."

"Following is the wrong word, Professor Finian," the female, Artemis, said, turning back to the window, "Dylan Howard has not moved for some time."

"Then why not send someone to fetch him, ancient one?" Oriana asked.

"Because it's not as simple as that," Finian said. "Whilst either Baccus or Artemis could leap straight to him, all they can give to anyone else is a direction and a vague idea of the distance. We believe him to be somewhere in the rather aptly named 'Warren'. As we have no wish to cause a panic across half of Dainnor we aren't sending the sethundra to get him unless we have to, there could be any number of people with him. I was hoping he would find his way back, but he hasn't moved for at least an hour."

"Could he be injured?"

"Unlikely," Baccus said, without moving or opening his eyes, "he is nervous, but calm."

"You can tell his emotional state?"

"Yes he can," Finian said, "and the moment it turns into anything like panic Artemis and Baccus will go to him, but until that time we have members of the royal guard looking for him."

Oriana shook her head. "They will not find him; the people of the Warren are renowned for withholding information. They keep to their own. The boy could be in any one of the hundreds of buildings there. What are they to do? Search every attic, every basement? It could take weeks, and during that time Melantha could decide she's less concerned about people knowing of her return than Artemis and Baccus are. If you wait until then before getting to him then it will mean a battle between three sethundra in the middle of the Warren. Panic will then be the least of your worries."

Finian regarded her over the top of his spectacles. "Do you think I have not considered these possibilities, Oriana? I have agents, guides if you like, within the Warren itself. They will make contact with the guard and know the right questions to ask of the right people. They will find him."

"If you will not accept my council will you at least accept my aid?"

"That would depend upon what aid you are offering."

"I also have contacts in the city, the Warren included. Collaborate our efforts and he will be found all the quicker. Also, should difficulties arise, a magi's presence could negate the need for sethundra involvement."

"She speaks the truth, Professor Finian," Artemis said.

Finian sighed. "You're right of course," he said reluctantly. "Very well, Oriana, I will give you the name of my contact in the Warren, however, I want you to take Olwyn with you."

The girl, Olwyn, blinked stupidly at the mention of her name. "Why would I possibly need her?" Oriana said.

"She herself is a magi of great talent and, more importantly, Dylan knows her and trusts her."

And he can have her keep an eye on me, Oriana thought bitterly. Alanson glared at Olwyn enviously. *Surely he doesn't want to come too? I'm hardly going to need someone to sweep the floor for me in the Warren.* "Very well," she said aloud, "but we have no more time for this pointless chatter. We leave now, girl." Finian wrote something down on a piece of parchment and handed it to Olwyn. "The name of the contact?"

"I have given it to Olwyn, she will speak to the contact directly."

Oriana held her tongue though almost bit it in two not spitting out an angry reply. Managing to keep her silence and preserve her dignity, she swept from the room, Olwyn trotting after her to keep up.

CHAPTER 16

Egan Burgess, Captain of the Royal Guard, leant against the wall, hand resting casually on the pommel of his sword. Not his usual royal guard sword, but a plain one of inferior quality. He also wasn't wearing his usual uniform, just plain brown garb, to make him look like a mercenary or merchant's guard, the exact type of person to be found in the Warren. He absently scratched at the scar on his cheek, a gift he had actually received in the Warren when he had been younger, less skilled and more hot-headed. A very painful lesson, but he still sometimes grinned to himself when he thought of the woman that had given it to him.

And now another woman had entered the Warren who sometimes made him grin. The Lady Oriana, a dangerous woman, Egan had little doubt, but the man who ever managed to snare her would be a lucky one indeed. Many a guardsman's head would turn from his watchful duty whenever she walked by. The younger woman, Olwyn, that she had brought with her was pretty too, though not a patch on Oriana. Both of them magi, both of them in the Warren, searching for the boy from another world who had caused so much trouble. *And likely a lot more if those other two sethundra don't put Melantha down soon.*

Egan wasn't an intellectual man, a fact he himself was happy to admit. All he really knew about was soldiering, he'd only risen to the rank of captain in the guard due to an act of heroism during the last war with the minotaurs. It hadn't been enough to save the king though; he had liked King Corann, had wept openly over his body on the battlefield. The fact that Egan had killed the minotaur that had slain the king had done nothing to console him. He didn't know anything about casting, or how the Heart Stones worked, but he knew that the boy was too young to be chosen. *I don't know much, but a boy should be a boy. It's too much responsibility on his young shoulders.*

His thoughts were interrupted when the women came out of the building in front of him. Oriana's face looked like she was ready to strike out at someone. Egan would still like to ask her for kiss, although he never would. *I'm not a complete idiot.*

"Did you learn anything, My Lady?" he asked, when they came close.

"We are to wait here for a guide," Oriana said, her beautiful mouth curling with contempt. "Who do these people think they are, don't they know who I am?"

"They do," Olwyn said, "they just don't care. People in the Warren find titles meaningless, they tend to live by their own rules."

Egan raised an eyebrow in surprise. "You're well informed for someone not raised here."

"I've read some books on the Warren and its people. It's really quite a fascinating subject."

"Do you ever do anything other than read?" Oriana asked dryly.

Olwyn blushed, looking a little embarrassed. "We did learn something that might be useful, Captain. There was another report of a minotaur running around the Warren."

"That makes three sightings," Egan said.

"It seems unlikely to be coincidence that a minotaur is seen in the Warren at the same time that Dylan goes missing here."

"You think we've been betrayed?"

Oriana shook her head. "No, they basically describe a minotaur little differently than they would describe a

166

sheep or a pig, they can't tell one from another as a rule, or at least they don't bother to try, however what they all agree on is that the minotaur was female."

"And this last sighting mentioned the name Peacekeeper," Olwyn added.

"Freya," Egan said, "what would she be doing here?"

"Exploring the city I'd imagine," Oriana said, "as that is what the queen gave her permission to do. It seems she took our young Terran Apprentice with her."

"Terran Apprentice? Now isn't that interesting." They all turned at the sound of the voice, Egan gripping the hilt of his sword, to see an old woman, her face lined with wrinkles, her grey hair pulled back into a tight bun regarding them with bright, blue eyes. "Information like that could fetch a very pretty price when sold to the right ear."

"You would be wise to forget anything you heard and be on your way, old woman," Oriana said coldly.

"And you would be wise to learn when to hold your tongue, girl," the woman answered back, just as coldly, "the Warren has as many ears as it does twists and turns. I doubt Finian would be pleased if the presence of someone from another world became common knowledge."

Oriana's lips curled contemptuously. "You are our guide?"

"I am. You can call me Ealga."

"Do you have information on where we might find our young friend?

"I do. There are rumours from reliable sources that a young lord is being held at an inn called The Spitted Boar. I trust you have not heard of it?" She waited as they all shook their heads. "Not surprising, it is not the sort of place decent people would choose to be in. A dangerous place, even for the likes of Ealga. I will lead you there, but

167

after that you are on your own." Without another word Ealga started off down a narrow street, giving the others little choice but to follow.

It wasn't long before even Egan, who had some knowledge of the Warren, was hopelessly lost. It was such a maze of twists and turns, dead ends and loops that an unwary traveller would often find themselves travelling along a street they had already been on, going in the opposite direction to the one they had been travelling in before. Egan began to suspect that the old woman, was deliberately leading them on an unnecessarily long route. He could also tell that Oriana thought the same, by the increasingly angry look in her eyes and clenching and unclenching of her fists. *Probably doesn't want anyone getting too familiar with her territory.*

Finally, the old woman brought them to a halt and pointed along the narrow alleyway they were on. Egan couldn't see very far as it ended in a blind bend. "Just around that bend is The Spitted Boar," Ealga said, "as I've said before, a dangerous place."

She turned to leave but Oriana stopped her. "Wait. How do we know for sure the boy is even in there?"

Ealga smiled slyly back at her. "You don't." And then she was gone, back down the alleyway they had just walked along.

"A curious woman," Olwyn said thoughtfully.

"That's one way to describe her," Oriana said, turning back towards The Spitted Boar. "Come, we have wasted enough time alre…"

A sound of an explosion cut her off midsentence, closely followed by a cloud of dust that swept around the bend ahead of them, blinding the three completely.

****

168

Artemis stared out of the arched window in Professor Finian's study, not really looking at the neat, well-kept gardens below, her mind occupied with other things.

Palmora is dead. No matter how many times she said it to herself it still sounded strange and impossible to her. *Palmora is dead, because I failed, I failed in my duty. Not the Terran's sin, my own.* She wanted her grief to consume her, to make her curl up in a ball and weep until she could weep no more, but the one thing Artemis had always excelled at was burying her emotions.

She glanced over at the still form of Baccus, his eyes closed in concentration, following the human boy, Dylan. As always, whenever she looked at Baccus, amongst the jumble of other emotions, she felt a stab of doubt. *Did you betray us, Baccus,* she asked herself for perhaps the thousandth time, *did you betray the will of the Hearts? Did you betray me?* And if he had then should she be trusting him to follow Dylan now. Artemis herself could easily sense his presence at this distance, but following his emotions as Baccus was doing required more concentration and Baccus was stronger than her, stronger than all of them except Melantha and Zotikos. *Why did the Hearts choose me if you were loyal, Baccus?* A question she had often pondered, even before the casting.

Someone had betrayed them, that much was clear. Artemis would cut off her own hand before she would believe Dardanus of treachery, but Baccus had always been grudging in his acceptance of the Hearts' decision to appoint mortal Guardians. He had never been of the opinion that the mortals should serve the sethundra, had even been kind to them in the beginning. But it was a kindness that a mortal might show to a horse or a dog, not one born out of mutual respect.

169

Then there was the question of why Dardanus slept on Terra at all? He should have been on Palmora. Had he come with new instructions for Artemis? To warn her of Baccus' treachery? Whatever the reason he had come too late. *Palmora is dead.* An involuntary shiver ran along her spine.

Suddenly, Baccus' eyes snapped open and he leapt to his feet, staff already in hand. Instinctively, Artemis reached for her own staff.

Baccus looked at her, a familiar fire in his eyes as he spoke. "We go to him, now."

CHAPTER 17

Freya smashed up her third chair and swung the single leg that had mostly survived her work in an experimental fashion.

"This should do," she said nervously, "I should be able to bash a few heads with this."

Dylan wasn't convinced. Instead of looking fearsome she looked clumsy and awkward. *Of all the possible minotaurs on Dainnor I had to pick the one that couldn't fight.*

It wasn't her fault, he admitted to himself. If he hadn't run off like he had, then neither of them would be in the mess they now found themselves. Dylan had been so happy to be out of the palace, exploring a new world and with the knowledge given to him by Freya that Katy was alive and well, he had completely forgotten about the possible dangers and ran headlong into trouble. *You need to learn to look before you leap, Dylan Howard.* One of his grandmother's favourite sayings.

Again Freya swung the chair leg, accidently knocking another chair in the process. Dylan shook his head despairingly; if they were going to get out of this then it was up to him. *I'm going to have to use magic, or casting, or whatever they call it.*

Jumping up onto the table he sat in a comfortable, crossed-legged position and closed his eyes. He did everything his grandfather had taught him, concentrated on deep, slow breaths, relaxed every part of his body. He pictured a light in front, allowed the light to travel towards him. Was it easier than before? Closer the light came, closer and closer, until it enveloped him completely. He felt powerful again, he felt as if he could do anything he wished. *But what?* He felt a little foolish for not thinking of that beforehand. He briefly thought of trying to wake up a sethundra, but quickly dismissed the idea, he had no clue as to whether one was close by anyway or even if it would do as it was told. *I can't make Artemis or Baccus do as I say and I could end up waking up someone like Melantha.*

Their first problem was to get out of the room. Breaking the door down was one thing, but there was bound to be someone guarding on the other side so he would need to act fast. He decided to practice first.

He looked to Freya who was still swinging her chair leg at imaginary enemies. That gave him an idea. Focusing on one of the unbroken chairs he tried willing it to break into pieces. Nothing happened. He tried again; and again nothing. Sighing in frustration he was about to give up when he heard his grandfather's voice in his head, *"the words are unimportant, they're merely a way of, shall we say, reminding yourself of what to do"*.

"You're trying to run before you can walk, Dylan Morgan," he said aloud, another favourite saying of his grandmother's. Freya looked at him curiously, but he ignored her. Taking a moment to arrange a spell in his head, he focussed again on the chair, took a deep breath, raised his hand, and began.

> "Enemies of Dylan, you must beware
> Feel my power as I destroy this chair!"

As he thrust his hand forward he felt something surge through him, it rose up from somewhere deep inside, filling him with energy until every part of his body tingled like electricity. For a split second he wondered what to do next when suddenly the energy rushed through him, out of his outstretched hand, and the chair exploded before him, showering splinters in all directions. Delighted, Dylan grinned widely at Freya who stared back, eyes wide with shock.

"What did you do?" she gasped.

"I used the power of a Heart Stone," he said excitedly, jumping up and standing on the table, "and now I'm going to use it to get us out of here."

"No, wait…" Freya began, but it was too late as Dylan had already begun to chant.

"I can't stay here, I have a mission
Power of the Heart Stone let me out of this prison!"

Flinging both of his hands forward, he again felt a surge of power, this time larger, much larger. He heard a huge explosion as he was hit by a wave of dizziness, nearly making him topple from the table. He shook his head, his vision taking a moment to clear, and looked up. Before him, a huge cloud of dust billowed, momentarily obscuring everything beyond a few feet in front of him, until it slowly began to dissipate; returning vision bringing with it groans of pain.

A scene of destruction unfolded before him. Where there had once been a wall, there was now just a hole into what was left of the common room of The Spitted Boar. Absurdly, the only thing left standing of their prison was the very door he had been trying to break down. Tables and chairs lay scattered about amid the tangled and battered bodies of patrons and serving girls alike. The upper floors of the building still stood, though for how long Dylan wasn't sure as he had appeared to have demolished half of the outside wall as well. He heard an ominous creak as the door to the prison lost its battle with gravity and came crashing to the ground.

He glanced across to Freya who stood, mouth agape at the destruction before her. Her head turned slowly towards Dylan, her eyes wide with fear, staring at him as if she wasn't sure what it was she was looking at.

Dylan didn't know what to say to comfort her, so he just went with the first thing that came into his ten-year-old head. "Oops."

"What happened here?"

They both turned at the sound of the shout to see Kelvin Doyle stepping into the remains of the common room, his once fine coat covered in dust, a pair of long knives held in his hands. He looked straight at Dylan standing upon the table top and snarled, "You!" Doyle pulled back an arm and flung one of the knives straight at him. The boy's mind desperately scrambled for a spell to save himself, but fear got in the way. He raised his arms in a pitiful bid to protect himself, knowing that there was nothing he could do. But then, at the last possible instant, a staff flashed across his vision, knocking the knife to the ground.

For a split-second Dylan thought it was Freya with her chair leg who had been his saviour, but the staff was too long and slender to be the minotaur's makeshift club. He looked across to see Baccus standing beside the table, staff in hand, face as grim as ever.

"Sethundra!" Doyle's terrified cry swept over the common room, rousing more of the patrons. Those that could, scrambled to their feet and ran. A few men stood with Doyle, nervously brandishing weapons, unsure of what to do. Doyle threw his other knife, but this time Artemis leapt into view, her staff easily knocking the blade harmlessly away.

174

"Yeah," Dylan yelled, punching his fist into the air,

"let's get them!"

"Let us not," Baccus growled.

"Baccus," Artemis said, "we are leaving, now!"

Baccus firmly grabbed Dylan by the shoulder; and then The Spitted Boar, Doyle, Freya and everything before him vanished from sight.

****

Freya gaped as Dylan and the two sethundra vanished from view. She had no idea whether the sethundra could have taken her with them or not, but she wished they hadn't just left her alone with Doyle and his men. Seeing that she was now unaided they regained a little of their courage, coming towards her, weapons raised.

"Doyle does not like having his prize taken from him," Doyle snarled angrily. "Doyle will demand a lot more from the minotaur princess for damages done."

Freya brandished her chair leg and tried her best to look fierce. She was under no illusions that she could defeat the men and a fervent wish that Prince Hrolf would suddenly come leaping into the common room to save her whirled around in her head.

My only chance is if I try to use my size against them. Maybe if I just charge, they'll scatter. But in her heart she knew it wouldn't work. Standing at nearly seven foot she wasn't that much bigger than some of the men and she had no fighting skills at all. But she could see no other options open to her. She took a deep breath, closed her eyes and prepared to charge the men.

"Get her!" Doyle yelled. But just as two of the men began to run forward an unseen force picked them both up and hurled them against one of the remaining walls. A scarred man leapt into view, sword in hand. One of Doyle's men swung at him with an axe, but the swordsman blocked it with ease. He then slashed his sword across the axe wielder's chest. The man screamed in pain, staggering backwards, away from the swordsman, toppling to the ground over a pile of rubble. Doyle and his remaining two heavies squared up to the swordsman, but before anyone could do anything, all three were suddenly slammed onto the ground, again by something unseen.

The man calmly sheathed his sword as two women emerged from the dusty air. Freya was shocked to see that one was Oriana, looking somewhat less pristine than she usually did, partly due to her plain attire and partly due to the thin layer of dust that covered her from head to toe. The other was younger, her blond hair cut short and with what looked like ink stains on her fingers.

Oriana's eyes surveyed the wreckage, quickly locking onto Freya, still holding her chair leg. "I might have known it would be you," she said with a contemptuous sniff. "Where is the boy?"

"Two sethundra just appeared from nowhere and took him," Freya said, hardly believing what she was saying.

Oriana's top lip curled up into a snarl. "So we have failed to contain the knowledge that sethundra are awake. Although we could of course limit the knowledge. I'm sure the people here would not be missed."

Freya didn't understand what she was suggesting until the younger woman blurted out, "You can't, Oriana, I won't allow it!"

"*You* won't?" Oriana sneered.

"No," the other woman said, visibly steeling herself against the other woman, "and neither will the professor."

The two women stared at each other for such a long time that Freya wondered if they were to come to blows. They broke off when the swordsman coughed politely. "If I could offer a suggestion," he said. "The cry of sethundra will already be going out in the Warren whatever we do here; several of the patrons ran past us before we could stop them. We can't hide that there were magi, but that's not unusual, but there is no evidence of sethundra. The claim will be laughed off and forgotten in a week, kill everyone and it'll look as though you're covering something up. It will lend weight to the claim that sethundra were here and the palace doesn't want anyone to know."

"He's right Oriana, it makes better sense to let them live."

Oriana looked at the other two for some time before nodding curtly. "Come," she said, turning back towards the alley way, "we can do no more here and I have no desire to spend any more time in this cursed place."

The swordsman followed her, the other woman smiled at Freya, indicating that she should join them. All four of them left behind the remains of The Spitted Boar and entered the twisted maze of the Warren.

******

Ealga hurried along the narrow alleyway of the Warren, cursing her old bones for not allowing her to move faster, cursing every bit of rubble and rubbish that got in her way and, most of all, cursing Finian for causing her so much trouble.

Bloody man! Why can't he leave me alone and find himself a younger agent? Thirty years in the service of the Guardian, barely a day had gone by when she hadn't wished she had never met Finian Pendaran. *Fetch this, deliver that, go there. Damn the man!* And now she had to somehow silence that rascal, Kelvin Doyle. It had been some hours since the incident at The Spitted Boar and already the whole Warren was talking about sethundra. Doyle had always liked the sound of his own voice, but now that he finally had something actually worth saying, Ealga had to try and shut him up in a way that wouldn't lend weight to his claim. *Bloody Professor bloody Finian bloody Pendaran!*

A woman's scream up ahead pulled Ealga to a halt. Without thinking she allowed the power of the Heart Stone to fill her, preparing herself to cast if she needed to. Not many people in the Warren knew that old Ealga was a magi, but those that did, knew to keep it to themselves. Betraying Ealga's trust was not the wisest of actions.

She continued forward more cautiously, until she saw a crowd of people gathered ahead of her. The alleyway opened out into a more residential area of the Warren, tall buildings filled with apartments rose up on either side of her, the cobbled square, normally a place where someone could stretch out, was now as cramped as the alleyway Ealga had just emerged from.

Dozens of people crowded the area, some talking in hushed, fearful tones, others looking pale, breathing heavily as if trying not to be sick, where some plainly already had. A few men stood with clenched fists, angrily snarling that someone would pay, although the fear in their eyes left Ealga unconvinced. Even a magi of Ealga's skill and experience wasn't sure she could make the perpetrator of the crime before them pay.

178

His once fine, black coat embroidered with colourful flowers now a torn, ragged ruin was the only thing that identified the bloodied thing hanging halfway up a wall as being Kelvin Doyle. His body had been ripped open, his internal organs grotesquely on display for all to see, his blood splayed out across the wall resembling so much a pair of huge wings that it must have been done deliberately. Ealga had always had a strong stomach but even she couldn't look at what had been done to Doyle's face for long without wanting to be violently sick. It was as if some huge animal had left deep claw marks through not just flesh, but through bone also.

Who could have done this? Only a magi could have done this, or possibly a…

"Sethundra!" Ealga jumped at the sound of her thoughts being spoken aloud. A man with a huge boil on his nose pointed at what was left of Kelvin Doyle. "Sethundra did that, I saw them with my own eyes!"

"He's been silenced," a young woman added, "he told everyone that he saw sethundra, now they've done this to him to shut him up."

"The sethundra have returned," someone in the crowd cried, then someone else repeated the cry, and again another.

Ealga couldn't contain it, there was nothing she could do. She could see people darting off down alleyways to spread the word, others entering the square for the first time to see the evidence for themselves. Ealga knew that by the end of the day every single person in the Warren would know that sethundra had returned and it wouldn't be long before the entire city had at least heard the story. On its own that wasn't a particularly worrying fact, in time it could all be quietened down, other explanations found, but what made a rapidly growing fear blossom within Elaga's belly was that she knew beyond doubt that panic spreading through the streets of Aldarris was exactly what someone wanted to happen.

CHAPTER 18

"How many?" Dunham asked Bevan, drawing his sword and taking his shield from off his back.

Bevan shook his head. "Difficult to be sure, the trees get pretty thick a little way from here. I counted seven for certain, but there could be more."

"How long before they reach us, Bevan?" Conall asked, also drawing his sword.

"If they keep heading straight towards us without stopping, ten minutes, maybe twenty. We'll hear them soon enough, Your Highness, they're not exactly stealthy."

"Find a good place to shoot from," Dunham commanded, "you too Brennan. Take down as many as you can, anything that gets through I'll have to deal with myself."

"Not alone, Captain," Conall said, expertly swinging his longsword.

"Agreed," Hrolf said, hefting his huge axe and earning a respectful nod from Conall.

"Fine," the captain said reluctantly, "but stand to either side of me and no unnecessary risks. I don't want to be the one having to explain to the queen and your father, Hrolf, why their sons have been killed on a peace mission."

Conall grinned back at the captain, until he realised that Hrolf was doing the same. He instantly buried his grin and turned away from them, making his way over to Katy who stood nervously by the horses. His face softened again when he looked at her. "Take up your bow," he said reassuringly, "find a good spot amongst the rocks. Keep back, don't panic, only shoot if you have a clean shot." He then smiled, excitement sparkling in his eyes. "This is my first battle too."

Katy nodded but didn't smile back, wanting to slap Conall instead. Fear pulsed through her at the thought of a battle and this idiot was actually looking forward to it.

Her mother's voice pushed into her thoughts. *"Fear will only conquer you if you let it, Katy. Push all other thoughts out of your mind and focus on what you need to do and your fear will never defeat you."*

She took a deep breath to steady her nerves, picked up her bow and quiver of arrows and looked for a place to make her stand. She found a large rectangular block of stone lying next to a pile of loose rubble. The wall of whatever building that had once stood there was at her back so no one could come up behind her. Once she had scrambled on top of the block she found she was quite a bit over the heads of the others, even Hrolf. Katy was confident she could make good use of her bow from where she stood without the risk of hitting her companions. She considered dropping the sword that hung awkwardly at her waist, having no plan to get close enough to a troll to actually use it, but then dismissed the idea. *Just in case one gets through.*

For the next few minutes it felt to Katy as if the whole wood was holding its breath. There was not a sound from the trees around them. No birds, no creaking branches or rustling of leaves. Unfortunately, they didn't have long to wait until all of that changed and they could clearly hear the approaching trolls. Bevan hadn't been wrong when he said that they weren't stealthy. They crashed through the trees, sounding almost as if they were deliberately trying to break every branch and twig that they came across. Soon, even their voices could be heard, clearly adding to the cacophony that had taken over the once peaceful woodland. Katy didn't know if

182

trolls could actually talk, but she couldn't discern anything that sounded like words from the grunts and growls that travelled towards them.

Soon the trees and underbrush ahead of them began to shake and the first troll blundered into view. It was large, alike in size to Hrolf, but that was where the similarity ended. It was completely hairless with greenish, grey, leathery skin. Its only items of clothing were a dirty loincloth and a necklace of bones that hung around a thick, short neck. It was an ugly thing that reminded her a little of a particularly hideous looking, hairless ape. It carried a crude and rusty looking sword which it pointed in their direction as soon as it spotted them with its small, piggish eyes. It roared a wordless cry of outrage as the others came bursting from the trees.

Five she counted in total, each little different from the first, carrying an assortment of primitive weapons. They roared as they rushed towards them, roars that turned into cries of pain from two as arrows thudded solidly into their chest, released from the bows of the twins. Katy saw with horror that this did little to slow them and with thick, black blood running down their bodies they came on with barely a pause. Two more arrows struck the same two trolls, one went down, gurgling with an arrow sticking from its throat, the other staggered and fell behind until a third arrow finished it.

The other three now reached Conall, Hrolf and Dunham and the three fighters leapt forward to meet them. Dunham fought methodically, there was nothing fancy in his sword play, just the cool efficiency of an experienced, professional soldier. Conall danced around his opponent, his longsword flickering faster than Katy could follow, it was almost beautiful to watch. Hrolf on the other hand was just plain terrifying. With a bellow that made even the troll hesitate the minotaur attacked the creature ferociously with his mighty axe, battering the thing to the ground with brute force.

We're going to win, Katy thought excitedly, until a thought occurred to her. *Bevan said he counted seven trolls. Where are the other two?*

Her question was answered when more trolls came bursting out of the trees. Not two, but four more, all of which rushed the fighters, howling at the top of their voices. The lead one went down, taken by two arrows, the next stumbled over its comrade's body, given Hrolf, who had just finished off his opponent the opportunity to leap upon it whilst it was unbalanced. Conall and Dunham quickly dispatched their trolls and turned to face the remaining two but then, to Katy's dismay, three more emerged from the trees and rushed to join the fight. The brothers, Bevan and Brennan fired arrow after arrow, picking their shots carefully so as not to risk hitting their companions who were now being hard pressed. So intent on his work, Brennan didn't notice a troll clambering up the rocks a little behind him, but Katy did. She cried out a warning whilst knocking an arrow and firing, missing the troll by several feet. She swore and fired again, this time taking a moment to actually aim properly, the arrow thundered solidly into the creature's shoulder. Hearing its cry of pain, Brennan turned, drawing his sword and opening up its throat with one swift slash of his blade. The twin spared a short nod of thanks to Katy before turning back to the battle before them.

Another troll had fallen, Hrolf faced off another, as did Dunham, whilst Conall danced around the other two, his sword little more than a blur in his hands, the trolls howling in pain every time his blade found its mark. Katy scanned the trees and the surrounding rocks looking for any signs that more trolls might be about to descend upon them, as she saw Bevan and Brennan do. She kept an arrow nocked, wanting to be able to fire as quickly as possible if anymore of the monsters appeared.

Catching a quick glance at the fighters she saw that they appeared to be winning their battles, even Conall was gradually wearing down his two opponents. She caught movement in the trees beyond them and two more trolls burst into view. Bevan and Brennan's bows went up ready to fire before they got too close and Katy kept an eye on the brothers' positions in case another of the creatures tried to take advantage of their distraction. It was then that she heard the crash from behind her.

She spun, facing the wall that she had assumed to be solid, but then a massive chunk of stone came crashing down, narrowly missing Katy and landing on the pile of rubble she had used to climb up to her current position. There was another crash, more stone fell and a huge troll, a massive hammer clutched in its monstrous fist, roared angrily at her. With a scream she released her arrow at it. At such close range she couldn't miss and it sunk into its belly. The troll staggered back with a grunt, but then with a snarl, blood and spittle flying from its vile mouth, it came on again. Katy tried to fire another arrow, but she panicked and dropped it amongst the rocks. The troll swung its hammer at Katy, she leapt out of the way landing on the pile of rubble. It shifted alarmingly and she struggled to maintain her balance. The troll lumbered towards her as she tried to draw her sword, but she got all tangled up with her bow still in her hand. The monster leapt onto the rubble and again it shifted. Katy thought she could hear a rumbling but was more concerned with getting away from the creature long enough for one of her companions to help her. The troll also struggled with balance on the shifting rubble and when it swung its hammer at Katy she easily managed to duck under the blow. Unbalanced, the troll nearly fell, giving Katy time to finally draw her sword and take a wild swing of her own, slashing across the troll's thigh. Howling in pain the troll brought its hammer down to crush the bothersome girl, but Katy managed to step back out of the way, the hammer smashing into the rubble at their feet.

The rumbling increased. The ground beneath them shifted alarmingly. Katy saw the danger, but the stupid troll didn't understand. As she turned to flee, the troll reached out and grabbed her painfully by the arm pulling her back towards it. An evil grin rose on its ugly face, thinking it had won, raising its hammer to finish its victim. But it was too late. With a horrifying crash the ground opened up beneath the pair and, with a terrified scream, Katy and the troll plummeted down, surrounded by stone, dust and darkness.

****

Conall opened up the troll's belly, spilling it innards onto the ground when he heard Katy's cry. He spun in her direction just as the troll leapt at her over the remains of the wall it had just smashed down. He was about to run to her aid when a roar behind him signalled the arrival of another brute. He raised his sword in defence, but it was unnecessary as an arrow flew over his shoulder and struck home into the monster's throat, dropping it to the ground. Turning back to Katy he heard the rumble, saw her trying to escape the clutches of the troll. And then, in a cloud of dust and stone they were suddenly gone, massive rocks from what remained of the wall crashing down onto the space they had once stood.

"NO!" Conall screamed. Leaving his companions to deal with whatever trolls remained he ran to the sight of the disaster. Dropping his father's sword, he began moving rocks, hurling them desperately aside. In moments Hrolf was at his side, moving even larger rocks, the minotaur searching for the girl as desperately as the human.

He heard others coming towards them, scrambling over the rocks until Dunham's voice stopped them. "You two, stand guard! Keep your eyes peeled and make sure we don't have any more visitors!

Dunham was then with the two princes, but he wasn't digging. He just looked at the pile of stones grimly. "Highness," he said, "Highness," he said again more loudly when neither of the princes stopped shifting stones.

"Don't say it, Dunham," Conall growled, "don't you dare say it."

"I have to, Your Highness. She's gone and we need to leave before more trolls find us."

Conall turned on Dunham angrily. "We're not leaving her behind, Captain! I am your prince and you will obey me!"

"Yes, Your Highness," Dunham said calmly, "I will obey you, but I will advise you as well. Nobody could have survived that rock fall, even the troll buried with her. The noise of the battle would have alerted any other trolls in the area and possibly Melantha herself is now aware of our presence. If we stay in this spot we will die, maybe not today, but tomorrow or the day after, but rest assured, we will die and this whole trip will have been in vain, Katy will have died for nothing. It's possibly Melantha has Katy's brother, that is why we came. If we die here, he will die, if we go on, we might be able to save him. Now, what are your orders, Highness?"

Conall stared at the soldier before nodding reluctantly. "We go on. Leave the horses, they'll only hinder us in these woods. Take the minimum we need, we're only a few hours away from the ruins anyway." He turned to Hrolf who stood glaring at the pile of rocks as if he could bore a hole through them to the girl. *Why can't I like him, we could be friends, but every time I look at him I see my dead father.* "Are you coming?" he said stiffly. "You fought well, a credit to your people. We will need you."

Hrolf fixed Conall with a hard stare and nodded once. "You fought well too," he added, just as stiffly.

We don't have to like each other, I just need his axe and his prowess in battle. He turned away from the minotaur. "Secure the horses, Dunham, if we survive I don't fancy having to walk all the way home." He walked away to be alone, waiting for the others, his thoughts filled with the girl from another world. *I couldn't save you, Katy, but I will die before I let any harm come to your brother.*

CHAPTER 19

"What did you think you were doing?" Finian shouted angrily again. "Is everyone on your world so woefully irresponsible? You could have been killed! By now there probably isn't a single person in the city who hasn't heard that we have sethundra walking around the place. Goodness only knows what trouble that will cause the queen. The very fact that you went into the city at all is inexcusable. What if Melantha had attacked? You would have been killed or taken, she would be free and all the worlds would be preparing for another sethundra war! And why? Because you wanted to go exploring! What have you got to say for yourself?"

Dylan looked up at the professor from his stool, not quite sure where to begin. "I'm sorry," he tried, a little lamely.

"You're sorry? Well I suppose that would be a start, if I could believe it, but I'm not sure that I can."

"But I can do magic now," Dylan said, "I worked out how to do it. Just take me to Melantha, I'll put her back to sleep, find Katy and go home."

"Pah! Just because any fool can draw a sword and stab someone with it doesn't make them a master swordsman. Casting takes years of training and discipline to achieve the necessary control. You have been lucky; extremely lucky. Half the city has been extremely lucky. You could have levelled the whole Warren trying to do what you did." Suddenly a flower that had been in a vase on the table rose up into the air and floated in front of Finian's face. "Using the power of the Heart Stones must be done delicately." One by one the petals came away from the flower until they were all free, they then spun around the centre of the plant in a beautiful dance. "It takes great skill and control to use properly." The petals stopped their spinning and reconnected with the plant, but now they constantly changed colour, from red to blue to yellow to pink and then back to red again. "One slip, one wrong move and..." There was a flash and the flower exploded into flame, earning a small yelp from Freya, who sat a few feet away and in moments nothing but ash fell to the floor.

"Cool," Dylan said, clapping his hands, "can I try?"

"No, you cannot try!" Finian roared.

Dylan looked to the others, hoping for some support, but found none forthcoming. Artemis stood looking out of a window, seemingly oblivious to what was going on, Baccus leant against a wall, his face unreadable. Olwyn looked a little sympathetic, but not much; the pretty woman, Oriana, fixed him with the same stare she had laid on him from the moment she stepped into the room covered in dust. Alanson openly smirked at him and Freya just looked very disappointed. She hadn't been happy at all to discover he wasn't supposed to leave the palace at all, let alone without someone to look after him.

Dylan had always had a temper. According to his grandmother it was one of the few things he and his sister had in common, inherited from their mother apparently and their father had done nothing to ease it. He had only added a far larger than necessary dose of sarcasm and some extremely colourful language into the mix. And it was that very temper that would send Nanny into an impressive tirade of her own that began to bubble within the scolded ten-year-old.

"You could have caused a diplomatic incident with the minotaurs," Finian went on, pacing up and down and waving his hands in the air. "The queen is involved in delicate peace negotiations with the minotaurs and you could have got one of their number killed! How would that have looked? You could have sparked another war!"

It was at that point that Dylan snapped. "Well how was I supposed to bloody know! I'm ten, stupid! I'm a ten-year-old boy from another world! I don't know how your ten-year-olds behave, but on my world we mess up sometimes, okay? It's not my fault Grandad told me about the sethundra, it's not my fault I can do magic, or casting, or whatever you bloody call it! I just want to put Melantha to sleep, find Katy and go home!"

The room fell deathly silent. Finian blinked confusedly, clearly not used to being spoken to in such a manner and was uncertain how to deal with it when a cough made them all turn towards the door to the study. Queen Arlana stood calmly regarding them all, the scarred soldier who had been in the throne room when Dylan had first arrived on Dainnor on one side, a minotaur, somewhat larger and more fearsome looking than Freya, on the other.

"Am I interrupting?" Arlana said.

"Of course not, Your Majesty," Finian said, "I was just discussing young Dylan's...erm, mistakes."

"Really? It sounded to me as though he was calling you stupid, Professor." She strode towards them, scooping up a stool as she went, placing it next to Dylan's and sitting down. "It is the same here on Dainnor as it is on your world, Dylan, sometimes ten-year-olds, "mess up" is the term I believe you used. You remind me a lot of my son, Conall. He was headstrong, still is in fact, you'd like him I think. He often rushes into things without thinking them through properly, as he has done by entering the Deadlands with your sister." She forced down a lump in her throat before continuing "But like you he needs to temper his impulses, look at every problem from every angle. He will have the burden of ruling a nation one day, you have the burden of becoming Guardian to an entire world. A heavy responsibility for anyone, more so for one so young. We have made mistakes in dealing with this entire situation, Dylan, we should have paid more attention to you and your needs. In all of this we have forgotten one very important fact; you are a ten-year-old boy, lost and alone in a strange world. On behalf of myself and all of the people of Dainnor, please accept my apology."

Dylan wasn't quite sure of the etiquette in responding to a queen apologising to him, but at that moment another thought occurred to him. *I'm Earth's Guardian, there might be another, but I have no idea who it is, that means Melantha is my responsibility.* Aloud he said, "I think we've all made mistakes, Your Majesty. Can we start over?"

"I think that's an excellent idea," Arlana said, smiling warmly at him. "Although, I hope you understand, that we will be taking extra precautions from now on."

"Oh?"

"You will have an armed guard everywhere you go, Dylan. This is not because I don't trust you, this is for your own protection." Dylan nodded, it didn't matter, he already knew what he was going to do. "Very good," the queen continued. "Captain Burgess will escort you back to your room where you will get some rest. In the morning Professor Finian will continue with your training. He will push you, focus your training on putting the sethundra back to sleep. It will be hard, but it needs to be, Dylan. It is time this business with Melantha was done."

"Yes, Your Majesty." Dylan stood and went to leave with the scarred captain, but stopped when he got to Freya. "I'm sorry I deceived you, Freya. I hope we can still be friends."

Freya smiled down at him. "Of course we can." Dylan smiled back and left the study with Captain Burgess.

Outside two guardsmen stood in the corridor, hands resting easily on the hilts of their swords. With a nod to his men to follow, Burgess, led Dylan through the maze of palace corridors to his room, the guardsmen following closely behind, making him feel uncomfortably like a prisoner. A feeling that appeared to be echoed by the numerous staff they passed, judging by the number of disapproving frowns he received.

They shortly reached his room and the captain opened the door. "You are to remain here," he said, "a maid will bring you a meal. If you require anything else you will speak to the guards. You will obey them. Is that understood?"

"Yes, sir," Dylan said, as meekly as he could manage.

"Good. In you go then."

Dylan stepped into the room and the captain shut the door firmly behind him, leaving him alone.

Which was exactly what he wanted to happen.

He jumped up onto the huge bed and sat cross-legged in the centre, wriggled around a bit to get comfortable and closed his eyes. He wasn't sure if what he was about to try was going to work but he could see no other option. *I have to stop Melantha and get home. People will be worried about us, they would have sent the police looking for us and everything.* He slowed his breathing, until he felt calm and relaxed, imagined the light, allowed it to come to him, embrace him, it seemed to happen easier than ever. He could feel it now, identify it, a power within him that hadn't been there before. *The Heart Stone,* he thought, *it must be.* He focussed on what he wanted to do, driving out all other thoughts, then took a deep breath, and spoke. "Artemis, Baccus, come." He felt something, a connection to the two beings that he hadn't noticed before. Something told him that the sethundra had heard the command, but there was resistance, as if they fought it. "Artemis, Baccus, come. I command you," he said more forcibly.

"This is unwise, Dylan Howard."

Dylan snapped his eyes open to see the two sethundra standing before him, Artemis, the one who had spoken frowning down at him, Baccus looking not at all happy about being summoned.

"You must release us at once," Artemis said insistently.

Fighting down his elation that his plan was working, Dylan refused to be diverted and maintained his focus. He hopped down off the bed and stepped between the two sethundra. "Artemis and Baccus, you will take me to the Deadlands."

With a great effort, Artemis shook her head. "You must not do this, you are not ready."

Dylan took a deep breath, he thought he felt more power pour into him, he couldn't be sure, there was still too much he didn't understand, but he spoke in the same way his grandmother spoke whenever she had had enough of arguments. "You will both take me to the Deadlands, and you will do it now."

A sethundra hand clamped down on each of his shoulders and Artemis and Baccus both stared at one spot in the room. At first nothing happened, and then it was as if everything in front of them stretched towards them, like paint that had begun to run. Just as the image was about to touch them, Dylan felt a tugging, a sensation of being pulled forward. And then, they were somewhere else.

They stood upon a hill overlooking a land of barren rock and it had to be the dullest place Dylan had ever seen. Nothing grew anywhere, not a tree, a bush or a single blade of grass, just mile upon mile of nothing to interest a ten-year-old, and everywhere around them there was a brown haze. Not of dust, that would have clogged his throat, although there was a dryness to the air, but like a dirty fog.

"Where...?" he began, but then, *flicker*. He whipped his head to the left, catching movement out of the corner of his eye, but he could see nothing. *Flicker*. This time something to his right, but even as he turned another movement caused him to look back again. *Flicker, flicker, flicker*. Again and again he caught movement, but every time he looked there was nothing to be seen. Any focus he had held to keep control of the two sethundra evaporated as he spun around looking for whatever it was that moved around them. "What is it?" he cried, shutting his eyes. "Make it stop!"

"We cannot, Dylan Howard," Artemis said.

"You are in the Deadlands," Baccus said, "you ordered us to bring you here, so that is what we did."

"The movement you are seeing are the sethundra. Our brothers and sisters are here in their thousands. You must learn to ignore what you can see on the edge of vision. It is difficult I know. Concentrate on my face. I am in front of you. Open your eyes."

Dylan did as he was told and found Artemis' beautiful face in front of him as she knelt on the barren ground and, amazingly, she was actually smiling, a warm, comforting smile that somehow manged to heighten her beauty. "You should smile more often," Dylan said, "it suits you."

"Perhaps I should," she said, chuckling, "but now we must talk."

Nodding, Dylan caught another flicker of movement out of the corner of his eye, but as Baccus moved up to one side of him he found that keeping his vision between the two sethundra kept the flickering at bay.

"What is your plan, Dylan Howard?" Artemis asked.

He was momentarily taken aback. It wasn't the question he had been expecting and he paused to arrange his thoughts. "I need you two to take me to Melantha. If you can keep her busy long enough for me to put her back to sleep again then we can find Katy and all go home. Katy's here somewhere, looking for me, we have to find her and help her. She'll be killed if we don't."

There was a long pause in which Dylan expected either Artemis or Baccus to scoop him up and drop him back down in the palace again. He was taken aback when Artemis finally spoke.

"It is a good plan, Dylan Howard. Simple, but effective, one we ourselves proposed to Professor Finian."

"With him at our side we would have increased our chances of success," Baccus said, "maybe even killed Melantha, but he will not take the risk."

"But why?"

"He has grown soft. Or perhaps always was. Guardian he may be, powerful, but I do not think he has ever had to fight anything or anyone his whole life. He sits comfortably in the palace; his biggest concern is training his apprentice."

Artemis nodded her agreement. "Even during the wars with the minotaurs he was never called to bring his power to bear. There is a rule in Dainnor that magi will not enter a battle for any single nation, it has made them weak I fear."

"Then we're going then?" Dylan said.

"Yes, Dylan Howard, we are going. The question is, how to proceed from here? Baccus, I would hear your thoughts."

"Melantha will be at her old fortress, that much we know, we also know that she is aware of our presence, she will know we are in the Deadlands. We can mask our presence, but can the boy mask his?"

"Mask my presence?"

"You are linked to Melantha as you are linked to us," Artemis answered, "which means that she can sense where you are. With a little concentration she would even be able to sense your moods. You can mask this in two ways; one, you could release Melantha, this would be unwise because you would not be able to return her to the dream and our only course of action would be to attempt to kill her, so I suggest the second way. Prepare yourself to cast." Dylan did as instructed, it took a couple of attempts this time, but finally he managed it. "I am unsure how exactly magi do this, I believe they picture themselves turning to one side and when they have done this they are not there. Does this make sense to you Dylan Howard?"

"Not really, but I'll try."

Dylan closed his eyes and tried doing what Artemis had said. He held an image of himself in his mind then imagined himself turning away and disappearing. Sometimes he vanished all at once, other times he faded gradually, he even tried physically turning at the same time as imagining it, but none of it seemed to work. He was about to give up in frustration when, on impulse, instead of vanishing he tried to imagine pulling the surrounding scenery around him like a cloak.

"It is done," Artemis said, "we can no longer sense you."

Dylan clapped his hands gleefully until Baccus said, "You are back again."

"It requires a small amount of concentration to maintain," Artemis said, "try again, but this time try to maintain it."

Dylan did the same again, this time masking himself on his first attempt. "What now?" he said, when he was done.

"We should not just jump straight into the fortress," Baccus said, "she will be expecting that, especially now that we are all masked."

"Agreed," said Artemis, "Melantha will be more on her guard than ever. The settlement of the minotaurs during the war would be a good place to start."

"Why can't we just go straight to her?" Dylan asked, confused.

"Melantha has masked herself as we have, she will know an attack is imminent. We have no way of knowing where exactly she is or what allies or defences she has gathered around her. If we jumped straight into her stronghold we could find ourselves in the middle of an army. By jumping a little distance away, we can approach with caution. Prepare yourself."

As in his room Artemis and Baccus placed a hand on each of his shoulders and immediately the surrounding Deadlands looked as though it were being pulled towards him, there was the same feeling of being tugged, and then they shifted to a new location.

I wonder if I can do that, he thought looking around him. Wherever they were, it didn't look like a minotaur settlement and it didn't look like the Deadlands either. They were in a wood filled with twisted trees that had grown into peculiar shapes around the large amount of huge moss covered rocks that lay about. The air was cool and damp, refreshing after where they had just been. An eerie silence hung over the place, not a bird sang anywhere in the leafy branches overhead.

"Where…?" Dylan began, but Baccus silenced him with a long finger to his lips. Dylan noticed the sethundra held his staff in hand and crouched as if expecting an attack, Artemis too held her staff. She indicated that Baccus should lead the way and with a silent nod of the head he began moving through the trees, Dylan following, Artemis coming watchfully behind.

CHAPTER 20

She wasn't even sure she had opened her eyes at first, the blackness was so complete. But then she moved and dust fell from somewhere above, stinging her eyes, making her blink. *Am I blind?* She waved her hand in front of her face, but could see nothing. She pushed herself up into a sitting position, every part of her body painfully protesting from multiple bruises and scratches, but as far as she could tell nothing was broken, although a sharp pain in her right ankle flared up when she moved it.

She tried squeezing her eyes shut in an effort to accustom them to the dark, hoping that some vision would return, until an idea suddenly occurred to her and she fumbled at her waist in the blackness. Finding her belt pouch, she reached inside, quickly finding what she was looking for. Praying the battery wasn't flat she turned on her mobile phone. There was a pause and then the screen illuminated before her, the sudden brightness making her squint painfully. *Not blind then,* she thought breathing a sigh of relief. She switched on the torch of her phone and looked around her.

Katy found herself sitting on a rough stone floor next to a pile of huge boulders. She almost screamed when she saw what remained of the troll she had been fighting, crushed by tons of stone. *I must have rolled out of the way when I fell.* She got stiffly to her feet taking a few more steps away from the rocks, just in case they weren't as stable as they now appeared. Her ankle protested but she found she could put a little weight on it. There appeared to be a tunnel stretching off into the darkness, the roof of which not much higher than her

200

head. As far as Katy could tell, she thought it was a natural tunnel. Judging by the oddly smooth shape of some of the rocks she guessed that an underground river must have run through here at some point, but to her dismay she could see no other way out.

"Hello," she risked shouting, hoping that Conall and the others would hear her. She listened but there was no reply. *If they're even still alive,* she thought, fighting back tears. "Stop it," she said to herself, wiping her eyes, "they were winning, they probably think *I'm* dead. The only one who's going to get me out of this is me. So stop feeling sorry for yourself and think."

She spotted her bow lying on the ground, picking it up and running her hands up and down it she saw, to her amazement, that it was undamaged. Three arrows lay on the floor, so she picked them up and returned them to her quiver. The others must have been buried under the stone, presumably with her sword, as she could see no sign of that either. With a final look around the place she began limping her way along the tunnel, not wanting to waste any more time. She was terrifyingly conscious of what would happen if the battery on her phone ran out before she managed to find a way back to the surface.

For a time the tunnel ran fairly flat, occasionally opening out into a slightly wider area, sometimes the ceiling coming down so low she had to duck, other times it stretched away beyond the light of her phone. At one point she found herself in a larger chamber filled with stalagmites and stalactites, making her feel as if she was trapped in the mouth of some monstrous creature. She paused for a moment as she tried to remember whether the stalagmites were the ones rising from the ground or hanging from the ceiling, when she noticed a movement in the gloom. She raised her torch, and then stopped when she saw a light. Without thinking she darted forward before immediately springing back again when her boot plunged into freezing water and sending a ripple through the light that had merely been a reflection of her torch. She studied the pool a little further with her torch, trying to get an idea of how big it was, but then something moved just beneath the surface. With a screech, Katy scrambled away from the pool, hurrying out of the cavern as quickly as she could.

As she hurried along the tunnel, dismay filled Katy's heart when she noticed that the ground appeared to be sloping downwards, deeper into the earth. The last thing she wanted was to get even further away from the surface. She briefly considered returning to the cavern to search it properly for another exit, but the thought of what may lay in the water there convinced her to continue along her current path.

It wasn't long before she faced another dilemma, this time in the form of an entrance to a side tunnel. Shinning the light from her phone into the entrance her heart sank when she saw that not only did it go deeper into the earth at an even steeper angle than the path she was on, it also narrowed considerably. She was about to continue along her current route when something made her stop. She stared down into the darkness of the narrowing tunnel, an odd feeling pulling her towards it.

Trust your instincts, Katy, her mother's voice pushed into her mind. She recalled clearly the time she had been given that little piece of advice from her mother. It had been her sixth birthday party, her mother had been heavily pregnant with Dylan and her father had arranged everything as apparently her mother hadn't been feeling up to it. Katy had been wearing her favourite princess dress like most of her friends, playing and laughing together until her mother had pulled her off a bouncy castle and began filling her head with stuff about responsibility and being strong for her brother. Katy had cried, wanting to just enjoy her party with her friends. Her father had pulled her mother away, until finally she had stormed out after they had a very loud, and very public, argument. Not long afterwards Dylan had been born and a few days later their mother had disappeared forever. Katy had never had another birthday party since.

Λ single tear managed to trickle down her cheek before she brushed it angrily away. "Fine then," she muttered, "I'll follow my bloody instincts." Holding her phone out before her to light the way she stepped into the side chamber and deeper into the earth.

After a little while of walking, the tunnel levelled out. Taking this to be a good sign she hurried forward, wanting to gain as much ground as she could. But then, without warning, the one thing she had been dreading more than anything happened. One step she could see clearly ahead of her, the next she was in total darkness as the battery on her phone finally ran out.

For a long time she huddled against the wall, sobbing uncontrollably, her imagination conjuring up all sorts of foul creatures waiting for her in the dark. Every story her grandfather had ever told her as a child suddenly seemed real, but twisted and more frightening. If Dainnor was real and minotaurs and trolls, then why not the other things. Could there be an underground lake here where the mer-people would be waiting to grab her, was that what had been in the pool earlier? Maybe a pack of vicious drakols would hunt her down, or even the mysterious cryn? *But the cryn were gentle weren't they,* a small voice in the back of her head said, *they would never harm anyone, they only wanted to help.* There was something familiar about that voice and then, cutting through her fear, a memory formed in her head.

Dylan's sobs woke her, pulling her from a pleasant dream, the memory of which was already fading.

Katy irritably sat up in bed, glaring across at her annoying, little brother in the twin bed next to hers. She hated him; well disliked him anyway. He had made her mummy go away and now this snivelling three-year-old was ruining the first holiday with daddy in ages. He complained about everything. He was too hot, too cold, hungry, thirsty, wanted a wee, scared of the dark. Katy wanted to spend time with her father, he was away so much and she missed him, but Dylan was ruining everything.

"What's wrong with you now?" she whispered. "Shut up, or you'll wake Daddy up."

"I had a bad dream," he snivelled back.

"It's just a dream stupid, it can't hurt you. Go back to sleep!"

"Mummy was in my dream, she was hurting."

Outrage blossomed within Katy's breast. How dare he dream of her, he never knew her! She was more her mother than his. "Go back to sleep," she snapped cruelly, "or the cryn will get you."

"But the cryn were gentle, weren't they? They would never harm anyone, they only wanted to help."

Should have said drakols, *Katy thought,* he was always scared of drakols. Why did I say the stupid cryn? *"Just go back to sleep,"* she snapped, rolling over and pulling the duvet over her head.

"Magic kiss?"

"What?"

"Nanny gives me a magic kiss to make bad dreams go away."

"She does that to take pain away, stupid."

"She takes bad dreams too," Dylan protested.

"Shut up, go to sleep! You're just stupid!"

Katy spent a long time lying in the dark, listening to her little brother's sobs before she drifted back off to sleep, but the pleasant dream wasn't there waiting for her this time, it was the nightmare's turn, the one where she screamed in pain.

She felt a pang of shame at the memory, she forced the thought of the nightmare away, that was the last thing she wanted to think about in the dark. She always felt ashamed when she recalled how she had treated Dylan back then. *He was a scared, three-year-old and I was so horrible to him.* She opened her eyes and stared bleakly into the darkness. For a moment she thought she could hear a child's sobs. Dylan had needed her and she had rejected him. *It was wrong, it's my duty to protect...* Her train of thought came to a sudden halt. "Why is it *my* duty?" she said aloud, her fear momentarily forgotten. "I'm his sister, not his mother. She left him and Dad is never around, why should he be my responsibility, I didn't ask for him." And yet, despite her thoughts she couldn't shake the feeling that Dylan was her responsibility somehow. *Duty, he's my duty.* That thought made no sense. *Since when is looking after your little brother a duty?* But now that the thought was with her, try as she might, she couldn't shake it.

Dylan was her duty.

She took a deep, calming breath, wiped the tears from her cheeks, her fear of the dark diminished to a small thing deep inside her. Now grim determination suddenly burned within her as she pulled herself to her feet. Her ankle protested, but she ignored the pain. Dylan needed her, desperately. She couldn't explain how she knew, she just did. *Hang in there, you little turd, I'm coming for you.*

Using her bow to feel her way, Katy blindly, continued along the tunnel.

CHAPTER 21

Conall ducked down behind a large rock that looked as though it may once have been part of a statue, as another band of huge trolls passed just a few feet in front of them. He counted twelve in this group, that made over a hundred they had seen so far. *How many has Melantha gathered?* It was a concerning thought. Even this part of the Deadlands didn't have much in the way of food for a large group of trolls. Melantha would have to move them soon or, sethundra or not, she would have a rebellion on her hands.

They had avoided killing any since the attack on their camp the day before and had spent a sleepless night in hiding, terrifyingly aware of just how much better troll eyesight was in the dark than human or minotaur. Despite several opportunities to reduce the number of trolls in the world, Conall, Dunham and Hrolf had all agreed that the noise of a battle could easily bring every troll in the area down upon them. *We're not here to fight a war,* Conall thought, angrily. *Find the boy and get out.* A sensible enough plan, although Conall would have liked nothing more than to kill as many of the beasts as he possibly could.

After the last troll had disappeared amongst the trees, Bevan dropped silently down from a branch, bow in hand, arrow nocked and at the ready. Brennan appeared around another tree a few feet away, signalling to the others that it was safe to come out. Brennan's hiding place had practically been in the trolls' path. It never ceased to amaze Conall how good the brothers were at hiding. The prince rose from behind his rock,

Hrolf and Dunham did the same from behind their own hiding places.

"The sightings are getting more frequent the closer we get to the fortress, Highness," the captain said grimly. "We should reconsider this course of action."

"We're not going back." Conall started hearing his own thoughts said aloud and looked up at Hrolf, who had spoken. "We're going in there for the boy, so there's no point discussing it."

Conall nodded to Hrolf. "What he just said."

"Very well then," Dunham growled. He signalled the brothers to lead the way and the five companions continued silently through the woods.

They walked along what Conall assumed to be the remains of a road as trees and undergrowth dominated their path rather than huge boulders or the remains of walls. It also followed a fairly straight path, where before they had twisted and turned around obstruction after obstruction. Being free of obstacles, the trees here grew straighter, looking far more natural. Also the undergrowth was a lot thicker, so Conall found himself tripping and stubbing his toes every few moments on hidden roots and rocks. He noticed, with some annoyance, that Hrolf wasn't having the same difficulty. They struggled on for about another half hour and just as Conall was thinking that if they didn't reach the fortress soon then he would suggest that they may be going the wrong way, Brennan raised a hand for a halt and crouched down, signalling that the others should do the same.

The two brothers stared into the woods, woods that Conall noted felt even more silent than usual.

Suddenly two shapes exploded out of the trees, both as tall as a troll, but slender and moving with the grace of dancers. They carried long staffs that spun in their hands,

208

knocking the bows harmlessly from Bevan's and Brennan's grasp. The brothers reached for their swords as Conall, Dunham and Hrolf drew their own weapons. The two creatures slammed their staffs painfully into the brothers' wrists, then, in perfect coordination, they used their weapons to sweep the legs from under their opponents, Bevan and Brennan falling to the ground, disappearing into the undergrowth. Dunham leapt forward, sword swinging at the one who Conall saw was female. She blocked the sword with her staff then spun, using the captain's momentum to push him away, bringing her face to face with Hrolf. Conall raised his sword and faced the second creature. *Sethundra,* he thought, putting a name to the scowling being before him. *Two sethundra, we haven't a chance!* Fear clutched his heart, but it didn't stop him from stepping forward. "If I die here, sethundra," he said, straining to keep the fear out of his voice, "then you will feel the bite of my blade before I fall."

The sethundra said nothing, only smirked, spinning his staff at Conall with astonishing speed. The prince barely managed to keep the weapon from crushing his throat, turning it away with his sword at the last possible second. He then blocked a swipe to his midriff, another to his head, had to suck in his gut to avoid another attack. Conall knew it was only a matter of time before the sethundra struck a blow, he had no chance at all to even think about a counter attack, his only hope was to keep the creature busy long enough for one of his companions to come to his aid.

"You fight well, human," the sethundra said calmly, not relenting in his attack at all, "but we both know the outcome."

Conall barely stopped the staff from sweeping his legs from under him, he desperately tried hopping back out of the way, but his back struck a tree. The distraction was enough, the sethundra jabbed with his staff, knocking Conall's sword from his hand. The prince knew it was the end, knew there was nothing he could do, he closed his eyes, waiting for the killing blow.

"Stop!"

That blow never came. Conall slowly opened his eyes to see the sethundra watching him, leaning casually on his staff. The prince risked a quick glance to see how his companions fared. Hrolf knelt on the floor, the female sethundra standing over him, Dunham, Bevan and Brennan were picking themselves up. All of them were staring at the small figure who had spoken, standing on a rock a little way off.

It was a boy of about eight or nine. *No, I think he's older than that,* he thought on reflection, *he's just small for his age.* Something in his face immediately reminded him of Katy, leaving no doubt in Conall's mind who the boy was. The one thing the prince couldn't comprehend was why the boy was wearing Conall's old clothes.

"Dylan?" Conall said.

The boy looked hard at the prince for a moment. "Do I know you?" he asked.

"Um, no, but I knew your sister. We were on our way to rescue you."

"Good job," the male sethundra snorted.

"You're Prince Conall," the boy said excitedly. "Where's Katy? Is she with you?"

He looked to his companions, but saw no help forthcoming from the soldiers. Hrolf was looking at Dylan, his face full of sympathy, knowing as well as Conall what it was like to lose a sibling. *And yet he doesn't hate humans. Why can't I feel that way?*

Pushing the minotaur from his mind, he turned to the boy. "I'm afraid I have some bad news, Dylan. We were attacked by trolls, your sister fought bravely." A lump rose in Conall's throat. "She fell," his voice cracked. "I'm sorry."

Dylan regarded the prince calmly. "What do you mean 'she fell'?"

"She's dead, Dylan. I'm sorry, there was nothing we could do."

The boy's face screwed up suddenly, tears welled up in his eyes.

"Dylan Howard, you must maintain your concentration," the female sethundra said, "you have dropped your mask." Dylan took a deep breath, pushing back his tears he stared at the sethundra before she said, "Good. I am truly sorry for your loss, but you must put aside your grief until our task is done." Dylan nodded silently, leaving Conall wondering at the odd exchange.

"Melantha is the reason she died," the male sethundra said, "focus on that. It will give you strength."

"She isn't dead," Dylan said, certainty filling his voice.

"How do you know this?" the female asked.

"I just do."

She studied the boy curiously. "Now is not the time to discuss this, we must move from this position immediately. Melantha knows where we are and may launch an attack. Baccus, lead the way."

"If you're going after Melantha then we're coming too," Conall said.

The female looked set to object until the one called Baccus spoke. "This one is good with his sword. Some extra fighters might be of use, against the trolls at least."

The female considered this before nodding her head. "Very well, but we go, now."

Baccus began leading the way, Dylan followed with the female sethundra, leaving the others to scramble in

the undergrowth for their weapons before hurrying to
catch up.

CHAPTER 22

Ignoring the two guards, Finian flung open the door to Dylan's room, already knowing it would be empty. He cursed the boy for his foolishness, but cursed himself more, knowing he had mishandled him terribly. And now he was gone. Off on some foolhardy adventure to face something he simply was not ready for, even with two sethundra at his back. And one of them not entirely trustful.

Olwyn crowded in behind him. "He's gone," she said needlessly. She turned to the two guards. "You were ordered to make sure he didn't leave the room."

"Think, Olwyn," Finian said, before either could respond, "Artemis and Baccus have taken him."

"But where? Why?"

"The boy has worked out how to control the sethundra, to a degree at least. Now I suspect he believes he can control Melantha too."

"Can he? Is he strong enough?"

"At his age? No. Even a fully trained Guardian would struggle to control Melantha. When I was Apprentice, quite far along in my studies, my Guardian ordered me to wake a sethundra he knew. She wasn't powerful, one of the weakest I've ever come across in fact. I did it, but it was like trying to wrestle a large snake covered in grease. Melantha would be impossible for Dylan."

"Then what are you going to do, Professor? You have to go after them, if Dylan falls then Melantha will be free."

"Do you think I don't know that!" Finian snapped. "I wish I could go to the boy, he'll need all the help he can get, but my duty is to protect the Heart Stone, not rush off into battle. If I fall then Dainnor will be unprotected. Do you think Melantha has been idle? She will have gathered allies, who knows what we would be walking into, trolls, minotaurs, possibly even magi. In one move, Melantha will have gained control of both Dainnor and Terra."

"So we leave him to his fate then?"

"No, *we* do nothing of the sort, *you,* however, will be going to his aid."

Olwyn's eyes went wide in shock. "*Me?*" she spluttered. "But how, I can't instantly transport myself anywhere, I would need a sethundra to do that and…" She trailed off when Finian raised his hand.

"There is a way, passed down by the Guardians to take yourself and indeed others to another place. It is believed that before the casting Guardians could transport themselves between worlds, but I've never managed to work out how they did it. Even so, transporting yourself around your own world requires a tremendous amount of power so, logically, taking yourself to another world would require even more. I doubt I, or anyone living, would be able to achieve this. So, I'm sending you to Dylan, I would consider sending Oriana too, but firstly, I don't trust her, and secondly, I can't find the damnable woman. However, you will not be going alone."

"I won't," Olwyn said, as Finian pushed past her, out of the room, "who will I be going with, Professor?"

Finian stood silently in the corridor, impatiently tapping his foot as he waited for the answer to Olwyn's question. They heard them before they saw them, the thump of heavy boots and the clank of weapons and armour was so loud in the palace corridors they may as well have blown trumpets. And then, from around a corner, they marched into view. Led by the fearsome

214

looking Alberich and General Macklyn were twenty heavily armed minotaurs together with the same number of Royal Guard. They marched in rows of four, two minotaurs and two humans, faces grim; whether at the prospect of battle or the whole idea of fighting alongside ancient enemies, Finian couldn't tell, but he noticed more than one set of eyes from both groups glance suspiciously at their new comrades. Much to Finian's annoyance he also noted the queen striding between Alberich and Macklyn, almost as if she intended to lead the lot of them into battle herself.

Finian bobbed a little bow as the group came to a halt before him. "Ah, Your Majesty, with the greatest respect, I said there was no need for you to be present at…

"With the greatest respect, Professor," the queen interrupted, coolly, "I am not in the habit of telling my soldiers, and guests, to prepare for battle without knowing the reason for it. So perhaps you would now care to enlighten me."

"Erm, yes, of course, Your Majesty." There was no way for him to keep what he was about to do secret from the queen, but he had hoped he could explain things more privately. The professor cleared his throat. "I will attempt to transport them all into the Deadlands."

Arlana's eyebrows rose in surprise. "You can do this?"

"Yes, Your Majesty, I believe I can."

Her eyes suddenly flashed with anger as she glared down at the small man. But it was Macklyn that spoke up. "You are capable of sending large numbers of troops to other parts of Dainnor instantly, and you are only revealing this to us now?"

"General, if I may…"

"How many men have died; women, children too? They could have been moved to safety in an instant. The king, the prince! How could you…"

"You know as well as I do, General, that all magi take a vow to not take part in the battles between nations."

"My husband, my son, both died…" the queen paused to swallow down a lump in her throat before continuing, her voice rising in anger. "You could have sent them aid, you could have stopped…"

"Enough!" The queen's mouth clapped shut at Finian's command, but her eyes blazed with fury. "Do you not think I would have saved the king if I could, Corann was my friend, and Conyn, I taught him from when he was little more than a babe. But I could do nothing. If I broke the vow of the magi then other nations would soon follow. Is that what you want, the power of the Heart Stone wielded in battle? Cities could be levelled in hours, innocent people killed in their thousands! That is why we take the vow, that is why we must hold to it no matter what!"

Finian was surprised when Alberich spoke up in support. "When a warrior armed with sword or axe attacks a town, even a small child may defend himself, his chance is slim, but he has that chance. When fire comes from above, even the mightiest warrior can do nothing against it. There is no honour in this. You did the right thing, Guardian, but now the fate of all worlds is threatened. You must aid us now."

Queen Arlana glared at Finian before reluctantly nodding her head. "Chief Alberich speaks rightly." She then stepped next to Finian and turned to face the assembled soldiers, Olwyn took the queen's place between Macklyn and Alberich.

"You are about to step into the unknown," Finian said, in a loud clear voice. "What we do know is that Melantha, a sethundra of terrible power, is free to trouble this world and indeed all worlds if we do not stop her. You must find the Terran boy, Dylan and keep him from harm. Also, your princes, Conall and Hrolf, may require your aid, but I cannot stress enough that it is the boy's safety that must be your first priority. If he dies, or worse, falls into Melantha's grasp, then I have little doubt in my mind that we will soon face a new sethundra war."

"Go," Arlana added, "go with the blessing of both our peoples and with the hope that minotaur and man will stand side by side forever more."

Finian half expected a rousing shout of some sort from the soldiers before him, but none was forthcoming, they stared grimly ahead, ready to see to the task that had been set for them.

The professor took a deep breath and prepared himself. He had only performed this cast five times in his life, only twice taking someone else with him and only once sending another elsewhere, he wasn't even sure if it was going to work with so many people. Long ago, when he had tested the limits of his power, he had worked out how many people he thought he could safely transport, but he had never actually tried anything close to this number. He blocked out all other thoughts from his mind, put all of his focus on the task ahead and cast.

The power of the Heart Stone flowed through him like never before, it was almost more than he could contend with, but he flung it across the warriors before him like a cloak. The air shimmered, he felt as if the whole palace wobbled and flexed. His vision blurred, he swayed, almost passing out, until he felt the queen's supportive hand on his shoulder. He shook his head, clearing his vision, suddenly feeling utterly exhausted, as if he had done a full day's hard labour with no rest.

"Forgive me, Your Majesty," he said, weakly, "that took more out of me than I had imagined."

"Then we must hope you were successful," the queen
replied.

Finian looked up, and to find that he and the queen stood alone in the corridor.

****

Oriana sat on the edge of her bed, confusion and frustration contorting her beautiful features. She had received many puzzling instructions over the years, but this latest one baffled her completely.

The boy had gone, again, but this time he had taken the two sethundra with him. *Surely I would be of more use in the Deadlands than here in the palace. Why not strike now?*

She stood up and began pacing back and forth across the room, mentally going over everything that had been said, looking for hidden meanings, something she may have missed. *Knowledge is power.* Something she had learned a long time ago to her advantage, but try as she might she could find no sense in the simple instruction, *"Wait"*.

Shaking her head she saw the chest sitting on the floor, and with barely a thought pushed it back under the bed with the power of the Stone. Not a frivolous use of her skills, she could barely move the thing without casting. It never ceased to amaze her how something so small could be so heavy.

With a hiss of frustration, Oriana lay down on her bed and stared up at the ceiling. Never in the years since discovering she could cast had she felt so utterly useless. She was a magi of great strength, so much so she had been certain she would become the Apprentice. In every one of Finian's lesson's she had excelled. She believed herself to be the most powerful magi on Dainnor, excepting Finian himself of course. And she could do nothing. *"Wait."* The order was foolish beyond belief, of that she was certain. But wait she did. Oriana lay on her bed and did nothing. She had no choice but to obey. For she knew that to disobey meant a very long, and very painful, death.

CHAPTER 23

Katy almost screamed when the hand trailing along the side of the tunnel suddenly felt only emptiness. She risked a step to her left but could find no tunnel wall within the grasp of her reaching fingers. She carefully did the same to her right, still no wall. She reached out with her bow; again, nothing. Panic rose within her and Katy forced it down before it could take a hold.

She was blind down under the ground, but she had other senses and she was learning to focus on them. The dark was as silent as it had always been, but there was a difference that she hadn't noticed before. The air felt fresher than it had, perhaps a little cooler. She reasoned that she must have entered another cavern. How large she had no idea. *But what if it has another pool in it? What if there's something living in that one too?* She pushed the thought away. The last thing she needed to think about was dark, slithery things crawling out of underground lakes.

She briefly considered firing an arrow into the darkness and listening to hear when it hit a wall, perhaps then she could work out roughly how far away it was. She quickly dismissed the idea though, only having three arrows left she didn't want to waste one and she was unlikely to be able to find it again in the darkness. However, she now had a dilemma. Which way to go? She could continue straight ahead, but unless there was another tunnel directly opposite the one she had just come out of and she somehow managed to keep to a perfectly straight line, then she was likely to miss a way out of the cavern. She could spend hours looking for one, could even end up unwittingly going back the way she had already been.

She decided to take a step back to where she entered the cavern, find the wall, and go along the edge. She was bound to come to an exit at some point, hopefully one that would finally start leading her upwards towards the surface. Katy had no idea how long she had been wandering around blindly under the ground, but it felt like forever since she had last seen the sun.

She stepped back, and with her left hand found the wall again. Quickly finding the place where the tunnel and the cavern met she began following the wall around, using her bow to feel her way along the ground. One step, two, three and then shock filled her as her bow struck only air. She stopped and carefully feeling her way with the bow she quickly discerned that she could go no further in that direction. *What is it? A hole to a lower level? A lair to some creature?* She shuddered at the thought. She warily backed away until she found the entrance to the tunnel again and repeated the exercise in the opposite direction. One step, two, three and again, nothing. She stepped back, her heart pounding in her chest as she tried to work out what was in front of her. Katy carefully used her bow to gently tap along the edge of the rock. It curved in front of her into the cavern and then her bow felt solid stone again. She continued her tapping for about a metre across and then again her bow found empty air again. She followed the edge along until she came back to the cavern wall where she had first found empty space. *Am I on a bridge? Why would anyone put a bridge down here?*

Katy stepped back into the mouth of the tunnel, her heart beating so loudly she swore she could hear it echoing off the walls around her. She crouched down on the floor as her body began to shake uncontrollably. She wanted to go back, to find another way, but something told her she had to go forward, had to cross the bridge in the dark, over who knew what.

Katy scrabbled around on the ground for a moment until she found a loose rock, then crawled hesitantly forward to the edge, dropping it over the side and waited to hear it land. It must have been over a minute before she finally admitted to herself that however far down the bottom was, the stone striking it was out of earshot.

If I fall I'm dead. A loud grumbling in her belly reminded her that she hadn't eaten for some while. *If I stay here or try to find another way, I'm dead.* There was no course open to her other than forward. She got unsteadily to her feet, her legs feeling like jelly beneath her. *Tap, tap* went the bow on the ground, her feet shuffling slowly forward. *Tap, tap,* nothing. She swung the bow back until she found the bridge again. She felt dizzy and stopped, trying desperately to clear her head.

Dropping heavily to her hands and knees, arms shaking so much she had to wait whilst she brought them under control, she cursed herself for not seeing the obvious before. *Crawl, you idiot!* She slung the bow onto her back and began moving forward. Her progress was slow, but it was better than walking. It wasn't long before Katy's knees began to hurt on the hard, uneven stone beneath them, but she crawled on, the pain a better alternative to walking in the dark. But the further she went, the greater the pain grew. The stone of the bridge wasn't smooth, it dipped into pits before rising up to ridges that, if she wasn't careful, would cut painfully into Katy's flesh. More than once she cried out in pain when her knees caught a raised point too sharply. On she crawled, until agony forced her to stop and she lay face down, sobbing at the thought of what she had to do.

You can do it, the bridge has run pretty straight so far, just take it slow. What if I fall, what if the bridge collapses? Don't think like that! But now that the thought was in her head, she couldn't shake it. How old was the bridge anyway? Could it take her weight? The more she thought about it the more frightened she became. The image of the bridge suddenly crumbling under her, dropping her into the abyss wouldn't leave her alone. And yet it was that very image that moved her.

Katy pushed herself up, her bruised and bloodied knees screaming in protest. She unslung the bow from her back, using it to feel her way once again. *Tap, tap, tap.* Step. *Tap, tap, tap.* Step. *Tap, tap,* nothing. She swung the bow back, taking a small step to her left away from the edge. *Tap, tap, tap.* Step. *Tap, tap, tap.* Step. *Tap, tap,* nothing. This time she had veered a little to her left and she moved to compensate. *Tap, tap, tap.* Katy moved her foot forward, but then she felt the stone under her bow suddenly shift. She froze, the stone shifted again. She felt a chunk break free and it tumbled down into the depths below.

With a whimper she picked up her pace, taking bigger steps, moving forward faster and faster. But then her bow struck air once again, at the same moment that her foot snagged a ridge in the stone. Katy stumbled forward with a scream, landing heavily on her front, somehow managing to keep the bow in her hand as it hung over the abyss. Her breath coming out in short, panicky gasp, she lay shaking on the bridge.

And then Katy heard a sound that made her heart freeze.

It was faint at first, but then it grew stronger. She couldn't identify it, but as she pulled her bow up from over the side her hand brushed the edge of the bridge and the stone began to crumble beneath her fingers.

Panic stricken, she scrambled to her feet and with the bow before her, moved as fast as she dared. A piece of stone fell under her foot, she nearly went down again, but she managed to somehow keep her footing. The bridge began crumbling away beneath her, she could hear it clearly now, the sound seeming overly loud after the long silence of the dark.

Katy had one choice before her. *Run you fool! Run or die!* She sprinted forward, praying she went in a straight line, praying harder the bridge also went in a straight line. As she ran, stones collapsed under her feet. She left it until the last possible second and then leapt. As she flew through the air, Katy was certain it was the end, that she would plummet to her death, but then, a split second later she crashed down hard onto solid ground once more.

For a long time she lay on the stone, breathing heavily and trying to get her shaking under control. Katy finally raised her hand to wipe the tears from her eyes and then stopped and stared. She could see her hand. Just barely, but wriggling her fingers just to be sure she could definitely see it. Light. There was light coming from somewhere. *And where there's light, there's a way out!*

She got painfully to her feet, a new sense of hope burning within her. Squinting in the dark it took her a moment to see it. An opening in the wall, another tunnel. She stepped inside and found it sloped gently upwards.

Without another thought, she hurried on out of the darkness. Up towards the light.

CHAPTER 24

Dylan stood silently amongst the trees between the two princes, Conall and Hrolf, a far more impressive minotaur than Freya in his opinion, as they waited for Artemis and Baccus to decide if it was safe enough to go through the gates. Or at least where there used to be gates, that's if it wasn't just a big hole in what was left of a wall. What wasn't covered in ivy and other vegetation was just piles of precariously balanced rocks, at least as far as the ten-year-old could tell. Beyond the wall there didn't appear to be any more trees, but neither could he see the brown haze that covered the Deadlands. *Maybe we're not in the Deadlands anymore.*

The grumpy looking old man and the brothers that he couldn't tell apart stood watchfully behind Dylan and the princes, keeping a sharp lookout in case anyone attacked from behind, a completely unnecessary precaution in his opinion. It wasn't as if trolls were little things good at sneaking up on people, the ones they had seen so far were huge and stank. Dylan's nose wrinkled at the memory, they smelt like the dead.

Thoughts of the dead brought his sister back to the forefront of his mind. *She's not dead,* he told himself angrily, *I don't care what the others say. I can...feel her.* That puzzled him. He had no idea how he knew, but Katy was somewhere close by and getting nearer, he was sure of it. He dared not dwell on it too much, in case he lost his concentration again. The last thing they needed was for him to lose his mask, leading to Melantha knowing exactly where to send all her trolls from wherever she was keeping them.

Finally, Baccus nodded silently to Artemis who in turn
motioned the others forward. Moving as quietly as they could to join the two sethundra, Dylan peeked around them through the hole in the wall, managing to get his first good look at what had once been Melantha's fortress.

He had expected to see something like the old castles that Grandad took him to see back home, all towers and turrets, but the building before him was nothing like those at all. At first he thought he was looking at a cliff face, but as he continued to study it he made out several openings in the face, spaced far too regularly to be natural and quickly guessed them to be windows. At ground level there was a much larger opening, presumably the main entrance to the fortress. The wall formed a huge rectangle that had obviously been recently cleared of vegetation and it wasn't until he saw the face of the fortress stretching off into the distance beyond the wall on either side of them that he realised his first thought had been correct. The entire fortress had been carved into the side of a cliff. The courtyard that had obviously been recently cleared of most of its vegetation was also littered with large rocks, presumably tumbled over time from the remains of the outer wall. All was silent, nothing stirred but Dylan couldn't help but think that many of the rocks looked plenty big enough to hide a troll or two behind. The doorway looked even more ominous, it was just an empty black hole. He could easily imagine a horde of monsters coming pouring out of it as soon as the companions stepped into the courtyard.

"I've heard so many stories about this place," Conall said quietly, "I've always wanted to see it. It would be a nightmare to storm it, but surely it would be easy to lay siege to. It's a trap, a dead end."

Hrolf shook his head. "Not so. When Melantha built it she created a network of tunnels underground, with secret entrances throughout the town. Any army besieging this place would soon find themselves being attacked from behind."

"Tunnels?" The prince said thoughtfully.

"A pity we don't know where any of those tunnel entrances are," Dunham growled, "it would be a far better route into the fortress than this. The moment we step in there, trolls are going to come pouring out of that doorway."

"You may be correct," Artemis said, "but we have little choice."

"We're walking into a trap!"

"Nevertheless, this is our route, Captain Dunham."

Baccus nodded at Bevan and Brennan. "Are they any good with those bows?"

"The best I've ever seen," Dunham said. "They could cover us from the wall."

"Agreed. You and the two princes stay beside the boy and quickly finish any trolls that get past Artemis and I."

The captain nodded. "Seems as good a plan as any".

Dunham quickly directed the brothers to find likely positions and the others watched as they scrambled up the crumbling wall, soon disappearing from site amongst the rocks.

"Forward then," Baccus said, once he was satisfied that the archers were in position.

Baccus stepped into the courtyard, Artemis following closely behind, both with staffs in hand. Next came Dunham, then Dylan flanked on either side by Conall and Hrolf. Dylan expected trolls to come charging out of the doorway as soon as they entered the courtyard, but the area remained eerily silent.

"I don't like this," Hrolf muttered, his eyes scanning the area for any signs of life.

"Neither do I," Conall agreed, "I feel like we're being watched."

Dunham glanced back at them briefly. "I still say we should leave, Highness, take the boy and get as far from here as we can."

"I have to put Melantha to sleep, she'll come after me if I don't," Dylan said.

"And Melantha will only get stronger if we leave, so we're staying to protect Dylan, Captain," Conall said.

"Even if it means our lives," the minotaur growled.

Conall regarded Hrolf a moment before nodding. "Even if it means our lives."

Dunham snorted. "Well if it ends up with you two getting along, it can't be that bad."

Both princes chortled quietly, Conall looking mildly surprised that he did so.

It wasn't until they reached the centre of the courtyard before the trap was sprung. Several trolls suddenly came roaring out of the main gateway, lumbering across the courtyard towards the companions. At the same instant there was the sound of huge stones being hurled aside and trolls clambered out of the ground from the entrances that that had been hidden underneath. Dozens of trolls surrounded them, too many for Dylan to count. Baleful glares were levelled at the companions for a few tense moments and then, as one, they charged.

****

Katy narrowly managed to suppress a scream when, stepping around a bend in the tunnel, she almost stumbled into the backs of several huge trolls in the gloom before her. She quickly ducked back around the bend, certain that the heart pounding within her chest was making enough noise to give her away.

The light had gradually grown since the bridge and Katy's pace had speeded up with it, an increasing sense of urgency pulling her forward. She had passed several turnings along her route, but hadn't diverted from the path she was on, a path that she noticed was considerably less natural than the tunnels she had passed through before. Now however, her way was blocked by several trolls.

Katy was lost for where to go; certain that she was on the right path she didn't relish the idea of finding another. She needed to get out quickly and not just for Dylan. She was painfully aware of how long ago it was since she had anything to eat or drink. The inside of her mouth felt like it was full of dust.

A cry of terror did escape Katy's lips when, without warning, an ear shattering crash filled the tunnel. She flung herself to the ground, her arms wrapped around her head, certain that the ceiling was about to come tumbling down upon her. The tunnel flooded with light, making Katy squint painfully after so long in darkness; but there was no rain of stone. The trolls roared, a deafening sound that reverberated of the walls, she couldn't be sure in the din, but Katy thought she heard other crashes, other roars from other tunnels. The sound was all around her and she crouched on the ground her arms covering her ears, eyes squeezed shut against the light, certain that at any moment a great, ugly beast would appear and end her misery. But then, as suddenly as it had begun, it was over. She could still hear the creatures, but the sound was muffled, like a door had been shut on them, it was as if they were no longer in the tunnels at all.

She opened her eyes, blinking in the light that shone down in a shaft from around the bend in the tunnel. Dust motes hung in the air that had a freshness to it that she hadn't realised she'd been missing. She cautiously got to her feet, peeked around the bend in the tunnel and saw that not only was the path now clear of trolls, but daylight was shining down from a square hole in the ceiling, illuminating stone steps leading up and out of the darkness.

A way out! Katy ran to the steps, squinting painfully as her eyes took a few moments to adjust to the glaring daylight above her. Then she saw it, something she had been desperate to see for so many hours; the sky, clear and blue. But she could also hear the trolls. Grunts and roars, screams of pain, metal clashing against metal, a terrifying cacophony of noise that could only mean one thing. *There's a battle going on up there!* The last thing she wanted to do was emerge from the tunnel into the middle of a battle with trolls and who knew what. To have freedom so close but still denied to her was frustrating beyond belief for Katy. She looked around to see what to do next and saw that the tunnel continued on past the steps, still sloping gently up. Seeing no option open to her, she ran on up the tunnel.

The sounds of battle diminished somewhat as she ran and it wasn't long before the tunnel finally ended at the foot of some wide, stone stairs. They didn't lead out into the daylight as Katy had hoped, but up into more darkness. Seeing no other choice before her, she nocked an arrow to her bow string and, with a deep breath to steady her nerves, silently began climbing the steps.

CHAPTER 25

Dylan had always imagined that a battle would be an exciting thing to be in the middle of, but the reality was simply the most terrifying experience of his life. He stood, helplessly in the middle of a triangle formed by Conall, Hrolf and Dunham, all three desperately beating back troll after troll. A fact proven by the impressive pile of fallen monsters in front of them, many with arrows sticking out of them, fired from the bows of Bevan and Brennan. It was Artemis and Baccus that impressed him the most though. They spun the staffs they carried so quickly that the slender weapons were just a blur in the hands of the sethundra. The creatures fell before the immortals, not one of the beasts able to get a weapon close to either of them, but despite that, Dylan judged that there were just too many opponents for the companions to defeat. It would only be a matter of time before they were overwhelmed. Conall, Hrolf and Dunham were beginning to tire and the arrows appeared to have stopped flying, leading Dylan to come to the conclusion that the brothers had either run out or met with an unfortunate end. He stamped his foot in anger, fear and frustration. *If only there was something I could do to help!*

The thought froze him to the spot as it suddenly dawned on him that there was something he could do. *You can do magic, you idiot! One blast and I can make all of these trolls go away!* He tried to think how he could do it, but with all the din of roaring trolls around him he found concentration hard, it was difficult enough just maintaining the mask. That thought stuck in his mind. Surely he no longer had need of the mask? All Melantha

231

needed to do was look out of a window to see where he was.

He let the mask slip, he started to form a spell in his head, but just at that moment a troll charged Conall, knocking the prince a pace backwards and bumping Dylan, breaking his concentration. Conall beat the troll back as Dylan's grip on the Heart Stone left him. He thought he heard Artemis shout something, but he couldn't be sure above the noise of battle. Suddenly the air in front of him shimmered and then, a creature of breath-taking beauty stood before him.

Clothed in a gown of black she stared down at Dylan with eyes that bore into the boy's soul and froze his heart with fear. Tears, unbidden, flowed down his cheeks as he realised his foolishness in thinking he could defeat this being; a creature that gave of an aura of terrifying power. No compassion showed in Melantha's cold face as she reached down and grasped his shoulder, her long fingers digging into his flesh, enough to make him cry out in pain.

And then the battle, the noise, his companions, everything before him, suddenly vanished.

****

Conall heard Dylan's cry and turned quickly to see what distressed him just in time to see him vanish with a black-clad sethundra.

"Artemis! Baccus!" he cried. He had just enough time to catch sight of the two before they both vanished too. They were the only hope for the boy's survival, but that now left the companions with their own problem. The only thing that had been keeping dozens of trolls off their backs had vanished. And now the creatures attacked with a new relish.

232

"Back to back!" Dunham cried, and Conall and Hrolf leapt to obey, both knowing the hopelessness of their situation.

"Never thought I die back to back with a minotaur," he said grimly.

"Nor I with a human," Hrolf said, tiredly hefting his axe.

"Just make sure the price for your lives is dear," Dunham muttered.

"'Just make sure the price for your lives is dear, *Your Highnesses*'" Conall corrected, earning a chortle from both his companions.

Their levity didn't last long as then the trolls charged in one roaring mass.

Conall killed the first with one wild slash across its throat, but then, before it had even hit the ground, he had two more to deal with and no room to move. He cut one across the thigh, but before he could even attempt to dodge or parry, the other smashed its club into the prince's arm. He heard a sickening snap as he dropped to the ground in agony. His arm hung uselessly at his side, a wave of dizziness swept over him, almost causing him to pass out. Confusion filled his head, for a moment he thought he could hear human cries amongst the din of the trolls. The one above him raised his club for a final killing blow. Conall weakly raised his blade, knowing it was pointless, knowing that this was the end. But then suddenly Hrolf was there, smashing the troll aside with his war hammer and then...

Conall caught himself, *wait a minute, Hrolf doesn't carry a hammer, he carries an axe.* Confusing images assaulted him. Men wearing the uniform of the royal guard, fighting side by side with minotaurs, were attacking the trolls ferociously. There was a roar and a massive fireball crashed into several trolls, scattering them as if they were children's toys. And then the pain in his arm finally became too much, as blackness enveloped him and he knew no more.

****

Katy ran up the stairs, a nagging sense of being needed pulling her ever forward, her already painful knees and ankle aching from climbing steps obviously made deeper for something taller than a human. She could still hear the faint sounds of battle coming from outside. They had faded almost completely for a short time, but now they were becoming louder again and that, together with the light steadily increasing, she came to the conclusion that she must be nearing the top of the stairs and hopefully a window onto the outside world. She desperately wanted to see what was going on.

Finally, her legs crying out in protest, she reached the top of the stairs, a wide, empty doorway before her. She cautiously poked her head through and found an empty, stone corridor, stretching out before her, featureless but for gaps where windows should be lining one side and what looked like more doorways on the other. The sounds of battle were much louder, so with another quick look around to check she was alone, she dashed to a window to see what was happening and found a scene of chaos.

Dead trolls lay everywhere, but many more still stood and fought in what appeared to be a courtyard. As far as Katy could tell the trolls were on the losing side of the battle, as several minotaurs and humans were fiercely beating them back from one point roughly in the centre of the courtyard. *Where the hell did they all come from?* Katy thought, wondering if they had been followed into the Deadlands by the prince's party.

A group of trolls charged forward towards some of the humans, but then fire suddenly burst out from the line of soldiers, smashing hard into the creatures, sending many scattering, screaming in pain. The men then leapt forward, quickly finishing the few that were left behind. More trolls ran towards the men, but some minotaurs rushed to intercept them. She briefly considered firing her three remaining arrows at the creatures, but then thought better of it. *I'm hardly going to make a difference, and besides, I might need them.*

Pushing the battle from her mind, Katy turned her attention back to her own problems. She assumed she must be in Melantha's fortress, but that left her with a dilemma. *Do I try to join up with the men in the courtyard or search this place for Melantha?* The thought of facing the sethundra alone with nothing more than three arrows wasn't an appealing prospect. *Soldiers then. Perhaps Conall and the others will be with them.*

She continued on down the corridor, quickly reaching the first doorway and peeked inside, finding nothing but a plain, empty room with no clue to its purpose. In fact, everything about the whole place was plain. There were no carvings on the walls, no beauty in the design, just functional and solid, cut into the very rock itself. Moving along, she passed more empty rooms, just as uninteresting as the first, until, about halfway down the corridor, she came to a wider entrance. This one led into a hallway, a huge, stone staircase in its centre leading up to a higher level, the opposite direction to the one she wanted to go in. However, the direction she wanted to travel was the least of her problems at that moment, for standing directly in front of the staircase was a particularly ugly looking troll.

Before Katy could duck back out of the way, the troll spotted her and, raising a wicked looking stone hammer, roared out in rage as it rushed towards her. Escape was impossible, she knew as she raised her bow and prepared to fire her nocked arrow. Knowing she only had time for one shot she let it draw closer, not wanting to risk missing, a curious sense of calm falling over her as the huge creature came crashing in. Then, when it was almost upon her, she let loose. The arrow thudded deeply into the monster's chest, right where she guessed its heart should be. The troll staggered back with the force of the blow, looking stupidly down at the arrow sticking out of its body and the precious lifeblood that seeped out of the wound. Katy immediately reached for another arrow and drew her bow, preparing for a second shot. But it was unnecessary, the arrow had found the creature's heart. The troll managed to raise its hammer again, take one step towards her, before crashing down onto the ground, dead.

Katy let out a long breath she hadn't been aware she'd been holding and considered what to do next. The staircase led upwards, but she felt she needed to go down to get to the humans and minotaurs and the battle below. *There must be another way out of this place that doesn't include the tunnels.* She turned back to try and find a way further along the corridor, but then she stopped, staring at the staircase.

"I need to go up," she said to herself, having no idea why.

She shrugged, stepped over the dead creature on the ground, readied another arrow and once more began to climb.

CHAPTER 26

They emerged in an unadorned room of stone, a throne cut from the rock itself at its centre as Melantha, mercifully, released Dylan from her painful grip on his shoulder. He scampered a little away from her, wanting to look to see if the sethundra had drawn blood, but too terrified to do anything but stare at the black-clad creature in horror as she casually extended the staff that had hung at her belt and waited.

She's waiting for Artemis and Baccus. I have to do something!

He tried to slow his breathing, tried to relax so he could use the Heart Stone, but Melantha's voice cut through his concentration, shattering his courage.

"You are more useful to me alive than dead, but if you attempt to cast then I will kill you." Something about the almost casual way she said it left Dylan in no doubt that she meant every word. His only hope was that Artemis and Baccus would come and either defeat her or keep her busy long enough for him to act.

Suddenly, the air in front of Dylan shimmered and Artemis and Baccus emerged, staffs in hand, moving cautiously to either side of Melantha.

"Artemis, Baccus," Melantha said, a cruel smile on her lips, "it is good to see the two of you again, after so many years. What? No Dardanus? I am insulted, the three of you together may have been able to defeat me, but just the two of you? Or are we to fight at all? Perhaps you would like to continue where we left off on Terra? Artemis, join us, or die alone."

"I stand with the will of the Hearts, Melantha," Artemis

said calmly, although Dylan couldn't help but notice a
touch of uncertainty in her voice.

"And she does not stand alone," Baccus growled.

Melantha laughed, a surprisingly musical sound, Dylan had half expected a laugh from her to be something akin to a pantomime villain. "Such loyalty, Baccus. Your sleep has obviously done you some good, you were so indecisive before."

"It is time you went back in your cage, Melantha."

"And what will happen after that? Do you really believe the mortals will allow you to roam free afterwards? Allow you to be with your precious Artemis for the rest of eternity? I am afraid not, your task will be done, and then you will be as much a prisoner as I, once more. You betray us all."

Baccus hesitated, his face a twisted frown.

"Remember the Oath, Baccus," Artemis said. The uncertainty in her voice was even more apparent now, together with more than a little fear.

"Oath!" Melantha sneered. "The Oath was sworn in ignorance. To serve the Hearts, to obey their will. We all swore it, but what did we receive in return? Betrayal! Our service meant nothing, they made us slaves to the mortals!"

"We were never the slaves of mortals, we were their protectors. You could never see that, Melantha, you only ever wanted to rule."

"We were born to rule! It is our right! Rid yourself of this fool, Baccus. Join with me. Artemis is weaker than you, kill her now and together we will begin a new awakening of the sethundra!"

With a roar of anger, Baccus threw himself forward at Melantha. His staff whizzed towards her throat, only to be knocked aside with almost casual ease. Artemis wasted no time in joining the fray, her own staff coming in low as Baccus' went high, but again, both were deflected easily, Melantha even laughing as she stepped out of their way. Again, Artemis and Baccus attacked, blow after blow being pushed aside or avoided by the stronger sethundra. For some moments Dylan watched, mesmerized by the display. It was like watching the most graceful dance ever created. It took Artemis' frantic shout to snap him out it.

"Now, Dylan Howard, do it now!"

Idiot, he thought scrambling to his feet, *this is what you were waiting for!*

He took a deep breath, his thoughts beginning to calm now that he had allies by his side. His body relaxed, the pain in his shoulder becoming a distant thing. A light appeared in front of his eyes, drawing closer, becoming brighter, more powerful. But then, Melantha suddenly moved with astonishing speed, the light vanishing as panic and fear again claimed victory over Dylan. The sethundra's staff slashed across Artemis' face, knocking her aside, in a blur of movement she then struck Baccus three times on his head, crumpling him to the floor and, in the blink of an eye, she crossed the room, lifting Dylan easily with one hand up off the floor by the throat. And then, she squeezed.

He couldn't breathe, he battered uselessly at her arm, but within moments all strength had left him. He felt tears on his cheeks, as darkness began to close in. *I don't want to die,* his mind cried out, *I'm just a boy! I want to go home! Mummy! Help me!*

It felt odd calling for her, she had never been part of his life, so why call for her now? He could barely see; the darkness had almost consumed him completely. Confusing images crossed his mind, but one thing he knew without any doubt. *I'm dying.*

An arrow thudded into Melantha's shoulder.

The sethundra hissed in shock and pain, her hand reflexively opening, dropping Dylan to the floor. He swallowed air hungrily, his throat feeling as though it was on fire. As his vision began to clear, he rolled away from Melantha, looking in the direction the arrow had come from and gasped in shock.

There, standing in the doorway, calmly fixing another arrow to a bow, covered from head to toe in a layer dust and muck, stood his sister, Katy.

She raised her bow, pointing it directly at the sethundra, and spoke, venom thick upon her tongue. "Get your filthy, bitch hands away from my little brother."

Without taking her gaze from Katy, Melantha pulled the arrow out of her shoulder, nothing more than a slight intake of breath to indicate she felt any pain. With a morbid fascination, Dylan noticed that there was only the tiniest trickle of greenish blood produced from the wound. She snapped the arrow in half, tossing it aside, contemptuously. A curious expression crossed over her face as she looked at his sister, her head tilted to one side. "So, it is you. Intriguing. I can feel the strength in you, but you are young, not yet ready. And you come to me now with nothing but an arrow. Foolish. You cannot defeat me this way."

"Maybe; maybe not, but I bet another one in your chest will hurt like hell. Dylan, come here." Dylan scampered over to Katy's side, for once more than willing to do as he was told. Melantha's eyes still did not leave his sister's face. "Now, I'm taking him out of here, we're going home and you people, or whatever you are, can continue to do whatever it is you are doing, but you leave us alone."

"No, Katy," Dylan said, "we can't. I have to put her to sleep again."

Melantha smiled cruelly. "You see, girl, there is no escape. If the boy will not aid me, then he will die."

Melantha shot forward, just as Katy released her arrow. The sethundra's staff knocked it aside with ease. Katy pushed Dylan behind her, raising her bow protectively across her chest. Melantha's staff swung, smashing the bow to pieces. She then sent the staff towards Katy's head, but then Artemis was there, an angry looking welt across her cheek, her own staff deflecting Melantha's. Artemis then leapt into the air, kicking Melantha in the chest, knocking her across the room. Allowing no time for her to recover, Artemis charged Melantha, her staff striking out in every possible direction. For a few moments it looked as though Artemis may have had a chance of victory, but the other sethundra recovered enough to gain the upper hand and it quickly became apparent to Dylan that Artemis was desperately fighting for her life.

Katy began pulling Dylan away from the fight. "Come on," she shouted desperately, "we have to get away from here, now!"

"No!" Dylan wrenched his arm free from his sister's grasp. It was now or never. If he couldn't stop Melantha now, then there was nothing to save any of them. He calmed his breathing, began the process to embrace the power of the Heart Stone, but then suddenly it was there. He didn't stop to wonder at the ease of which he had done it, but focussed everything on Melantha. And the words poured out of him.

"Sleep Melantha, be gone from this place
Sleep and become unseen
For the sake of worlds laid to waste

I banish you to the dream."

Dylan felt power flow through him, and he hurtled it towards the sethundra. He felt it wrap around her, enveloping her completely. He thought that was it, she was beaten, but then Melantha fought back. She tried to push the power of the Heart Stone away, with a tremendous heave of her mind, she pushed back at Dylan, making him stagger, his focus wavering, his head throbbing in pain. Somehow Dylan pulled more power into him, throwing it as hard as he could at his opponent, making it Melantha's turn to stagger. Her eyes went wide with surprise at Dylan's strength and he wasted no time in seizing the advantage. He threw everything he had at her, more and more power flooding through him, wrapping around the sethundra. There was nothing she could do to escape; Dylan was too strong for her. She reached out to Artemis as if trying to pull her in with her, but the nimble sethundra managed to dance out of the way. A howling wind sprung up, nearly knocking Dylan off his feet. Melantha had just enough time to throw back her head and scream in anguish before, as swiftly as it had started, the wind died, and Melantha was gone.

CHAPTER 27

Katy let out the long breath she been holding as she stared at the spot where Melantha had disappeared. *Did Dylan do that?* She looked down at her brother in wonder. He looked pale, his eyes dark, like he hadn't slept in some time. As she watched, he swayed, as if about to fall and she placed a supporting hand on his shoulder.

"Easy there, Shrimp," she said, not unkindly, "I don't know what you did there, but I think it took a lot out of you."

"I'll be fine," he protested, but exhaustion was as evident in his voice as it was in his face.

"Your sister is correct, Dylan Howard," Artemis said, "you drew upon a lot of power to do what you did, more than I would have thought one of your age would be able to use, but you must rest." She then looked at Katy, curiosity in her eyes. "I am pleased to see you well, Katy. Melantha was correct about one thing, there is great strength in you I think." She then crossed over to kneel down next to Baccus, who still lay unmoving on the ground.

"Is he alright?" Dylan asked, worriedly.

"He will recover." Katy was surprised by the note of tenderness in Artemis' voice.

She didn't have time to ponder as the sound of several approaching footsteps arose from behind them. Katy span around, pushing Dylan protectively behind her, although she wasn't sure what she was going to be able to do. A fraction later, Artemis was beside her, staff held ready. She quickly scanned the room, searching for anything she could use as a weapon. She spied Baccus' staff lying beside him and was about to dash over and grab it, when a familiar figure leapt into the room, huge axe in hand.

"Hrolf!" Katy cried, running forward, throwing her arms around the startled minotaur.

"Y...you're alive," he stammered, "but how? You fell."

"I don't know. I'm just lucky I guess. Where's Conall and the others?"

Hrolf grimaced as more figures entered the room. Minotaurs mainly, with a handful of humans including Bevan and Brennan. Dylan's face split into a grin when he saw the one woman amongst the newcomers.

"Olwyn," he said, "how did you get here?"

She smiled briefly at Dylan, her eyes scanning the room nervously. "Melantha?"

"She's gone, we beat her."

"That is not entirely correct, Dylan Howard," Artemis said, "we did indeed defeat her, but she is not gone, she is still here, merely held in the dream."

As Artemis spoke, Baccus began to stir, a pained groan escaping from his lips. Artemis immediately went to his side, her staff shrinking with a flick of her wrist and hung back onto her belt. Dylan stared hard at the spot where Melantha had disappeared for a moment before muttering quietly to himself. "There's something missing; it's weird, but it's like there should be something there."

"What's happened to Conall?" asked Katy, more concerned with the fate of the prince at that moment than the mysteries of magic and sethundra.

"He's been hurt," Hrolf said. "It looked bad, but we didn't have time to see to him properly. Once we routed the trolls we came here. Dunham's with him, with General Macklyn and a few of the palace guards."

"I should go to him," Olwyn said, "I might be able to do

something to help."

The party began moving out, the soldiers and minotaurs forming a protective ring around Katy, Dylan and Olwyn, just in case any trolls remained. Hrolf helped Artemis support Baccus, who could barely walk with his injuries. Katy, to Dylan's obvious irritation, put a protective arm around his shoulders and led him along. He tried telling his sister that he was fine, but Katy wasn't about to let him go again now that she had found him. *Besides he looks almost ready to fall flat on his face.* An opinion reinforced when he stumbled on a step and it was only Katy's support that stopped him from falling.

They reached the courtyard without incident and mercifully quickly as Katy hurt everywhere and felt even more exhausted than Dylan looked and found Dunham, Macklyn, Alberich and the remaining soldiers standing protectively around their prince, who sat propped up against a rock, clutching his left arm in pain. He gaped in disbelief when Katy went running to his side.

"You're alive," he said joyously, until he remembered how much pain he was in and an agonised groan escaped his lips.

"And in better shape than you it seems," Katy said. "What happened?"

"A troll thought it would be a good idea to break my arm. Don't worry though," he added with a grin, "I've got another."

Olwyn knelt beside him and placed her hand gently on his broken arm, concentrating.

Conall blinked in surprise. "I didn't know you could do that."

Olwyn smiled shyly. "We don't really let it be known. No magi would be given a moments peace if everyone knew we could heal. It's not our greatest talent and I'm not very good at it anyway. Your arm is still broken, but I've taken much of the pain away. We'll have to put it in a sling until we can get you to Professor Finian, or let it heal naturally."

"How are we going to get back? How did you get here, anyway?"

"Something the professor did. Quite remarkable really. I think I saw how he did it, but I would never be able to replicate the feat. Not without aid anyway."

"We have a long march ahead of us then," Macklyn said grimly.

"Not so," Artemis said, easing Baccus onto the ground next to Conall. "I can take you all back. Not all at once as the professor did, but it will not take long. It would be quicker if Baccus was well, but..."

"I am fine," Baccus grumbled, a little groggily in Katy's opinion.

"You are not, you are weak and require rest. I will take you back as well."

Baccus made as if to argue, but then he grimaced in pain, slumping on the ground in silence.

"The princes should go first," Alberich said, "they're important to the future of our nations." He then glared at Hrolf critically. "Well, Conall is important to Lors, Hrolf's future remains to be seen."

Hrolf glared back defiantly. "I am my father's heir, Alberich, the Horned Crown is mine by rights."

"You are not ready to lead our people, this jaunt into the Deadlands has proven that."

246

"I did what I believed was right."

"You 'believed' wrongly. If we had not arrived when we had, then you would be dead."

Katy stepped up in defence of her friend. "If Hrolf
hadn't come with me into the Deadlands then my brother
would be dead and Melantha would be free."

"I agree," Conall said, unexpectedly sticking up for the minotaur. "Hrolf fought with valour, a credit to your people, Alberich."

"It's not his prowess in battle I question," Alberich said, "it's his judgement to rule. We have many warriors, just as capable of this trip to the Deadlands, *if* it was necessary at all. One good warrior's death will be mourned by a few, but the death of a good king will be mourned by all."

"Alberich speaks the truth," General Macklyn said. "You nearly died, Conall. If you had, your mother would have no successor, leading to uncertain times for the realm. Prince Hrolf's irresponsibility may lead to the tribes splitting whatever he does now. However, there will be plenty of time for us to dwell on the consequences of your actions later, for now, it is time we left, before the trolls have time to regroup and find their courage. Artemis, I suggest you take Dylan and his sister first, followed by the princes."

Artemis nodded once before placing a hand on Katy and Dylan's shoulders. Katy gasped as everything in front of them appeared to stretch towards them and then their surroundings changed.

CHAPTER 28

It didn't take long to transport them all back to the palace. After she had transported Katy, Dylan and the two princes, Artemis concentrated on the wounded before bringing the others, finishing with Baccus and Olwyn. So it was about twenty minutes later that Dylan found himself standing beside Katy in Professor Finian's study, Conall sat in a chair refusing to budge. Freya was there and Dylan couldn't help but giggle at the shy looks she kept casting in Hrolf's direction. *If she smooths her hair and dress down anymore she'll wear them both away.* Hrolf on the other hand seemed to be taking great pains to ignore her completely, that is when he wasn't glaring at Alberich

Suddenly, Finian burst into the room accompanied by the queen who went straight to Conall, her face caught somewhere between fury at his irresponsible behaviour and relief. Finian opened his mouth to speak until he caught sight of Katy. He looked at her oddly for a moment, surprise and confusion on his face.

"Professor," Dylan said, "this is my sister, Katy."

"Your sister?" Finian shook his head. "Of course, of course she is. Welcome, it is good to see you survived your ordeal." Katy nodded and smiled as Finian turned away, but Dylan noticed that he occasionally eyed her strangely. "Well, Dylan, I don't think I have to tell you that what you did was incredibly foolish, dangerous and irresponsible beyond belief. Saying that though, you have been successful, unbelievably fortunate, but successful nonetheless and I suppose, for that, we must be grateful."

"And now that Melantha is held here on Dainnor she can be properly guarded," Queen Arlana said coming forward. "I feel we should have some sort of celebration, but time will not allow for this. It is time for you both to return home."

"What," Conall blurted from his chair, "now? Shouldn't they at least rest for a few days?"

"They have both been gone from their home for many days already, their family must be beside themselves with worry. As a mother," she eyed Conall, "I know exactly how that feels."

"But we will see them again?"

"Unlikely," Finian said, "I fear Terra's knowledge of their own history is woefully inadequate. I can hardly see us beginning a new era of communication between our worlds. However, I cannot stress enough, Dylan, you must find your Guardian. Your grandfather will help." He handed a folded-up piece of parchment to Katy, his gaze again lingering on her face a moment longer than necessary. "Give this to your grandfather, it is a letter from myself to him."

"I'll give it to him," Katy said, folding the letter into her belt pouch.

"We must leave," Artemis said. Baccus was at her side, still leaning heavily on her. He held his staff, but this time for support rather than battle.

"Just like that," Dylan said, "can't we say goodbye to everyone first." He looked around desperately at Conall, Hrolf, Freya and Olwyn, even the grumpy looking Alanson, sullenly dusting shelves across the room. He couldn't believe he wasn't going to see any of them again.

"We will meet again, Dylan," Conall said, "I don't care what the professor says." The prince's gaze lingered on his sister, she held it before blushing, looking shyly away. Dylan made a mental note to tease her about it later, when he wasn't quite so tired. Putting Melantha to sleep had completely exhausted him.

Artemis stared at a spot in the room cleared of people and suddenly a hole appeared in mid-air, just as it had in his grandparents' garden what seemed a lifetime ago. The same kaleidoscope of colours spun away down a long tunnel. Finian and Olwyn studied it intently as if attempting to understand how it worked, Dylan noted with surprise that Alanson appeared to be doing the same.

"Hold on to me," Artemis said, "do not let go, no matter what."

Katy and Dylan each clutched tightly to one of Artemis' outstretched hands, Baccus held her arm. And then, without another word to anyone in the room, she leapt into the pathway.

Down the tunnel they sped, colours whizzing silently past them. Dylan hadn't noticed the first time around; but the pathway was eerily quiet. The thought of speaking felt wrong somehow. He also felt a curious sense of loss. *I'm probably just missing Freya and the others already. I hope I can go back to Dainnor one day.* He glanced across at his sister to see that she looked like she wanted to be sick and immediately wished that he hadn't, the head movement making him feel the same way. He concentrated on keeping his eyes front and then suddenly, it was over.

Artemis came to a halt, landing gracefully as Katy and Dylan were flung forward, landing on their faces on wet grass. Baccus landed with a grunt and lay on the ground, breathing heavily.

250

Dylan looked around, it was night time and he instantly knew where he was. "We're back," he shouted, "we're in Nanny and Grandad's garden!"

"I can see that," Katy said, "but what do we do now? They've probably had the police looking for us, we need a convincing story of where we've been."

"That must come later," Artemis said, "firstly you must cast Baccus and I back into the dream."

"Now?" Dylan said. "But I don't want you to go."

"We must, Dylan Howard. Baccus requires healing and in the dream he will heal quickly."

"I'll miss you," Dylan said, suddenly fighting back tears.

Artemis smiled warmly down at him. Dylan had thought her beautiful before, but when she smiled like that it took his breath away. "And I will miss you. You will make a fine Guardian one day, Dylan Howard. Do what Professor Finian said, find Terra's Guardian; learn." She then turned to his sister. "He will need you, protect him well."

"I will," Katy said, nodding.

Dylan resisted the urge to point out that he was perfectly capable of looking after himself and turned to Baccus instead. He hadn't really been expecting the sethundra to say anything nice, but he smiled when Baccus nodded, respect showing in his eyes before he lay back and closed them.

Dylan breathed deeply, quickly finding the Heart Stone. It felt different somehow to Dainnor's and curiously, he noticed, the sense of loss was gone. He focussed on the two sethundra and spoke the words he had used before, but for a small difference.

"Sleep Artemis and Baccus, be gone from this place
Sleep and become unseen

For the sake of worlds laid to waste
I banish you to the dream."

As before a wind emerged, though not as violent as before, it wrapped around Artemis and Baccus, but unlike with Melantha there was no resistance, only acceptance and a sense of pain and sadness that he was sure came from both of them. And then they were gone. Dylan stared at the spot where they had been, sensing the same wrongness that he had felt when he had looked at where Melantha had been. *Something's missing.*

"Katy, Dylan?"

They both turned at the sound of the voice to see their grandfather standing at the backdoor to the house, relief on his face, tears pouring down his cheeks. He rushed to them as they ran to him, sweeping them both up in a fierce hug. Dylan expected a hundred questions about where they had been, what they had been doing, but none came. He just held them tightly and wouldn't let go.

It wasn't until much later that, despite his exhaustion, Dylan, lying awake in bed, finally figured out what had been bothering him about his grandfather's face when he had greeted them. Not so much when he looked at Katy, but when he looked at Dylan himself.

They had not been tears of joy that had flowed down Bryn Morgan's cheeks; they had been tears of grief.

CHAPTER 29

Paul angrily threw the mobile phone across the room; it struck the wall before falling harmlessly to the worn, carpeted floor. Such a cold message. Almost nine years of searching, he finally discovered something worthwhile and then he finds one heartless message left on his phone three weeks ago, telling him it had all been for nothing.

It is confirmed. Aelwen is dead. Return to Carreg-y-galon, the children will need you.

Carreg-y-galon. Just the very name of the place filled him with hatred. Paul had travelled the world in his search, met thousands of people from hundreds of communities and never had he encountered such a nest of self-important, opinionated busybodies. He wished he had never set eyes on the place.

But then I would never have met Aelwen.

He sank down onto the floor of his hotel room, his head buried into the carpet and gave into grief. Years of hope of finding an answer, shattered in moments.

It was some time before he looked up again. He pushed himself to his feet, feeling wearier than he had ever remembered feeling before. He caught his reflexion in the cracked wall mirror. Handsome, in an unkempt sort of way, a thin beard decorated his chin, grown from not bothering to shave rather than a choice of look. It had been a long time since he had last cared anything for his appearance. He made a small effort for the kids, but not when he was travelling. He was still only a young man, being only sixteen when he'd first become a father and attracted looks from women not much older than his

253

daughter. Only earlier that evening the waitress in the restaurant downstairs had made a point of letting him know what time she finished her shift. He had politely refused of course. He always politely refused. There had never been anyone for him other than Aelwen.

It is confirmed. Aelwen is dead.

How could Bryn be so cold-hearted about his own daughter?

He's spent too long living in that damned village.

He needed to get Katy and Dylan away from the place before they ended up the same. There were no more excuses. It was time to settle down. Start a new life. Create a proper home for the three of them. Maybe even move them back to England. He had family there still, a few friends. And it would be a long way from Carreg-y-galon.

Can I move on that easily?

Again the tears came and he sat on the edge of the bed, his head in his hands. When he finally managed to bring his grief back under control he turned his eyes towards the old, brown rucksack, lying on the bed next to him.

Could it really be hers? She had one like it?

But what had brought her to Canada in the first place, to some town he hadn't even heard of? Kamloops, in British Columbia. He had got the rucksack from some toothless old woman who had spent the entire time going on about Aelwen taking Thera away. Whoever the hell that was. The explanation had been vague at best.

"Who's Thera?" Paul asked, as patiently as he could manage.

The old woman's eyes took on a faraway look as she rocked back and forth in her rocking chair, a worn blanket keeping her frail body warm on the chilly Canadian night.

"I saw her once," she said after some time, "I mean properly saw her, when I was young."

"What do mean, 'properly saw her'?"

The old woman suddenly stared at him intently, her voice lowering to a whisper. "Everyone can see her when she sleeps, if you're standing in the right place, but only for an instant." The old woman smiled, revealing a mouth full of red gums, devoid of any teeth. "But I saw her when she was awake. Beautiful she was, so tall and beautiful. She was talking to a woman." She chuckled. "Her name was Aelwen too. Although, not as pretty as yours."

Paul looked up sharply at that. Aelwen had been named after her grandmother on her mother's side. He shook his head. The old woman was confused, her mind was failing her. He stood up from the old, threadbare armchair, scooping up the rucksack the old woman claimed belonged to his wife. "Thank you for this," he said, "you've been a great help."

The old woman nodded, her eyes closed, her smile clearly remembering happier times. "Aelwen had somebody with her when she was here."

"My wife? Who?"

"No, not your wife." She waved a spindly hand dismissively at him. "The other one, from long ago."

"Who?"

"A boy, a student of hers I think. At least he seemed to be, going by the way she made him fetch and carry. What was his name?"

The old woman fell silent, her breathing deepened. Paul sighed and made for the door as quietly as he could, leaving her to her sleep. He turned the handle and immediately felt a blast of cool air from outside.

"Bryn."

"What?" Paul said, turning back to the old woman.

255

"That was his name," she said, sleepily, *"the boy was called Bryn."*

Paul stared at the rucksack, lying on the bed beside him. It couldn't possibly be a coincidence, but what the hell had Bryn been doing here with his future mother-in-law?

He dragged the rucksack over to him, opened it up and looked inside. There were just some clothes that may or may not have belonged to her. He smelled them, breathing in deeply to try to get some scent of her, but there was nothing.

Aelwen is dead.

Instead of answers, he had found only more questions.

He was about to push the rucksack away when he felt something tucked down at the bottom. He reached inside and pulled it out. A journal! Aelwen's journal in fact! Paul recognised it immediately, he had bought it for her years ago, when she had become pregnant with Dylan. Surely in here there would be something that would tell him what had happened to her? He opened it and began flicking through the pages, curiosity turning to confusion. It was unmistakably Aelwen's handwriting, elegant and beautiful, just like her. But every page was exactly the same. The same few words written over and over; hundreds, thousands of times.

Paul lay back on the bed, staring up at the ceiling. Had Aelwen been going mad? It was the only explanation that he could come up with and it might explain her sudden disappearance. Perhaps he would get some answers in Carreg-y-galon. Bryn must know something of what had happened to his daughter, otherwise how would he know she was dead? He could also confirm what the old woman had said. That must have had something to do with why Aelwen had come here.

256

Paul's eyelids began to droop and soon he drifted down into sleep.

It was that *dream again. He had it every now again,*

but never as regularly as he had for the past few nights.

He stood before a door, carved with vegetation, so lifelike, he felt he should be able to reach out and pluck one of the many flowers decorating its surface. Seven curious symbols rose in an arch over an eighth, a circle with a star at its centre, and eyes, malevolent and cruel, were hidden amongst the foliage.

"Come."

The voice, he hadn't recognised it when he had been here before, but it was clearer now.

"Aelwen?"

"Come."

The door stood open, there was nothing but blackness beyond it, but he stepped through nonetheless.

He stood on a small green, on a warm, sunny day, chocolate box houses with bright, colourful gardens surrounding him on all sides. A pole was beside him and he looked up to see the Welsh flag fluttering in a gentle breeze. He knew where he was. Carreg-y-galon. But instead of the usual locals, moving about their business, and poking their noses into other peoples, the village was eerily quiet.

Flicker.

He whipped his head to the left, catching a movement out of the corner of his eye, but could see nothing. But now things had changed. The gardens had ceased to bloom; the once bright flowers were now sick and dying.

Flicker.

He spun to the right. Still nothing, but now the once pristine houses were crumbling in ruins.

Flicker.

Again he turned and he could hear his wife's voice.

Flicker. Flicker. Flicker.

Each time he turned the village decayed even more. Flicker. *The trees became dead, twisted ruins.* Flicker. *The grass beneath his feet turned to hard barren earth.* Flicker. *The flag pole lay broken on the ground, the dragon banner, torn to shreds and soaked in blood.* Flicker. *And as he turned, he could hear her voice, whispering the same thing, over and over again.*

"Aelwen?"

Flicker.

"Aelwen!" There was no answer to his shouts.

Flicker, flicker, flicker.

He wanted it to stop, the voice, the movement, everything. He squeezed his eyes shut and put his hands over his ears, expecting to wake as he always did; but then the dream changed and there was silence. He slowly removed his hands, cautiously opening his eyes. The village had returned to normal, the flowers bloomed, the flag fluttered on its pole, the houses looked warm and inviting. But now, before him on the green, stood an intricately carved door.

"Come."

He took a single step forward and the door swung silently open, but instead of seeing a view of the village through the doorway, he saw a familiar looking room. Shelves, heavily laden with books and curios lined the walls, the Welsh flag hanging between two of them, a sword hanging over a fireplace; and at the large writing desk, head down as she wrote, dark hair obscuring her features, sat Aelwen.

Her belly was swollen, Paul guessed she was just a few weeks away from giving birth judging by her size. He took another step forward and could see that she was writing in her journal.

"Aelwen?"

She stopped, slowly raising her head. And Paul screamed in horror at the nightmarish vision before him. Her face was hideously burned, glowing embers crisscrossing what was left of her features. She stared at Paul, her eyes burning a fierce intensity and then, through cracked and bloodied lips, she spoke the words she had been writing.

"It is time to wake."

With a wave of her hand, the door slammed shut in Paul's face, and blackness consumed him.

18400654R00156

Printed in Poland
by Amazon Fulfillment
Poland Sp. z o.o., Wrocław